THE
WIDE
STARLIGHT

ALSO BY NICOLE LESPERANCE

The Depths

The Nightmare Thief

The Dream Spies

THE
WIDE
STARLIGHT

NICOLE LESPERANCE

RAZORBILL

RAZORBILL

An imprint of Penguin Random House LLC, New York

First published in the United States of America by Razorbill,
an imprint of Penguin Random House LLC, 2021
First paperback edition published 2022

Visit us online at penguinrandomhouse.com.

LIBRARY OF CONGRESS CATALOGING-IN-PUBLICATION DATA
Names: Lesperance, Nicole, author.
Title: The wide starlight / Nicole Lesperance.
Description: New York : Razorbill, [2021] | Audience: Ages 12+. |
Summary: Eli was six when her mother disappeared off a frozen fjord in Norway under the
Northern Lights and now, at age sixteen, she returns, determined to discover what really happened.
Identifiers: LCCN 2020049753 | ISBN 9780593116227 (hardcover) |
ISBN 9780593116241 (trade paperback) | ISBN 9780593116234 (ebook)
Subjects: CYAC: Mothers and daughters—Fiction. | Missing persons—Fiction. |
Storytelling—Fiction. | Auroras—Fiction. | Supernatural—Fiction. | Norway—Fiction.
Classification: LCC PZ7.1.L4732 Wid 2021 | DDC [Fic]—dc23
LC record available at https://lccn.loc.gov/2020049753

Manufactured in Canada

1 3 5 7 9 10 8 6 4 2

FRI

Design by Rebecca Aidlin
Text set in Arno Pro

For my mother, Lynn

THE
WIDE
STARLIGHT

PART ONE

CHAPTER 1

You're not allowed to be born or to die on Svalbard. On this tiny archipelago halfway between Norway and the North Pole, there's no cemetery because the bodies freeze solid and never go away. And the hospital isn't equipped for all the messy and terrible things that can happen in childbirth, so women fly down to the mainland before their babies are due. No beginnings or endings of life, just the in-between.

Once upon a time, in a green house at the top of the world, my mother and father were waiting for me to be born. It was almost time, and my mother had bought her plane ticket and packed her suitcase: books, pajamas, toothbrush, diapers, more books. Everything was ready and she was supposed to be sleeping, but an ache in her lower back kept nudging her awake. She left my father snoring in bed and stole outside.

Even at midnight, the sun was bright, the air scented with cold sea and wind over stone. On an improvised clothesline behind the house, my mother had hung three pairs of tiny footed pajamas that she'd bought for me. She wanted them to absorb that night-sun smell so I'd know it as soon as I came into the world.

As she reached up to unpin the first sleeve, the whispering

of wings filled the air. Claws grasped the shoulders of her robe, her hair, her wrists and fingers. White feathers flew like snow as the birds flapped and pulled and rose. Up my mother flew over the little town of Longyearbyen, its rows of candy-colored houses cradled by flat-topped mountains. Down through a fjord with water like blue stained glass. Over a craggy glacier with waterfalls pouring into the sea, then up, up again to the top of a snow-covered peak.

I used to ask my mother if she was scared when she flew all that way, but she told me the birds were so gentle with their claws, and besides, she'd never been afraid of heights. As she flew, she said, the pain in her back grew deeper, fiercer, until it felt like she might turn inside out. Finally, the birds set her down in a nest made of down feathers, softer than clouds. Moments later, she pushed me out into the world, wet and steaming in the cold.

She pulled off her bathrobe and wrapped me in it, put me to her breast. I asked her once if she was cold without her bathrobe, but she said she felt nothing but wild elation singing through her veins now that she finally could hold me in her arms and see my face. She said she could have walked home naked and not shivered once.

But she didn't have to walk home. Once I'd dropped off to sleep and my mother tucked her robe closer around my shriveled face, the birds took her again, this time by the shoulders of her nightgown. She wasn't worried about dropping me—she was physically incapable of letting me go, she said.

The birds flew my mother across the fjord and back into the town, which was now slowly waking up, though it had been light all night long. She pointed to our house, the green one at the end of the row, in case the birds had forgotten. As they put her down, her feet slid right into her slippers where she'd left them. The door had latched shut, and she hadn't brought her keys, so she knocked. When my father answered, bleary and tousled, there she was, holding the child he hadn't been expecting to see for weeks. Sometimes as I'm just about to fall asleep, I can almost remember it, the confusion in his face fading to love as he drank me in.

It didn't matter how or why.

We were back. We were home. We were safe.

But it wasn't the only time my mother flew away.

CHAPTER 2

Wellfleet, Massachusetts

I find the letter one slushy February afternoon, stuck in the holly bush beside my front door. Setting my bag of library books on the steps, I crouch and fish the envelope out of the jagged branches. Judging from the dark splotches and water lines on the paper, it's been there a long time. Someone has printed my name in pencil, crooked and hasty, with none of the *i*'s dotted and the faintest hints of crosses on the *t*'s.

Eline Davis
Massachusetts, USA

There's an official post office sticker across the bottom. RETURN TO SENDER, it says. NOT DELIVERABLE AS ADDRESSED. But somehow it made it here anyway. The postmark is smudged; I can only just make out the word *Norge*. *Norway*. Oblivious to the icy rain pattering into my hair, I tear the envelope open. Somehow, the paper inside isn't wet.

Moren din er nær. Jeg hører henne, men hun kan ikke høre meg. Du må prøve. Kall på henne.   —M

6

I never learned to read Norwegian, and it's been years since I spoke the language. Whenever I try, the words feel like rocks in my mouth. Squinting at the paper, I whisper them out loud.

Moren. Mother.

My scalp begins to prickle. It's been ten years since I last saw my mother, ten years I've been waiting for her to come back, even though my dad and I live on another continent now and she'd have no idea how to find us. I mutter the rest of the words, hating how awkward and foreign I sound. It says something about hearing but not hearing, something about calling.

I glance across the street: Iris's truck isn't in her driveway. On Saturdays she meets up with other incredibly intelligent people from all over Cape Cod and they solve math problems for fun. She should be home any minute now.

Moren din. Your mother.

A bead of ice slips inside my collar, sending a wash of goose bumps across my skin. With trembling fingers, I unlock the door and step inside, where I'm enveloped by the smoky scent of chipotle layered over rich, salty beef. My dad left the house while I was out, but he must have put dinner in the Crock-Pot first. Pulling out my phone, I sit on our ancient couch and type the note's words into an online translator.

Your mother is close. I hear her, but she cannot hear me. You must try. Call her.

Every inch of me goes shivery. I used to get lots of letters after my mother disappeared and we were all over the news, but those letters tapered off years ago. The last one came when I was twelve, and I burned it like all the others. But this one is different. This one hums with an almost imperceptible energy.

I send Iris a text:

Me: *Found a weird note in my bushes. Where are you?*

The response is instantaneous:

Iris: *[Auto-Reply] I'm driving right now—I'll get back to you later.*

I hope that means she's on her way home. Aimless and unsettled, I wander into the kitchen. On the counter, the Crock-Pot bubbles and simmers. Beside it is a note from my dad, written on the back of a receipt.

Out with Helen for the rest of the day. Help yourself. It might need more cumin.

I haven't met Helen. My dad stopped bringing his girlfriends home years ago because I kept trying to wrap myself up in them, even though they never quite fit. The last one I met was named Clara. She was from Germany, tall and lean and red-haired. She taught me how to knit, and it still hurts my chest to think about her.

The chili does need cumin, so I add a bit more, then head for my room, which is crammed full of bookshelves and bins of fabric and yarn. Gertrude, my headless dressmaker's dummy, stands beside my bed, piled high with half-sewn clothing. Setting the note on my desk, I press the creases to lay it flat, and I write the English words underneath their Norwegian originals.

Your mother is close. I hear her, but she cannot hear me. You must try. Call her.

As if it were that simple. As if I haven't tried. Even in my dreams I'm calling her. Screaming her name, whispering it, sobbing it. Finding phones and dialing over and over, always getting one number wrong and having to start again. Sometimes in my dreams, I call and scream and plead and she actually, finally comes and I see her face again, those dark eyes and sweeping cheekbones, and her soft body folds around me and I'm home. Nothing is dangerous; nothing is bad. It's the way I wish I could remember her always. Those are the most heartbreaking dreams because when I wake up, she's gone all over again and the loss is a thousand times sharper.

I hear her.

I'd laugh if this weren't so creepy. Reaching up, I pull a binder from the shelf above my desk. It's been years since I've opened this, and the paper is musty. The first page is a printed-out article, and beside the headline is a black-and-white photo of my mother with her long, dark hair—one of the few features we share—draped over her shoulder. She's caught in an expectant half smile, looking like she just asked a question and is waiting for whoever took the photo to answer.

SPITSBERGEN POST

LONGYEARBYEN WOMAN MISSING, DAUGHTER FOUND ON FROZEN FJORD

Early Friday morning, an expedition group found a six-year-old girl on the ice of Ekmanfjorden, nearly fifty kilometres from the town of Longyearbyen. The child was taken to the hospital, where doctors pronounced her in perfect health and said it was a miracle she'd survived.

The girl's mother, twenty-nine-year-old Silje Lund, has

been reported missing by her family. The girl is being cared for by her father, American marine biologist Peter Davis, and her grandmother, Astrid Lund. Local officials have mounted a massive search effort, but with temperatures hovering at negative twenty degrees, Lund's chances of survival are dwindling. She is 1.75 metres tall, with dark hair and brown eyes, and is believed to be wearing a light blue coat and black trousers. Police urge anyone with information about Lund to contact them as quickly as possible.

Ten years later, parts of that article still make my skin crawl. *Lund's chances of survival are dwindling.* They have no idea what she faced that night, what she had to survive. What we both had to survive. She promised nothing bad could happen as long as we were together, but it turns out that was a lie.

The rest of the binder is filled with articles, some in English and others in Norwegian, the language I'd be reading in if we'd stayed on Svalbard—if she'd stayed. Each article is a story about my mother and me, crafted in the imagination of someone who wasn't there. As they go on, it becomes clear that my mother isn't coming back, and the tone of the stories changes. The authors speculate on why she did it, they dig up details from her life and childhood, they interview people who knew her. Never me, of course, and never my father or grandmother, who refused to speak to reporters. I've printed out all of those articles, but I don't like to read them. The facts may be correct, but they're fiction.

From out in the living room comes an enormous crash; I drop the scrapbook and race down the hall. The front door is swinging on its hinges, wind pouring inside. I poke my head out, but there's no one there. The sleet has stopped, and the cold air smells of wood smoke. The sun has dipped lower than the trees now, casting everything in slanted golden light.

I hear her, but she cannot hear me.

I haven't felt this aimless, flighty sense of anticipation in a long time. Something is coming; something is building, but I don't know what. Today feels upside down, crooked somehow.

An engine chugs in the distance, and a big blue Suburban comes lumbering up the road and turns into the driveway across the street. A tiny figure hops out. Iris Pells is a whisper in human form. She's barely five feet tall, she's got bird bones and fidgety fingers, and she doesn't make a lot of eye contact. Even her hair is whispery: it's white-blond and so fine it floats around her head when the air gets too dry.

"Hey!" I call. "How was genius club?"

I can't quite see her rolling her eyes from this far away, but I know she's doing it. "Super."

"Did you get my text?"

"Yes." She hefts open her garage door. "I'll be over in two seconds. Just have to feed the birds."

Iris runs a makeshift animal hospital in her garage, and people from all over town bring her sick and lost creatures when the real shelter is closed or won't take them. I knit blankets for Iris's foundlings: tiny sweaters for the shivering ones, nests for the birds, mother-shaped pillows for the babies.

Call her.

I shut the door and slump on the couch. There's something I'm supposed to understand here, something the letter writer thinks is obvious but isn't. There must be some way to call my mother that's not as literal as using a phone. But I don't have all the pieces to figure it out.

The door bangs open again, making my heartbeat skitter, but this time it's Iris, breathless and grinning. "Did you see this?" She holds her phone up. "The Northern Lights are coming. Tonight."

Again, that upside-down sensation, that fist-squeeze of anxiety weighted with nostalgia. The Northern Lights have never come this far south before. I haven't seen them since that night on the fjord. The night she called them down.

The night she *called* them down . . .

My skin tingles with possibility.

"There's a solar storm happening right now," continues Iris, reading off her screen. "The strongest one in over a hundred years. Apparently the lights could be visible as soon as it gets dark, and there's a ninety percent chance we'll see them over the Cape. How cool is—"

My face must look something like the tornado that's tearing through my brain, because Iris catches my hand and stands on tiptoes to peer into my eyes. "Are you okay, Eli?"

Call her.

The missing piece clicks.

The Northern Lights are coming, and I think I know what I have to do.

CHAPTER 3

Once upon a time, in a green house at the top of the world, there lived a girl and her mother. They spent every minute of every day together, from the time the girl woke and climbed into her mother's bed to the last moments of consciousness as she drifted away on stories and dreams. They watched the world through identical eyes the color of strong-brewed coffee, and sometimes it was hard to tell who saw what, where the girl ended and her mother began.

In summertime, they lay in fields of cotton grass, puffs of downy white brushing their faces. When it was dinnertime, the girl's mother would carry her home on her back, and the girl would lay her cheek on her swaying shoulder and watch the world drift. Sometimes it was hard to tell who was walking and who was carrying whom.

We're two branches of the same tree, her mother said. The girl had never seen a living tree; their island was too far north for them to grow. She thought of the Christmas trees that people set up each December, glowing with lights and decorated with tiny, beautiful things, and that seemed like a perfect way to describe her and her mother.

In wintertime, they waded through snow that was smooth as

cake frosting. The girl liked to step in her mother's footprints; she knew the exact size and shape that her boots made: medium-size with rounded edges, patterned with hundreds of diamond shapes. The girl's own boots made simple, horizontal lines. When she laid her lines over the diamonds, the shapes would twist and swirl. The diamonds became triangles and trapezoids, flowers and fish, stars, moons, and planets.

One late-winter day, the girl was following her mother's footprints home from the store. The snow was tinged blue from the twilit midday sky, and the prints were waves that made splashing sounds each time the girl stepped into them. The girl's canvas shopping bag bump-bumped against her back as she leapt from one tiny ocean to the next. Then the footprints ended at her mother, who had stopped to talk to an old woman at the corner of their road.

"Spare me some food," croaked the woman, pointing to the mother's bag full of groceries. The girl didn't know who this crone was, didn't understand why she hadn't flown south to be taken care of like all of the other old people. The mother pulled out a loaf of bread and gave it to the old woman, who turned her squinty eyes to the girl's small bag.

"And you?" Her dusty black dress smelled of mold, and her fingernails were filthy. The girl had only one thing in her bag: a packet of ginger cookies shaped like hearts. They had been her reward for behaving in the grocery store. The girl cast a quick glance at her mother, who nodded. She pulled out the packet, intending to give a cookie to the old woman, but the crone snatched the entire bag, ripped it open with her spindly fingers, and began cramming the hearts into her wrinkly mouth. The girl wondered how she could chew when she was missing so many teeth.

When she had eaten the entire packet of cookies, the crone pulled a lumpy handkerchief from her sleeve and wiped the crumbs from her mouth. She gave the empty paper bag to the girl and bent low. The sour reek of mildew made the girl's eyes water. The old woman snatched up a lock of the girl's long, brown hair, and the girl let out a yelp.

"Mamma," she said, but her mother stood immobile, keen interest flickering in her eyes. The girl wished desperately that her mother would pick her up or hold her hand, but she always chided her for feeling nervous in situations like this. *Nothing bad can happen as long as you're with me*, she would say.

Murmuring a low, haphazard song, the crone pulled a plain gold ring from a pocket in her dress, and she wound the girl's hair through it, around and around until it was firmly stuck. It burned cold against the girl's scalp.

"This will give you two wishes," she whispered. "Be careful how you use them."

The girl couldn't thank the woman because her voice had flown away, but she nodded. The old woman's back made a rusty creaking sound as she straightened up.

"I'm cold," she said. "Let me come to your house."

"We've given you enough," said the mother. "It's time for us to go now, and you may not come with us." She stepped between the old woman and her daughter, and the girl sagged with relief. Nothing bad could happen, after all. The old woman grumbled, but the mother picked up her daughter's hand and brought her close into the shelter of her body. "Goodbye," she said firmly.

Without another word, they began to walk toward the warm light of their house. The girl turned back to see if the old woman was watching, but she was gone.

CHAPTER 4

Pebbles ping the underside of Iris's truck as we follow the dirt road that winds through our neighborhood, tucked in a forest of stunted pines. Our houses and the Franklins', a few doors down, are the only other homes that are lived in year-round. The rest are summer cottages, silent and sleeping since the last of the autumn tourists trundled back over the bridge. My own red-shingled house is little more than a glorified summer cottage, but it's plenty of room for me and my dad.

"So what does the note say?" Iris asks.

I pull it out of my pocket and read the Norwegian, then the English, and she gives a little shudder. "Who do you think could have sent it?" she says.

"I have no idea."

Iris slows and we thump up onto the paved road that leads into town. "Is there a return address?"

"Nope. The postmark says it's from Norway, but there's a big sticker on the bottom that says the post office couldn't deliver it. Somehow it got to my house anyway."

Iris drums her fingers on the steering wheel. "Maybe somebody at the post office knows you and where you live? Or they looked you up."

"Possibly," I say. "But that still doesn't explain how it got to Wellfleet or why it ended up in my bush, not in the mailbox."

"Maybe your dad was carrying a bunch of mail and dropped it?" says Iris. "Maybe the wind blew it into the bush?"

When I was little, my mother told me stories about the North Wind. He was the strongest and fiercest of all the winds. Sometimes he helped people on their quests, flying them to faraway lands, or sometimes he brought them things they needed. But he was erratic and mercurial—there was no way of knowing who he'd help, or when or why.

"Maybe," I say.

Between this letter and the Northern Lights, it's too much of a coincidence. The person who wrote this letter knows something. And tonight I'm going to find out if they're right. Tucked in my bag is another book from the shelf above my desk. Blue and cloth-bound, it's full of stories that I wrote myself. Stories from my childhood on Svalbard. These stories are nonfiction. They're pieces of my heart made of paper and ink.

"Try not to worry about it," says Iris, even though that's impossible.

In late winter, Wellfleet is a ghost town. The setting sun washes everything in orange-pink as Iris's truck rumbles alongside the sloshing harbor, past gray-shingled houses and up toward Main Street. The engine clanks and clunks, and my heart lurches along with it. Belching out a cloud of exhaust, we pass the expensive grocery store all the summer people shop at, the closed-for-the-season ice cream parlors, the gift shops that sell straw hats and pastel paintings of dunes.

"Must you do that?" Iris inclines her head toward my knee, which has been jittering so hard it's squeaking the springs in my seat.

"Sorry." I tuck my hands under my legs, which stops the shaking but does nothing for my nerves. "Does it look like it's getting cloudy to you?"

"Not at all."

"Good." Because if there are clouds, it'll ruin everything. "It's been a strange day. First the letter, now maybe the lights. I have this itchy feeling, like anything could happen."

"Anything?" Iris flicks on her blinker and we turn away from the sunset and into the growing dark. "Like my superpowers will finally manifest and I'll be able to leap tall buildings in a single bound?"

Iris has a knack for pulling me back just as I'm about to spiral into self-absorption. "That must be it," I say with a reluctant smile.

"Or teleportation," she says wistfully. "That would solve all my problems."

"What problems?"

"Nothing." She fiddles with the silver hoop in her ear as we coast up to a red light. "What powers are you getting?"

"Time travel."

As we wait for the light to change, Iris keeps taking sharp little breaths like she's about to say something, but then doesn't. Finally, she swivels in her seat and lays her doll-size hand on my shaking knee. "Seriously, though. Why do you look like you're going to throw up?"

"I'm not, I'm just . . . distracted," I say. "I'm thinking about the story I'm going to tell you tonight."

I decided on this story because I don't know how else to explain what might happen. Iris needs to know the background in case my plan works, and if it doesn't work, then it was just a story. No harm done.

"A story under the Northern Lights," says Iris. "I love it. Where should we go? Newcomb Hollow?"

"Not a beach," I say. There's too much chance of running into other people. "How about the baseball field?"

"Perfect," she says, cutting a left that takes us farther still from town.

I unzip my bag and tuck the book inside the front of my coat, hunching my body around it. These stories are mine, and they're nothing like my mother's. Still, I've never read one of them aloud before.

Surrounded by deserted athletic fields, the baseball diamond is silent and boggy with mud puddles. Iris drives up over the curb, skirts around home plate, and stops beside first base. As she cuts the engine, darkness folds around us and cold seeps into the truck.

I'm not sure if I can do this, if I'm supposed to do this. I'm not sure if this wild beating in my chest is terror or elation or some combination of both. The sky is perfectly, emptily black. Moonless. No sign of the aurora yet. Clutching the lumpy front of my coat like it's a life vest, I climb out of the truck.

"These mittens are amazing," says Iris as we squelch across the half-frozen grass. "My hands are the only part of me that's not freezing right now."

"Glad you like them," I say. "Alpaca's one of the warmest natural fibers." I'm knitting her a matching hat, but she doesn't know that yet.

As Iris clambers up the bleachers, I pace the line between home plate and first base, trying to build up some momentum and courage. With shaking fingers, I unzip my coat and pull out the book.

Midway up the bleachers, Iris sits and tucks up her knees, which makes her look even more childlike than usual. "I'm ready for your story."

Am I?

It's not so much the telling of this story that scares me, but the reliving of it. Mud slurps under my heels as I rock back and forth a few times and then open the book. Chilly wind whispers around my face, urging me on. It's too dark to see the words, but I don't need to. I take a deep, night-scented breath and begin.

CHAPTER 5

Once upon a time, in a green house at the top of the world, a girl woke in the middle of the night. From her parents' room came thumps and bangs, drawers opening and cupboards closing. The mother's voice, fast and frantic. The father's, low and even. This was how it always went: her mother's words would grow sharp and piercing, and her father would grind them down with his slow, calm reasoning until they were dull again. But tonight, the ragged fear in her mother's voice crept over the girl's skin like insects.

The mother began to threaten; the girl heard her pacing like a caged tiger. She burrowed under the blankets, but the words knifed through the fabric. Still, the father's voice came soft and low, and the girl clung to his calmness like it was a rock in a churning ocean. Something crashed and shattered, and the girl slid under her bed, found a crack between the floorboards, and slipped inside it.

After minutes or days or months, the girl felt a tug on her toe. But she didn't want to hear any more, didn't want to leave her hiding spot. As her mother dragged her out, the girl became wild like a tiger too, with claws instead of fingernails.

The mother wiped three parallel threads of blood from her cheek.

"Come with me," she whispered as she slipped two pairs of woolen socks over the girl's feet. Long underwear, leg warmers, snowpants, sweater, fleece, coat, and two hats. The girl wanted to ask where they were going, but her tongue had turned to a fat slug in her mouth. As her mother turned to put on her own warm layers, the girl shuffled to the window and wiped a circle in the frosty glass.

The blizzard that had groaned and swarmed around their house all day was over, and fresh snow gleamed under the moon. A black-and-white muzzle appeared in the window, and its hot breath fogged up the other side of the pane.

"Mamma," the girl said, pointing.

The mother glanced at the window and nodded. "Let's go." Taking the girl's hand, she eased the door open and led her into the breathtaking cold.

On the steps stood the largest reindeer the girl had ever seen. The ones on her island were the size of goats, but this creature's shoulder was level with the top of her mother's head. The creature snorted and snuffled and bent its head low to look into the girl's face. When she saw the simple kindness in its brown eyes, she was no longer afraid. The girl let her mother lift her up onto the animal's back; she buried her red-and-white mittens in the shaggy fur around its neck. She felt her mother's arms wrap around her from behind, and the reindeer set off down the sleeping street.

The creature's loping stride grew wider as they reached the outskirts of town. From the hazy space between two buildings came a tiny silver flash, and the girl turned to look, but then it was gone.

The reindeer's run became a glide, and soon they were skimming across the surface of the snow faster than a bird in flight, then veering out onto the fjord, which was frozen solid. As they flew down the corridor of ice flanked by looming, jagged mountains, the sky began to fill with color and light. A long line of ectoplasmic green, its edges hinting at pink, wavered from one horizon to the other.

Finally, the reindeer slowed, its panting sides pressing into the girl's legs. Her mother helped her down, then reached up to stroke the animal's velvet nose.

"We'll go from here on foot," she said. But the girl didn't want to walk; she felt cold and afraid again now that the reindeer was leaving. She pulled off her mitten and stuck her fingers in her hair, searching for the wishing ring the old woman had given her. But before she could grasp it, her mother put the girl's mitten back on her hand, hoisted her onto her hip, and set out again.

This wasn't right, whatever was happening, wherever they were going. The girl had heard the dagger words her mother hurled at her father, even buried down between the cracks in the floor, and they filled her veins with cement. Things her mother had threatened to do, things that couldn't possibly be true. The girl shivered and tucked her face into the hollow of her mother's shoulder, tried to leach some comfort and warmth like she was a radiator. *Nothing bad can happen*, she thought. *Nothing bad*. But it was hard to make herself believe that. Through her mother's coat, she felt frenetic energy. Fear and guilt and fierce, furious love.

The Northern Lights had filled the night sky so completely that no black was visible. No stars, no moon. A million dazzling shades of emerald and amethyst, swirling so slowly that it felt like the earth was moving while they stood still. A whizzing, crackling static filled the air. The girl closed her eyes, but the green filtered through her eyelids, and still the colors drifted. For a long time, the only sound was the creaking of the mother's boots on the snow and the slow rhythm of their breathing.

Miles from nowhere and nothing, the mother stopped.

She dropped to her knees and pulled the girl tight to her chest. She buried her nose in the girl's hats and whispered her love. Then she tipped her head back and whistled at the sky. It wasn't a song; it was a call.

The wave of electric light curved down. The girl wanted to scream, but her breath was stuck. She clung to her mother's hand like she was drowning, but her mother's fingers squirmed. The girl's hair lifted off her shoulders; one of her hats slipped off and tumbled up into the streaming sky. The ring tied in her hair came loose, but it fell down instead of up. Frantic, she dropped to a crouch, ripped off her mittens, and dug her bare hands into the snow. The nail of her littlest finger caught the ring's metal edge.

"I wish for the lights to—"

Eyes wide, the mother gasped the girl's name as the lights swept her up. They took her. Mid-wish, the girl choked.

"—to—to go away," she stammered as her finger slid inside the ring.

As one, the lights in the sky winked out. They left the girl there, alone on the ice.

CHAPTER 6

Dead silence. Iris is staring at me, and I can't tell if she's spell-bound or horrified.

"Uh . . . the end," I say.

"What kind of ending was that?" Iris's voice almost reaches shouting volume as she leaps down the bleachers, her boots ring-ing on the metal. "What happened to the poor girl?"

She stood on the frozen fjord and cried until she had no voice left, but her mother never came down from the sky. The girl lives on Cape Cod now, with her father.

"I guess it's open to interpretation," I say.

An odd look drifts across Iris's face, like she's seeing me for the first time despite being my best friend since we were seven. As far as she's concerned, my mother abandoned me in a more tra-ditional way, though I've never elaborated on the specifics. Sort of like her dad, who we also don't talk about in too much detail. My mother always warned me not to tell people about the strange things that happened to us. People see what they want to see, she said, and there's usually a good reason for that.

"Look!" Iris points at something behind me, and I whirl around. Just above the tree line, the sky glows green. It all comes flooding back, even more vivid than when I was telling the story. I can smell my mother, feel the warmth of her breath through my hats. The stark Arctic cold on my cheeks.

Slowly, almost imperceptibly, the glow brightens and smears across the sky. The pieces are all fitting together.

I hear her, but she cannot hear me.

As a smokelike tendril of electric green unfurls, I strain for traces of her voice, her breath, her heartbeat. The air fills with the same tingly, static electricity I remember, and when I shut my eyes, my mother's face appears, more vivid than it's been in years. I can see her individual eyelashes, frosty with cold. Fear gusts up through my chest.

Call her.

I have to whistle those lights down. But there's no guarantee they won't sweep me away like they did my mother. I should have brought a rope and tethered myself to something, but it's too late now; the lights could vanish at any moment. This is my only chance.

Are you up there? The words form, soundless, on my lips. My need for her goes beyond anything rational or sane. It feels like my skin's peeling away, my nerve endings exposed and raw.

The whispery green aurora hovers straight over us now, and I'm scared it'll disappear, scared it'll stay, scared it'll snatch me away, scared nothing will happen and I'll just be standing here whistling at the sky. My throat is tight; my eyes stream chilly tears. There's a stone in my gut and a flapping moth in my chest, and this is it, this is it, this is it.

"Go stand over there and I'll take a picture of you." I nudge Iris gently toward the bleachers to keep her safe from what I'm about to do. It's almost impossible to resist the urge to scream or cry or run back to the truck, but I don't know how much longer these lights will last. It has to be now.

I suck in a breath, fill my lungs with the static air.

The first sound that comes from between my lips is almost inaudible. I rub my mouth on my sleeve and try again. This time it comes out shaky and warbling, but louder.

"I swear they're coming closer," murmurs Iris.

And maybe they are; maybe they're curling lower. I swallow, take another quick breath, and whistle. It's not even a song, just a note that wanders up and down a haphazard scale. Then my breath is gone and the note dies. In the silence, Iris's teeth chatter.

The wave in the sky pulses and leaps straight down.

My head lolls back; my hands stretch skyward. I haven't felt this dizzying blend of fear and elation and whispering magic since my mother disappeared. The air is full of magnets; it whistles and pops and hums, and even with my eyes shut I see the lights zapping gold and fuchsia and scarlet. My hair lifts up from my scalp, and a giddy laugh burbles up my throat.

Then everything goes black. The sky is empty.

I'm standing in a muddy baseball field.

Without her.

"Eli, can you talk to me?" Iris pours hot chocolate out of her thermos and folds a cup into my hands. I have no memory of walking back across the field, of getting into the truck. It didn't work. *It didn't work.* Blinking hard, I command my eyes to stop leaking but they're useless.

"I don't think so." It comes out as a squeak, and I hate myself even more for being so embarrassing. I hate that I can't tell her the exact truth, but it's better that I didn't. If I'd told Iris my mother was coming back from the sky and then she didn't, her pity and disbelief would have been unbearable.

My mother was right when she said we were two branches of the same tree. But we weren't just flimsy twigs that could snap off without causing any damage. We were a single trunk forking into two thick boughs, and when one of us broke off, when she flew away, there was barely enough left of me to survive. The gash she made was jagged and splintery and oozing sap. It cut all the way down to my roots, and it should have killed me.

Somehow, though, over years and years, the wound scarred and dried, and new bark grew to cover it. I learned how to balance myself without the weight of her, how to grow toward the patches of sun that only she could reach before. But the phantom sense of that missing limb never went away.

Iris swings her legs over the center console, crams herself into the footwell on my side of the truck, and sets my hot chocolate in the cup holder. She wraps both arms around me, rocks us both, and kisses my hair, and I'm sure her mother holds her exactly like this when she's upset. I'd give anything to have a mother like Iris's, even if she was always dragging me to garden shows and nagging me about dressing nicer. Iris's mother would never have taken her out on a frozen fjord at night and let herself get swept away.

"Did you write that story?" says Iris.

Before I can stop it, a sob lurches up my chest, and I'm bawling like a toddler, crying for my mother who's never given me a curfew, who's never taken me to a garden show, who hasn't let me sleep in her bed for ten years, who hasn't listened to my secrets. Who hasn't been anything to me for a decade. I can't believe I thought that letter meant anything. I can't believe how stupid I am.

Once I'm dried out and hot-faced and heaving, Iris hands me a wad of napkins. "That was a beautiful way to describe what happened to you." She pauses. "I mean, it was utterly horrible, but also beautiful. Does that make sense?"

I nod. She thinks it was an allegory for what happened, a metaphor for my mom going out for a loaf of bread and never coming back. Given how stupid I was about the Northern Lights just now, I'd rather she believe that.

Iris hands me another napkin and then climbs back into the driver's seat. "Did you ever set a date for that trip to Svalbard?"

I swab at my raw eyes and nose. "Not yet."

For my sixteenth birthday, my dad offered to buy me a plane ticket to Svalbard. He said there was no pressure and to let him know when I was ready to go. That was almost a year ago, and neither of us has mentioned it since.

"Doesn't he want to go back?" says Iris.

I lower my window to let the cold soothe my burning cheeks. "I think he's still a little . . . traumatized."

After they called off the search for my mother, my dad went out to look for her by himself. He lost half his toes and two fingers to frostbite before they finally dragged him back. He stayed in the hospital for several weeks, and I think when he lost those parts of himself, he lost something else too.

"Well, I think you should go." The engine chugs as Iris turns the key, then motions for me to put on my seat belt. "Maybe talk to your mom's family."

"Yeah. It's just . . . I don't know, I'm nervous."

"Why?"

Because despite having been born there, I can barely understand Norwegian anymore. I'm not who I used to be, but that's who everybody on Svalbard will expect. The Eline they used to know. The sweet little Norwegian girl who never raised her voice, never said anything rude or hurtful. Not the almost-grown, almost-American girl named Eli who broke and couldn't put herself back together in quite the same way and always says the wrong things. And although some of my memories of Svalbard are beautiful, many aren't. Some of them make my skin crawl.

"It's complicated," I say.

"Just because it's complicated doesn't mean you shouldn't think about it."

I roll my eyes. "Do you have to be so rational all the time?"

Iris flips on her blinker. "Yes."

As we rattle back through town, I hate that I'm still looking for my mother in the streets, on the sidewalks, in the shadowy shop fronts. I'm furious that I ever believed a sketchy note from a nameless stranger, furious that I still care this much about her when she's the one who left me.

A shadow moves between two parked cars. A tiny silver flash.

"Stop!" I yell, and Iris slams on the brakes, crushing us both into our seat belts.

"What?" she says, chest heaving. "Did we hit something?"

"No. Can you back up?" I point to the cars behind us. Throwing me a worried look, Iris shifts into reverse. I lower my window and switch on my phone's flashlight, but there's nothing between the two cars. Nothing on the sidewalk behind them. Nothing in the road.

"Sorry," I mumble, closing my window and slumping back. It was just another ridiculous delusion to add to tonight's list. Disappointment mixed with humiliation rolls over me, shoves me under for a long while, and then we're pulling up my driveway even though I could easily walk home from Iris's.

My dad's car still isn't back. I'd been hoping we could stay up and watch a movie together, even if he sat with his laptop open the whole time and only pretended to pay attention.

"Thank you," I say as I climb out of the truck, and it's for more than just dropping me off. I'm grateful to Iris for not asking any more questions about my story. And for giving me a nudge in a direction I don't want to think about but probably should.

"Come over if you need anything," she calls out her window as she backs out of the driveway. "I don't care what time it is. Wake me up."

I hate myself for checking the gap beside the steps for more letters, for crouching to peer among the roots of the holly bush, for scanning the sky, which is now full of silver pinprick stars. Although it felt like anything could happen today, nothing did.

A lump of white nestled in a tree's bare branches catches my eye. It moves, swiveling its head all the way around to peer at me. A snowy owl, its feathers practically glowing in the darkness. The bird watches me with unblinking eyes as I hold perfectly still, afraid even to breathe. Its claws scritch on the branch, and then it stretches its wings impossibly wide and takes off into the empty sky.

I can't help but feel the aching echo of my mother.

CHAPTER 7

Once upon a time, far from the green house at the top of the world, a girl stood alone on a frozen fjord under an empty night sky, clutching a ring that had turned from gleaming gold to dull silver.

"I wish for my mamma to come back!" she screamed until her voice was ragged, and even then, she screamed until the shreds of voice became threads and frayed to nothing. She tore the ring off her finger and hurled it onto the ice, as hard as her little body could throw.

A fist-size hole opened up, tunneled all the way down to the water underneath. The ring rolled down the tunnel and disappeared. With a soundless shriek, the girl shoved her hand inside the hole. Her shoulder went in, then her head, and down, down she slid.

Gray-blue light filtered through the ice above as the girl sank. A lumpy little fish swam up and stopped beside her face. Its body flashed silver, then muddy brown, then silver again. The fish opened its mouth so she could see all the way inside, and deep down in its belly was the ring. The girl's watery shout sent bubbles bumping up against the ice. She kicked off after the fish, but she was too slow in her winter clothes, and then it was gone and she realized she'd lost the hole she'd come down through. The ice was a vast continent overhead, and the girl was going to drown. Alone.

Tiny blue orbs began to glow around the girl's head. They sang a wordless lullaby, a sleeping song, a letting-go song. But the girl didn't want to let go. She wanted her mother. She pounded with her fists on the ice until the skin on her knuckles broke, and then she flipped upside down and kicked with her waterlogged boots. The lights swarmed closer, their music filling her ears and her sinuses and her eyes.

One final, convulsing kick. Both feet. Both fists.

The ice shattered.

The girl shoved her head into the air and gasped it down. The Northern Lights were gone, replaced by useless stars, and the girl had no strength left to climb up onto the ice. She dug her fingernails into the edge, hung there, and sobbed. All across the sky, the stars began to fall.

Hot, fishy breath blew down the back of the girl's neck. A wet mouth full of teeth closed around her shoulder and pulled her up onto the ice. She lay there, too destroyed to care that she was staring into the face of a polar bear ten times her size. The girl's heart was too broken to beat fast. She curled up fetal, just as she'd been inside her mother's body, and wished she could be there now. She wished to go back, back, back.

With a groaning sigh, the massive animal lay down beside the girl. It tucked its body around her—furry belly against fragile, shivering spine—and the lullaby wafted out of the water and into the still air. The girl closed her eyes. As she slept, the ice closed over the hole in the fjord.

CHAPTER 8

My bedroom door bangs open, crashes me awake. Cold gushes in, and snowflakes sprinkle my blanket. Grabbing my sweatshirt off the floor, I dash into the hallway, which is full of whirling snow, the carpet coated in white. My dad's snores rumble through his closed door as I steal past, toward the living room and the source of this wind.

The front door is wide open. I slide my bare feet into boots and step out into the night. Again, the upside-down sensation hits me, the otherworldly nostalgia. Snow covers the yard, but there's a clean line where it stops at the street and the perimeter of the property. As I make my way down the steps and the brick walkway, the wind stills and the snow slows to a gentle, sinking float.

A low, grunting hoot filters down through the trees. I hear the owl's feathers rustling, the scrape of its nails on bark, its breath puffing from its beak. Then it's silent; we're both silent. Waiting. For what I'm not sure.

"Eline."

A woman's whisper cuts through the snowy stillness. Every hair on my body goes rigid. In a cluster of leafless beech trees stands a figure. A tall woman, lean, with dark hair streaming over her shoulders and ghosting around her torso. A breath of wind sends the clouds tumbling away from the moon, and its silver light pours down over us.

It can't be her. It has to be her. I can't look. I can't not look.

The falling snow switches direction, begins to float up into the sky, the flakes like stars returning to the galaxy. I choke down my fear, let myself see this, accept what's happening. This thing I've waited for, imagined, dreamed. It's so overwhelming that it hurts.

The woman pauses, her angular face caught somewhere between joy and terror, and I'm sure mine looks the same.

"Mamma," I say.

She says something and looks at me like her heart is breaking to hear my answer, and my heart is breaking too because I can't understand my own mother.

"Sorry, I . . ." I don't know how to finish the sentence. Snow filters up onto my face, catching on my earlobes and chin. My mother frowns, and her disappointment hits me like a sledgehammer. "It's . . . it's just that we live here now," I stammer. "Dad and I do, I mean, and people only speak English."

And you left me, you left me. And after we gave up on looking for you and moved away, I didn't want to hear anything that sounded like you for a long time.

My mother drops her gaze. "It's fine if we speak English."

She used to speak English with my father, but never to me, not once, not even if the three of us were having a conversation together. Now that I'm hearing her with my American ears, she has almost no accent at all, just a slightly different cadence to her words. She holds out her hand, long fingers outstretched. The same fingers that wormed in my grip, that didn't keep me safe like she'd promised. All those years I spent longing for her to come back, and now that it's happening, I can't bring myself to take that hand.

Why did you do it? The words are caught in my throat. My mother takes a cautious step forward. She's wearing the same clothes she had on the night she flew away: a white cable-knit sweater with frayed cuffs and black weatherproof pants that gape at her knees and hips, though her coat is gone. There's something strange about her face, like I'm looking at a mirror reflection of her. Still the same, but everything is reversed, the eyes switched to opposite sides. Tiny leaves and twigs are caught in her dark hair, snow rings her nostrils, and her eyes are blacker than the deep brown I remember.

"How old are you?" she says.

"Seventeen in June."

Her hands flutter like moths; she traps one inside the other and pins it to her chest. "Ten years I was up there? How is that possible?"

"I . . . don't know."

"Where are we?" She's exactly on eye level with me now. The last time I saw her, she was carrying me. I don't want to look at her because she's pulling me in and I don't know if I want to be pulled. It's too much, too much. Invisible wisps of her curl around me, soft on my cheeks and light on my lips.

I scrub my face with the cuff of my sweatshirt. "We're in Wellfleet. Cape Cod. Massachusetts."

She makes a small *hmm* sound. "That's what the hook was."

"The hook?"

"I felt something pulling me down from the sky, and there was a little hook of land jutting out into the ocean and I wanted very badly to go there."

"Cape Cod," I say. "It's shaped like a hook."

She nods. "Your father used to show me with his arm how it was shaped." She holds up her own arm in a muscle-flexing pose. "A story floated up to me, about a woman and a girl and a reindeer. And it all started coming back. That night when . . ." My mother's moth fingers flutter again, landing over her mouth.

That night when you abandoned me.

"Then there was a sharp wave of sound," she continues. "It pierced right through . . . whatever I was when I was up past the sky, and it grabbed me and I started to fall. I fell and I fell and I had a body again and it was burning up."

With a shiver, I hold my hand out, palm down, and snowflakes patter against it. The thought of her burning up makes me queasy, though she seems perfectly intact now, if a bit . . . strange.

"Someone whose name starts with an *M* sent me a letter about you," I say. "Do you know who it is?"

"A letter?"

"Yeah, I . . . found it in the bush." I don't know why this feels like a strange detail to reveal, considering the strangeness of everything right now.

She screws up her face. "Everything's so foggy still. What did it say?"

"It said '*Moren din . . . er nær . . .*'"

Her dark eyebrows arc at my awkward pronunciation, and shame burns my cheeks. I switch to English. "'I can hear her, but she cannot hear me. You need to try. Call her.' So I did. I waited for the Northern Lights and I whistled, and you came."

My mother's breath hisses in. "You whistled?"

"Yes. After I read a story I wrote about the night you . . . left."

Her brow creases. "Eli, that was very dangerous."

"Lots of things are dangerous. But I'm fine. Nothing happened." I glance at her too-dark eyes and shift half a step backward. "To me, anyway."

We're supposed to hug now. We're supposed to cry and cling to each other and be so incredibly happy to be together after all this time. My mother keeps moving forward like she might want that to happen, but there's worry in her eyes. And even though this is everything, everything I dreamed of for ten years, I don't think I want to hug her. There's something about this mirror-image-her that frightens me. I wasn't expecting to be afraid.

"Aren't you even sorry?" I blurt out.

The lamp in front of the house flicks on, and we both cringe away from the flooding light. My mother looks gaunt under the yellow glare.

"Eli?" My dad's sleep-slurred voice floats through the open door. "Are you out there?"

In the cone of lamplight, the snow soars up, up, up.

"I forgot something in my car," I call. "Be right back."

He mutters something and is gone. When I turn back to my mother, she's gone too.

"Mamma?" I whisper.

"Here." Her voice slides out from behind a beech tree. Up wafts the snow, whirling and dancing in a cloudless, starry sky. This is all too much, too much at once. Wrapping my arms around my middle, I peer into the shadows. "Do you want to come inside?"

"Not yet."

"Why?"

She leans her tired face against the tree's bark and sighs. "I can't face him."

The snow's upward drift makes me feel like I'm sinking. "But you can face me?"

"Yes. It's always been easier with us, hasn't it?"

Again, I feel her pull, the invisible threads I thought had snapped years ago. "Where will you sleep?"

A wisp of her long hair wraps around the trunk of the tree. "I'll stay out here."

"Just . . . there? Behind the tree?"

Her laugh brings back whispers of the soft mother I remember—the safe, calm one. Steaming cups of cocoa at our old kitchen table, flannel pajamas, flushed cheeks.

"Hang on." I slip into the house, pull the knitted afghan and a throw pillow from the couch, and switch off the outdoor light. As I sneak down the front steps and into the powdered-sugar snow, I wonder if she'll still be there. If she was ever there. But that long wisp of hair is still clinging to the tree, and as I draw closer, her face appears, pinched with sorrow.

"I didn't answer your question," she says. "I am utterly devastated by what happened."

An ember sparks in my chest, and I cup my hands over it. It could warm me or burn me to ashes, save me or kill me. I'm afraid she can feel it too.

"This way," I say, leading her around the back of the house and into the woods. The trees gather around us, their branches clacking and groaning in the cold. At the foot of an old oak, I stop and point to a platform six feet above the ground. On top sits a crooked shack made of nailed-together boards and shingles. Against the tree rests a ladder that Iris and I borrowed from her mother and never returned.

"You can sleep up there," I say. "Sorry, it won't be very warm."

"It will be perfect." My mother reaches for my cheek, but she must see the fear in my face, because her hand switches direction a hairbreadth away. With an awkward cough, I hold out the pillow and blanket, which she accepts. From above the tree house comes the owl's soft, looping call.

"Will you promise not to tell your father until I'm ready?" she says.

It doesn't feel right, not after all the years he's taken care of me, all the time he's ached for her too, but I can't refuse her, not after she came back from the sky.

"I promise."

"Thank you," she says, and there's more than that in her expression.

"Good night, Mamma," I say, backing away from the tree house. I can't handle any more of tonight. My brain feels like it might be dissolving.

"Good night, Eline." Tucking the blanket and pillow under her arm, she climbs the ladder. The wind sings through the bone-bare trees and slips inside the neck of my sweatshirt. With a shiver, I turn and run back through the woods.

CHAPTER 9

Once upon a time, in a green house at the top of the world, before any of their troubles had begun, a girl and her mother sat at their kitchen table. The mother was reading the girl's favorite story aloud: the tale of a brave young woman who agreed to marry a huge white bear in order to save her family from poverty. The young woman climbed onto the bear's shaggy back, and he carried her to his castle in the far, far north.

As the mother read, the girl's father wandered into the kitchen in his coat and socks. He kissed his wife and daughter on the tops of their heads, then stepped into his boots and left. The mother gave the girl a conspiring wink and continued reading.

The brave young woman was lonely during her days in the castle, but every night a man came to lie beside her in bed, though she never saw his face because he disappeared by daybreak. The young woman became increasingly curious, and one night she fetched a bit of candle stump and shone its light on the sleeping man's face. He was the most beautiful thing she'd ever seen, and as she leaned over to kiss him, drops of wax fell onto his chest and he woke.

The little girl always gasped at this part of the story, at the fact that such a tiny, clumsy mistake could have such grave consequences.

The handsome young man revealed that he was a prince under the spell of a wicked sorceress, cursed to live his days as a bear and his nights as a man. But now that the young woman had uncovered the truth, he must go away to the sorceress's castle, which lay east of the sun and west of the moon. He disappeared in a blink, and so did his castle. The brave young woman was alone.

"But she will find him," whispered the little girl, and the mother smiled.

"As the young woman journeyed, she met three old crones," said the mother. "Each one gave her a gift: a golden apple, a golden carding comb, and a golden spinning wheel—"

"And then she rode on the North Wind's back!" cried the girl.

The mother tutted. "You're rushing, just like the wind yourself. First the girl visited the East Wind, and he carried her as far as he could, but he couldn't reach the place that was east of the sun and west of the moon. Nor could the West Wind or the South Wind. But the South Wind took her to his brother, the North Wind, who was the strongest and the fiercest, and when she knocked on his door, he called out—"

"BLAST YOU BOTH!" bellowed the little girl in her deepest voice. "WHAT DO YOU WANT?"

Both mother and daughter burst out laughing, and the pages of the book fluttered and flipped as the mother let go of it to clutch her stomach.

"Can we?" said the little girl.

The mother crept to the front door and peered into the street. There were certain things they could only do when the father was out. Things he didn't understand or want to see. With a quick nod, she picked up the book, and she and her daughter slipped into their shoes and coats. Past the rows of candy-colored houses they dashed, the summer sun beaming down like a smile, until they reached a quiet spot full of cotton grass and breeze.

The mother opened the book again. "'Aren't you afraid?' asked the North Wind, and the young woman cried out, 'No!'"

Arms outstretched, the little girl leaned into the gathering wind. "I'm not afraid either!"

"'Well then, you may ride on my back,' said the North Wind, and he puffed himself up until he was massive and ferocious, and still the young woman was not afraid, for she knew what needed to be done."

As the mother continued to read—as the young woman in the story journeyed east of the sun and west of the moon, used the gifts given to her by the crones, and rescued her true love—the little girl sank backward and let the wind catch her up. She squealed as it swooped her softly along, her shoes trailing over the fluffy tops of the cotton grass flowers.

The mother kept one eye on the book and one eye on her daughter, making sure that the wind didn't get carried away—or carry her away. Once the story was finished, she closed the book, and the girl landed in a gentle heap on the ground.

"More, Mamma!" she pleaded. "Please!"

"That's enough for now," said her mother, for she knew it wasn't safe to let these things go too far. "Let's go home and make some stew for when your father gets home."

"Thank you, wind," whispered the girl as they walked back toward their house.

The wind tickled her cheek with a strand of her hair and blew away into the sky.

CHAPTER 10

In the morning I find my dad sitting at the kitchen table with his laptop and an empty plate. Scribbled-on drafts of his latest scientific paper lie scattered all over the table. He's wearing one of his seven identical Wellfleet Oceanographic Institute T-shirts, and the computer screen casts a bluish glow on his shaved head. Even with the pinky and ring fingers of his left hand gone, he's typing nine hundred miles an hour.

"Look at this." He holds up a shiny, pockmarked rock, his eyes still locked on his screen. "Found it when I went to get the paper. It cracked the whole front step where it landed." He turns his computer so I can see a photo of a black stone just like it. The caption says IRON METEORITE.

It's not the only thing that fell out of the sky last night. My secret feels like a giant flashing neon sign on top of my head. I haven't checked for my mother yet this morning, but I feel the threads of her.

"Pretty cool, huh?" My dad twirls the stone between his fingers. "Most of these things don't survive their trip through the earth's atmosphere." He glances up. "You cold?"

I rub the goose bumps off my arms. "A little."

Even though all the snow was gone when I woke up, the temperature has dropped twenty degrees since yesterday. The wind is moaning and howling around the house like it wants to get in.

The toaster dings, and while my dad busies himself getting out butter and jam, I slide into the chair beside his and run my finger over the stone. It's the temperature of ice.

She's back, she's back, she's back. My mouth forms the words that I'm not allowed to say.

"Let go, for crying out loud." My dad jiggles the toaster handle, slams it up and down, but it won't release his bread. He tips the machine sideways, scattering black crumbs everywhere. No toast. With an annoyed grunt, he yanks out the plug and fishes out a charred slice of bread with his butter knife. A wisp of smoke trails out, curling in on itself as it wafts toward the ceiling.

She's back, she's back, but it's not like I expected, and I'm afraid.

"Did you catch the light show last night?" His tone is falsely casual.

"Uh, no." I duck my head and pretend to be examining the meteorite. "Iris and I went to a movie and we missed it."

He pulls open the junk drawer and rummages until he finds a screwdriver. "I hadn't seen the aurora since we were on Svalbard."

My dad never believed my story of what happened the night my mother disappeared. He said I had a false memory—apparently that's common when children experience traumatic events. Not that he's an expert in psychology, just in rationality. My father needs facts to support every hypothesis, and his facts told him that my mother took me out onto a frozen fjord, left me, and then disappeared. She must have fallen through the ice, he said, or slipped inside a glacier or gotten lost in the mountains.

With a sigh, he sets the screwdriver beside the toaster and gazes into the space above my head. "I dreamed about her last night."

My earlobes start to tingle. "About Mamma?"

He nods slowly. "I thought she was in bed with me for a second. I could have sworn the mattress was sinking under her weight."

"Maybe she was—" I begin, but my dad snaps out of his daze and snatches up the screwdriver.

"Classic case of sleep paralysis." He jams the screwdriver into the back panel of the toaster, less than an inch from his remaining fingers, and I cringe. "It's a mental state somewhere between consciousness and unconsciousness. People think they're awake and there's a ghost or a demon in their room. They swear up and down that it really happened."

But it wasn't a ghost or a demon. It was her. I squeeze the meteorite until its cold little edges dig into my palm.

"Guess I should lay off the chili before bed." My dad scoffs and twists the screwdriver until the panel pops off. Though the toaster is unplugged, the coils inside are still bright orange. He waves away the little curls of smoke and peers into the machinery. "Looks like this thing is shorting out. You'd better have cereal."

I set the meteorite down and push my chair back. "Actually, I'm not that hungry."

"Take a banana for later." His broad shoulders hunch as he leans over the toaster, which is now emitting a low, rattling buzz.

"Okay." I pull a banana and an apple out of the jumble in the fruit bowl. "See you tonight."

He mumbles something resembling goodbye as the toaster fizzles and smokes.

The front steps of our house have been cracked nearly in half. A narrow gap runs all the way down to the dirt underneath, and I shudder to think what might have happened if a person had been standing there when the meteorite fell. There's nothing inside the crack, and no letter beside the holly bush. I'd been hoping that M would write again and tell me what to do next.

The wind dances around me, tossing wisps of my hair as I follow the haphazard path that leads into the woods. A frost covers the tree-house roof, making the edges sparkle in the sunlight. I'm not tall enough to see inside the dark doorway and I don't want to climb up, not yet. In a hole in the tree trunk just above the roof, something stirs. The snowy owl ruffles its feathers and fixes its steady, yellow gaze on me. "Is she still there?" I whisper.

It bobs its head twice, then tucks its beak into its chest and closes its eyes. I could wake her, but there's something reassuring about the fact that she's here and I don't have to say anything. She must be exhausted. I'll let her sleep, and hopefully by this afternoon, I'll have figured out how to act around her. Sliding my foot onto the ladder's lowest rung, I hoist myself up just long enough to set a green apple on the edge of the platform. Then I slip back through the woods, heading for my car.

CHAPTER 11

It's snowing in Sophia Hernandez's locker, and she's too busy trying to get her hat back from Kevin Thompson to notice. I peer around the edge of my own locker door as the two of them scuffle, Sophia giggling and swiping at the pink pompom beanie that Kevin's holding just out of her reach. Meanwhile, specks of white whirl in the narrow metal space, coating her textbooks and papers. Sophia finally manages to grab her hat, swats Kevin in the face with it, and slams her locker shut. I close mine too, then drift down the mob-scene hallway toward English class.

If I have to look at one more person's pictures of the Northern Lights this morning, I might cry. It's all anybody's talking about, it's all over the news, it's the greatest light show ever seen in New England. In Mr. Frome's classroom, I find a desk in the back corner and pull out my phone.

Silje Lund Longyearbyen

The same old photos of her appear, the same archived articles. I didn't expect to find anything new—it's not like she'll have joined any social media sites since last night—but it feels like the internet should know more. There should be something I can type into this little box that will help me understand, but I'm fairly sure

I'm the only person on the planet who's ever dealt with this situation. There are no online support groups for girls whose mothers unexpectedly returned from the sky.

Mr. Frome bangs into the classroom, smelling of leathery-sweet pipe tobacco. Mercifully, he says nothing about last night, just asks everyone to open their copies of *A Separate Peace* to page forty-nine. With my book propped up like a screen, I set my chin on my folded arms and hide from the world.

I am utterly devastated by what happened, she said. It's like something a newscaster would say after a natural disaster. The region was utterly devastated by the earthquake.

Unexpectedly, *I* am devastated by the avalanche of jumbled feelings that hit me when she came back. In all those years of dreaming about her return, imagining exactly how it would happen, I pictured myself as a six-year-old fitting into the curves and hollows of her body. Not my awkward, itchy, mostly grown self. I expected to feel more like her daughter. It's strange to be the same size as her, and it's unsettling to see the uncertainty in her face that was never there before. She was always in charge of us, and now she's waiting for me to decide what happens next. I don't know what's supposed to happen next.

I should have hugged her, though.

The bell rings, and the rushing swarm of students pulls me along toward the cafeteria. Maybe I'll just stay at school forever. I'll make myself a fort in the drama club's costume closet, pile up bins and boots and bolts of fabric and props, and eat food from the vending machines and never have to figure out what to do about my mother.

Eline.

I feel the word fizz in my head rather than hear it, and I jolt to a stop. Everyone around me keeps swarming, jostling my backpack and bumping my arms.

From somewhere in the crowd comes a tiny flash of silver. A long, dark cloak swishes, heading away down the hall. All of the sound around me goes syrupy and muted. I can't see a face, but I keep catching glimpses of an embroidered hem trailing on the floor, lost in a jumble of sneakers and boots.

"Hey," I call, weaving through the chaos as quickly as I can.

A gust of wind whistles down the hallway, and three lockers bang open in quick succession. Nobody notices but me. I start to jog, nudging people out of the way and muttering apologies. Away swishes the cloak, and an eerie laugh cuts through the clanging din.

"Stop," I whisper, but it doesn't and I'm not sure I want it to.

We round a bend, spilling into the wide corridor by the principal's office, and the crowd begins to thin. Bells ring and people disappear into classrooms, down other halls, into the gym and the cafeteria and out into the parking lot. Then the hall is empty.

I stand, blinking in the silent fluorescence. The person in the cloak is gone.

CHAPTER 12

Iris sits at our usual table in the cafeteria, hunched over her phone, and I hope she's not looking at photos of the lights because I really will cry if I see another one. She doesn't look up, doesn't even move until I drop my tray of spaghetti and wilted salad on the table, and then she almost falls off her stool.

"Eli!" she gasps, sliding the phone inside the wide cuff of her sweater. "You never texted me back. Are you feeling better today?"

"Yes," I lie. "Sorry I didn't write back."

More than anything, I want to tell her what happened last night. Even though I promised not to tell my dad about my mother, I never said anything about my friends. This is too massive to not share with Iris, and maybe there's a way I could explain without giving her specific details. I shuffle through the words in my head, searching for the right combination. Another story, perhaps.

"So, I was thinking," says Iris, slipping her phone from her sleeve into her bag and zipping it shut. "We should try sitting at a new table today. Branch out a little."

"Are you serious?" Iris never talks to other people unless it's strictly essential.

"We're like hermits. Let's go sit with Maisie Maddigan for a change." She inclines her head at the long, noisy table full of drama kids.

I tuck my ankle around the leg of my stool. "But you hate Maisie."

"Of course I don't hate her." Iris lets out a nervous laugh. "I just don't know why she speaks with a British accent when she's from Marshfield. But she's not that bad. And it's probably not healthy for me and you to be so codependent all the time. What if one of us got sick or had to go away or something?"

I narrow my eyes. "What do you mean, go away?"

"Nothing. Just come on," she says, heading across the cafeteria. This is so utterly unlike Iris that I'm more fascinated than annoyed. Gathering up my tray and bag, I follow her.

Surrounded by chattering chaos, Maisie looks up from her silver container of kiwi slices and beams at us. She's wearing a purple velvet Victorian-style jacket that she sewed herself. Maisie takes her role as the school's costume designer very seriously— co–costume designer with me, that is. A monocle dangles from a silver chain around her neck.

"Darlings!" she cries, and I can feel Iris cringing beside me. Maisie drags over two empty stools from a nearby table and squeezes them in on either side of her. "I'm so glad you popped over. We need a plan of attack for the fur on those god-awful wolf costumes."

A draft slithers up the back of my neck. I scan the cafeteria, searching among the tables for a glimpse of that cloaked person I saw in the hall. Straining my ears for that whisper that spoke my name . . . if it can even be called a whisper. On Maisie's other side,

Iris is absorbed in her phone again, her wispy blond eyebrows creased with worry.

". . . but that should be the last of it," Maisie is saying. "Worst-case scenario, we can split them up and take them home."

"Okay." I'm not sure exactly what I'm agreeing to, but it doesn't matter. Iris is still focused on her phone, lips moving silently, and I want to ask her what's wrong, why she dragged us over here in an effort to be more social but is now ignoring everybody.

"As I was saying." Maisie leans forward to block my view of Iris. "We should also think about—"

There.

A cloaked figure stands alone in the back corner of the cafeteria. Tall and slim, with their head dropped low so the hood covers their face. Nobody's looking at them; nobody seems to care that there's a stranger lurking here while we all eat our lunches. Slowly, the figure's head lifts, and from deep inside the hood comes a silver flash.

I'm halfway out of my seat when a thunderous bang sends me reeling backward. The emergency exit doors have flown open. Napkins and paper wrappers soar off the tables, caught and swirling. People are jumping up, yelling, chasing their tumbling lunches, but as the pandemonium grows, my body stills and the noise fades to a dull hum. A single, unfolded napkin flutters up, up, up toward the ceiling.

"Poppet, are you all right?"

I don't understand why Maisie is looming over me. Then I realize I'm sitting on the floor, surrounded by napkins and trash. As she and Iris take my elbows and help me upright, I notice a french fry caught in the pocket of her jacket.

"Did I fall?" I say.

"You stood up and then just sort of . . . sat down on the floor." says Iris.

"I didn't eat breakfast," I say, like that explains anything.

She turns to Maisie. "Can you keep an eye on her while I go get a Coke?"

Maisie helps me onto my chair like I'm a frail old person while Iris hurries over to the lunch line, where perplexed ladies in hairnets are leaning over the counters. The exit doors are shut now, the wind is gone, and Mrs. Janowski is waving her arms and shouting at everyone to help clean up the mess.

The figure in the cloak is gone. It's colder in the cafeteria now, and conversations are hushed. Maisie picks a wayward straw wrapper out of my hair and presses two fingers to the inside of my wrist.

"Are you taking my *pulse*?" I say.

"Shh." She points to the clock over the lunch line and holds up a finger every time I try to talk until the second hand makes half a revolution. "Thirty-three, thirty-four . . ."

Iris's phone lies forgotten on the table, its screen still lit.

"Forty-one, forty-two. Hey, don't move," warns Maisie as I reach for it.

Leaving my right arm with her, I stretch out my left and slide the phone closer. The screen's beaming so bright, it's like it wants me to look. Over in the cafeteria line, Iris is arguing with the lunch lady for some reason.

"Bloody hell, I lost count again," says Maisie. "Will you please hold still?"

I scroll to the top of the message on Iris's screen.

Dear Ms. Pells,

*We are pleased to welcome you as a member of the
Dickinson School . . .*

"Dickinson School?" I mutter. It's not a place I've ever heard of. I know I shouldn't be reading Iris's email, but my finger scrolls down, down, down anyway. The message talks about character and merit and the importance of hard work, and it makes no sense whatsoever. Even if the Dickinson School were a college, we won't start applying to those until next year. Iris and I still have more than a year left together. And there's a good chance we might both go to college in Boston. Iris is a million times smarter than I am, but we could still see each other if we went to different schools in the same city.

We look forward to welcoming you to Amherst this fall, says the final line of the email.

I set the phone down carefully like it's poisonous and rub my eyes hard, wishing I could unsee everything.

A can plunks down beside me. "They can't sell soda during school hours," says Iris. "The lunch lady said apple juice would work, but if it doesn't, I'll go back." Her brow furrows as she picks up her phone. "Why is this . . ." She trails off as she sees the email that's still on the screen. "Oh, Eli. Oh, shit."

"Sorry, I shouldn't have been reading that." I start piling napkins and random trash onto my lunch tray, but there's such an enormous mess everywhere and I just want a trapdoor to swing open and swallow me away forever.

"No, it's fine." Iris's voice is small and quavering. "I was going to tell you."

"What's the Dickinson School?" I want her to tell me it's spam, it's a joke, it's some random program that invited her to join and there's no way she'd actually do it. But I saw the worry in her eyes earlier. She wouldn't be worried if it didn't mean something.

Iris catches my sleeve. "Let's go somewhere quiet so we can talk."

I don't want to go somewhere and talk about this like it's something rational we can form words and sentences about. I don't want to know what's going on if it means Iris is leaving me *this* fall. It's all too much, too much after everything that's happened in the past twenty-four hours. My hearing is starting to fade out again.

"My cousin went to the Dickinson School," says Maisie, but I don't want to hear it, don't want to acknowledge that it's a real place. Leaving my tray, I grab my bag and run out into the hall, and I don't stop until I'm in the parking lot.

The darkening sky sags with the weight of unreleased rain, and the wind is working up to gale force. Halfway across the lot, I have to stop and bend over, hands on knees, because I can't breathe. It's not the running that's killing me; it's the betrayal.

"Hey!" Iris staggers up to me, one arm inside her coat and the rest of it flapping behind like a broken wing. "Eli, please talk to me."

"Why didn't you tell me?" I say through gasping breaths.

Iris struggles with the other sleeve of her coat, but it's inside out. "Because I haven't decided yet if I'm going."

A fat drop of rain splats onto my nose and I wipe it off. "What even is the Dickinson School?"

"It's for high school kids who want to start college early," says Iris. "I've been so bored here, Eli."

I know she's bored, but we have plenty of AP classes here. Those are college-level. Not that they're exactly difficult for Iris. The wind falls away, like it's taking a deep breath. Then with a huge gust, it spits sideways splinters of rain all over us. Neither of us moves.

"And you would live there?" I say. "In Amherst?" It's over three hours away. My dad will never let me drive that far by myself.

Iris zips up her coat and hunches inside it. "If I decide to go. There are a couple of other places I applied to."

There are more than one. She really does mean to leave me. On any other day, I might have been able to handle this news more gracefully. I might have tried to remember that Iris is wasting her time going to high school when her brain is light-years ahead of everybody else's. On any other day, I would have tried to be happy for her, to figure out how to make this work.

But not the day after my mother fell from the sky.

Sudden, irrational fury bubbles up through my insides, molten and steaming. Poisonous words form on my tongue, words I'll hate myself for if I let them out. I bite my lips together and unlock my car.

"I'm so, so sorry," Iris says as I climb inside. "But listen, there's—"

I shut my door and she stands there in the pelting rain, not bothering to pull up her hood as I reverse out of my parking space. I don't look back as I head for the exit and then veer out onto the road. The wind is heaving now, hurling sheets of water at my windshield. My speed keeps wavering between crawling and careening, and I can't seem to pull anything together. I should go back and tell Iris everything, explain that it's not just her—it's everything at once and I'm falling apart. But I can't do it. She must have applied to that school months ago and kept it a secret all this time.

As I pull onto a back road lined with scrubby oak trees, the car wobbles across the center line and I tug it back into the lane. Between the rain and my streaming eyes, I can barely see the edges of the street. It wouldn't matter if I went back to Iris anyway. She'd never understand what's happened. No one can help me.

Something lurches out into the road. I cut the wheel hard, and the car skids and spins. For what feels like a lifetime inside one second, everything goes silent and slow and surreal. Then the car stops, facing the wrong way on the wrong side of the road. Once I'm able to pry my hands off the steering wheel, I throw the door open. A figure huddles in the ditch on the opposite side of the road.

If I've hit a person, if I've killed somebody, I don't know what I'll do. There's nothing but woods for this whole stretch of road, no cars in sight. Leaving my engine running, I dash into the road.

The huddled shape twitches, and I freeze in the middle of the street, not daring to blink. Slowly unfolding its long limbs, the figure stands and shakes out its long cloak. As it pulls off its hood, all the breath goes out of me.

The girl's face is striking, with silver eyes and rosy lips. Her corn-silk hair is braided and coiled on top of her head, and a thin circle of gold gleams among the braids.

"Are you all right?" I say. "Did I hit you?"

She licks her lips, her pale face glowing with delight, and

climbs out of the ditch. Her cloak isn't muddy—it doesn't even look wet.

"Why are you crying?" Her voice is gritty as ashes.

"It's nothing," I say.

"What could you possibly have to cry about?" Her empty silver eyes bore into mine, making me feel exposed. Like she already knows the answer and just wants me to say it.

"My best friend is moving away," I say.

She drifts closer, her feet invisible under the cloak. "Of course she is. Everyone leaves you, Eline."

My mouth drops open. I can't comprehend the level of ugliness it takes to say something like that out loud.

The girl smiles, teeth flashing like broken glass. "But that isn't a bad thing. Good riddance to all of them."

Dread washes through my gut. "How do you know my name? Were you the one who sent that letter?"

She shakes her head. "Don't you remember us?"

I peer into the trees behind her, up the street in both directions, but there's no one else here. There's nobody to help me, nobody to witness this whole disturbing, nonsensical interaction.

"I have no idea who you are."

But maybe that's not exactly true. Maybe it's more that I don't *want* to have any idea who she is. I keep edging backward until my legs hit the fender of my car. "Leave me alone. Don't come to my school again. I don't want anything to do with you."

The girl lets out a sandpaper laugh that sets my teeth on edge. Without waiting for her answer, I get back in my car, lock all the doors, and hit the gas.

CHAPTER 13

Once upon a time, in a green house at the top of the world, a girl woke shivering, with burning eyes and a head that felt like a fried egg. Her mother felt her forehead and sighed.

"We'll stay home today," she said.

The girl began to cry because they were supposed to go see a puppet show and she'd been thinking about nothing else for the past three days.

"It's all right," said her mother, sweeping her up, blankets and all, and carrying her to the living room. "Make yourself comfortable and we'll have our own puppet show."

The girl's body was too full of aches and groans to get comfortable, but she tucked herself under her blankets on the sofa. Her mother made her a cup of bitter tea that warmed her stomach but nowhere else. As the girl sipped and shivered, her mother swished around the room, stoking the fire in the fireplace until it roared and threw out a wall of hot air. She stretched a sheet flat between two chairs so that the fire cast its orange-gold light on it like a screen, and then she sat beside the girl and opened a book.

The shadows on the flickering sheet began to swirl, then form into images. A silhouette of a woman wearing a crown sat on the ground, sobbing for babies she could not have. A crooked old woman appeared, holding a two-handled cup.

"Put this upside down in your garden." The old woman's voice creaked out through the snaps and crackles of the fire. "Tomorrow at sunrise, you will find two flowers underneath, one red and one white. Choose one and eat it, but only one—or you will be sorry!"

The queen took the cup, her movements jerky and puppet-like, and the shadows swirled and danced and covered the entire sheet in glowing red. Then they cleared, and two vines wormed out from either side, twisting and writhing. A bud appeared on the end of each vine, then opened into a blossom. A dainty hand reached down and plucked one, and the sounds of chewing and swallowing crackled out from the fire. A groan and a sigh, and the hand snatched the other flower as well, and the sounds of gulping and smacking filled the room.

"Oh no," gasped the little girl.

"She's going to be sorry," said her mother with a smile.

The vines withered and shrank, and the queen appeared, lying in a bed. She gave a sharp cry, and a tiny bundle emerged from between her legs. It wailed, and a nursemaid picked it up.

"A boy!" she cried, and handed the bundle to the queen. But the queen gave another scream, and out came another bundle from between her legs. This one grew longer and longer, unfurling until it was larger than she. The nursemaid screamed as the serpent grew horns and opened its sharp-toothed mouth.

A man appeared with a pointed hat. He wrestled the writhing creature into a sack and disappeared. On the bed, the queen held her baby and crooned a lullaby.

"That's the same song you always sing to me," said the girl. Her mother nodded and pointed to the screen.

The baby grew into a man. He mounted a prancing horse and called to his parents, who sat on their thrones: "I am off to find a bride!"

The girl squirmed. "Isn't the queen going to be sorry?"

"Just watch," murmured her mother, transfixed by the jumpy images.

The horse trotted across the screen and reared up on its hind legs. From the bottom corner, a creature came slithering, with a wide mouth and rows of pointed teeth.

"It's Prince Lindworm," whispered the mother.

"A bride for me before a bride for you." The lindworm's voice was cinders and knives.

The prince tried to skirt around the lindworm, but it grew longer and fatter, blocking every direction but the one he'd come from. With a huff, the prince wheeled his horse around and disappeared. Grunting and laughing, the lindworm coiled itself up and waited.

Crack, crackle, went the fireplace. *Blink, blink, snick*, went the lindworm's glowing eyes.

The king and queen appeared. Between them they held a willowy girl with a long veil trailing behind her.

"Do you, Prince Lindworm, take this princess to be your bride?" said the king.

"I do," snarled the lindworm, and the queen pushed the girl forward and then dashed away with the king. The lindworm opened its mouth wide, wider, widest. The princess moaned and cowered and pleaded.

Snap.

The princess disappeared into the lindworm's gulping mouth. Drops of black blood flew off the screen and onto the blanket covering the girl and her mother. The girl screamed.

The door flew open, and the girl's father appeared in a cloud of snow, wearing a heavy coat and an earflap hat. He yanked down the sheet, where the lindworm had frozen in the midst of devouring the princess. Behind the screen, the fire had spilled out of the fireplace and was creeping across the carpet. The smoldering arm of a chair had turned black. Quickly, the father tugged his daughter's blankets off. She sat paralyzed and shivering in her nightgown as he smothered out the flames. When it was finished, he turned his terrified fury on the mother.

"Silje, what have you done?"

CHAPTER 14

My mother sits on the edge of the tree-house platform, legs dangling. She's wearing her old brown boots, the ones that make diamond prints, and I wonder if my now-size footprints layered over hers would make the shapes change again. But there's no snow left to try. A cautious smile appears on her face as she catches sight of me, and though my fingers itch to climb up the ladder, I hold back. The rain has turned to mist, the chilly, dense kind that crawls inside your clothes and sinks into your bones.

"I'm not ready to just . . . be your daughter again." I tug a dead leaf from a branch and crumble it to powder.

"I understand." Her eyes are even darker today, the pupils like two black buttons.

"I'm glad at least one of us understands this."

My mother makes a sad *hmm* sound and gathers her knees up under her chin, ankles crossed. It's exactly the way I sit when I'm trying to process something, and I wonder what other gestures we share without knowing. Things I wouldn't even notice if she'd stayed because she wouldn't feel like a stranger.

"But I've been thinking about this, and I need you to know me," I say. "No matter what happens. Even if you fly back into the sky tonight."

"I won't." Her voice wavers.

"Just in case." I pull the blue book of my stories from underneath my coat. She kneels at the edge of the platform to reach for it, and her fingernails glitter blue-white. I don't remember her ever wearing nail polish like that.

"I can't watch you read it," I say.

Her gaze hovers on me, her expression unreadable. Then she gives a little nod and ducks inside the crooked hut, clutching the book to her chest. Numb, I walk through the woods and around the house. Iris's driveway is empty, and the lights in her house are off. I need to talk to someone, even if it's just about something dull and safe like school or sewing. But not someone who's been lying to me for months. My dad won't be home for hours, and in the dimming light, my house feels emptier than usual.

After steeping a cup of blackberry tea, I make a nest of pillows on the couch. The afghan is still in the tree house with my mother, so I get another blanket from the closet and a bag from my bedroom. Inside is my worry scarf, something I knit when I need to keep my fingers busy but don't have the emotional energy to invest in following a pattern. The scarf is at least fifty feet long now, in more colors than I've bothered to count. Switching on the TV, I curl up in my pillow nest and let my fingers push-loop-pull, push-loop-pull. My mother is reading my words now, peering inside my brain at the darkest memories and deepest secrets. There's no way of knowing what will happen next. There's nothing to do but wait.

My phone pings with a message from Iris.

Iris: *Will you please talk to me?*

I switch the phone off, pick up my needles again, and sink into a nervous daze until my father's key in the lock jerks me into the present.

"You all right, Eli-bug?" He drops his keys into the clay bowl and crosses the room.

I'm ready to crawl out of my own skin right now, I'm thinking about her so much.

My dad gathers up the massive worry scarf and piles it in his lap as he sits.

"Are you staying home tonight?" I say.

"Helen and I were thinking about seeing a movie." He presses his hand to my forehead like I'm six years old and might have a fever. "But I'm probably going to cancel."

"You don't have to do that." My voice doesn't quite convey the nonchalance I was aiming for.

"It's been a long day," he says, pulling out his phone. "Wouldn't want to fall asleep in the middle of the theater and start snoring. We'll reschedule—no big deal."

He goes into his room for a few minutes to call Helen, then returns in sweatpants and slippers. "Do you want to talk about it?" he says.

I do. I can't.

"Iris applied to go away to school next year and didn't tell me. And she got in." It's not the thing I really want to say, but it's not nothing.

His bushy eyebrows lift. "What school?"

"Some place in Amherst. Dickins Academy or whatever." I know the real name, but I won't use it.

"Wow." He rakes his fingers through his nonexistent hair,

fingers sliding over his smooth skull. "Let's heat up the chili. I can make corn bread."

My dad's not great with emotional things, but he's cooked me food through a million and one disasters and heartbreaks over the past ten years. I'm not sure I can swallow anything right now, but the gesture means more than the actual eating.

The toaster lies in pieces on the kitchen counter, a yellow wire here, a circuit board there. The floor crunches with burnt crumbs, so I get the broom while my dad pulls ingredients from cupboards. He measures out the cornmeal and pours it in a thin stream into the bowl.

"Her mom mentioned they were looking at options for next year," he says. "She said Iris is bored sick at school."

"You knew about it too?" The broom scrubs the tile a little too hard as I collect the crumbs in a messy jumble. "When was this conversation?"

He whacks an egg on the counter and drops its gloopy contents into his mix. "Couple of months ago. I told her it sounded like a good idea. Iris could easily be doing graduate-level coursework, expanding her horizons. Maybe teaching the rest of the world a thing or two."

Crumbs fly in all directions as I misjudge my broom swipe. "Why didn't you tell me?"

"I just assumed it was a couple of online courses." My dad pulls a whisk from a drawer and begins to stir. "And I figured Iris would've told you all about it."

"She didn't." I jab the broom into the corners under the cupboards, not even looking at what's under there. "She's been hiding it for months."

He rummages through the pots and pans in the drawer under the stove. "Why do you think she'd do that?"

"Because she's a coward?" The word leaves a sour taste on my tongue. When you're as shy as Iris, packing up and moving to a new place all by yourself is the opposite of cowardly.

"She's probably just been trying to figure out how to tell you." My dad extracts his favorite blue Pyrex baking dish. "I'm sure she knew how upset you'd be. And it can't be easy for her to leave you either."

"Then she shouldn't." My voice quavers, and my dad pulls me into a hug.

"Nothing's set in stone yet," he says. "See how it all plays out. Worst-case scenario, you take a lot of weekend buses to Amherst."

I clean up the rest of the crumbs while he finishes the corn bread, and then I take the leftover chili out of the fridge, along with some vegetables for salad. We work in silence for a while, moving around each other like planets in orbit, and by the time the corn bread is out of the oven, I'm feeling slightly less frantic. He's right about all of this. I can't be angry about Iris wanting more. The things inside her brain are far vaster than this small place where we live.

"I'm sure you two will figure it all out." My dad sets a steaming slice of corn bread in front of me, and in spite of all the achiness, the worry and the anger, my stomach growls. I haven't eaten all day, and this corn bread smells like home and love. By the time the chili is served, I've finished my slice and am cutting a second one.

"Can I ask you a completely hypothetical question?" I say.

He wipes a string of melted cheese from the corner of his mouth. "Go for it."

"What would you do if Mamma came here?" I keep my gaze steady on my bowl. "Like, what if she really had been in your bed last night and she was just . . . back?"

He drains his entire glass of water, probably so he doesn't have to answer right away. "She'd have a lot of questions to answer, that's for sure."

She does. So many I don't even know where to start.

"Do you think you could let her be part of our family again?" I say. "Could you forgive her, no matter what her answers were?"

He mashes what's left of his chili flat with his fork. "I don't know."

"If she was really, really sorry?" I don't know why I'm defending her all of a sudden. "If she had a valid reason for what she did, for being gone so long? Would that change anything?"

"I . . . don't know." When he finally looks at me, my dad's eyes are a little glassy. "I spent years taking care of your mother, pretending I could keep everything together, pretending she actually listened to me." He sighs. "Maybe if she agreed to go to therapy again."

I wonder what kind of therapy could possibly help her problems. If there aren't support groups for girls whose mothers unexpectedly returned from the sky, there definitely aren't any for the mothers either.

"She was seeing a therapist before you were born." says my dad. "For anxiety and depression and some other stuff. I thought it was helping, but apparently there were a lot of things I didn't realize."

More than you can imagine.

"What if what happened was out of her control?" I say.

He piles his utensils into his bowl and crumples his napkin on top. "It was in her control to ignore me, over and over, when I asked her to go back to that therapist. She said she didn't like him, but he was the only one in Longyearbyen at the time. And it was *absolutely* in her control to keep you inside the house that night."

I know, I know, I know. But there was more to it than that, so many more pieces that had nothing to do with my mother's mental health. He never saw the magic hidden in the edges of the world. The things that appeared from out of nowhere—sometimes lovely, sometimes gruesome, sometimes terrifying.

Like that girl in the cloak.

The wind gusts outside, moaning through the eaves. I glance at the black windowpane over the sink and wonder if she's out there. Creeping through the night, her silver eyes glinting. Before I go to bed, I double-check that all the doors and windows are locked. I hope my mother is sleeping safe in the tree house. I hope she'll come inside to us soon.

CHAPTER 15

Once upon a time, in a green house at the top of the world, there was a blackened carpet and a scorched chair and a little girl in tears because her father was packing her suitcase.

"You could have killed her," he said in a tight voice to the mother, who was sitting on the hearth, wrapped in the sheet that had held the shadow puppets. Her expression, blank as a wall, did not change as the father's words splintered around her.

Irresponsible.

Dangerous.

Foolish.

Unfit.

The girl's broiling head throbbed; the ceiling warped down and the couch bent up, and she clung to the cushions so she wouldn't be thrown off. Her father pushed boots onto her feet, tugged a coat around her shoulders, and lifted her onto his hip.

"Never again," he said. "Not until you stop this."

He flung the door open, and the girl expected her mother to stop him. She was far too sick to be outside—her mother had taken her temperature and fought to keep the worry out of her face when she read the number. But now her mother sat like a statue beside the fireplace, didn't look up as the girl cried out. Not a blink, not a twitch.

Then the girl was outside in a cloud of water and ice, and her father was running, slipping and gasping.

"Put me down." She planted her palm on his cheek and pushed. His skin was wet with tears or sleet, and he didn't let her go. The mountains leaned in closer, groaning in disapproval. The father ran down the main street of town, past the grocery store and the library, past a gray-shingled bar. The girl realized where they were going, and her chest grew tight.

HOTEL LUND, read the sign in straight black letters.

"Pappa, no." The girl's voice was a frog jumping in her throat.

The father carried her up the steps and into an austere lobby that was only slightly warmer than the outside. The entire space reeked of pine-scented cleaning liquid. A woman with short, gray hair stood behind the desk, arms folded over her thin chest.

Mormor. Grandmother.

The father set the girl on a straight-backed chair and leaned over the counter to whisper to the grandmother. The girl strained to listen, but the fever made her head so thick that the words sounded like they were underwater.

". . . almost burned the house down . . . can't leave her alone . . . frankly terrified."

The grandmother's gray eyes matched her hair. They fixed on the girl, and the girl felt as though she were a circle of cork and they were steel-tipped darts. Where the girl's mother was soft edges and whispered secrets, the grandmother was titanium plates and factual statements. She gave a sharp nod.

"Your mother is sick," she said to the girl. "You'll stay here until she's well again."

"But I'm sick too," moaned the girl. She pleaded with her father, begged him to take her home. Trails of salt and mucus ran down her face, but he seemed unable to see her. The girl fell to the floor and wrapped her arms around his muddy boot. With an irritated huff, the grandmother pulled her off, pinned her arms to her sides, and carried her, kicking, through a doorway behind the reception desk and into a small, sparsely furnished apartment.

"You've got one night to cry," she said, pointing to a narrow cot beside a woodstove. "Tomorrow, sick or well, you will help me with my work."

CHAPTER 16

Tap tap tap.

With a start, I sit up, groggily trying to figure out what woke me. Everything's fuzzy and crooked, like I'm watching an old black-and-white movie on TV. The dressmaker's dummy lurks beside my bed, looking more real than not in the shadows, and maybe there's a head under that pile of clothes after all. One with shining silver eyes. Shuddering, I pull the covers over my head.

Tap tap tap.

The sound is coming from the window beside my dresser. In the stuffy under-blanket air, I pray for it not to be that girl.

Tap tap.

Dread weakens my limbs as I ease out of bed. My bare feet hush through the carpet, through the reaching shadows. White moonlight edges the window shade, and I'm not sure I can bring myself to lift it and look outside.

Tap.

Pulse pounding in my ears, I lift the shade and press my forehead to the glass. My mother's face takes shape on the other side, made foggy by my breath on the pane. She's wearing a pair of cheap, wire-rimmed sunglasses and that same white sweater. No coat or hat or gloves. With something like relief, I ease the window open, and frigid air gusts in.

"What are you doing here?" I whisper.

"I couldn't wait until morning." Her voice is tinkling icicles as she holds up my book. "I finished reading this."

I hug my arms around my chest, like I can hold back the pieces of myself that are trying to fly toward her like magnets, despite everything she's done. "The whole thing?"

She steps closer to the window, and it's hard to resist the pull of her. "Can you come outside?"

I glance at the clock. "It's three thirty. I have school tomorrow."

"Just for a little while."

I rock on my heels, leaning back into the warm safety of my room, then tipping forward into the white-streaked night filled with her, with her, with her.

"Why are you wearing sunglasses?" I say.

"The moon's too bright."

I wait for her to laugh, but she doesn't.

"Is something wrong with your eyes?" I say.

She hesitates a moment too long. "They're a little sensitive."

"Did you hurt your head when you fell?"

My mother folds her arms and doesn't answer.

"Hang on." My coat is hanging in the living room, and I don't want to risk waking my dad, so I take two from my closet: my ski parka and a long wool dress coat. It's the nicer of the two, so I hand it through the window to her before pulling on the parka. Then I get us each a hat and gloves and clamber through the window. The cold makes me shrivel in on myself, and quickly I zip my jacket and pull the hat on. She looks regal in my coat, in a way

I'm sure I never do. Even wearing five-dollar sunglasses and a pink knitted beanie.

"How far is the beach?" she says.

"Less than a mile."

"Can we go there?"

I'm not just going to fall back into being her daughter again, but this is the woman who made me and carried me inside her body and fed me with her own blood, who held me and cried with me and whispered her love into my baby seashell ears. Back when she wasn't a mirror image of herself. When we lived in the snow and the cotton-grass summers. I'll never share that with anyone else. And I need to know why it all happened, how she feels, where this leaves us now.

"For a few minutes," I say.

Everything's cast in black and silver as we sneak to the path that runs through the woods to the beach. Somewhere in the branches high above us, the owl is looping through its melancholic mantra.

"My best friend lives there," I say, pointing to Iris's house. Her giant truck slumbers in the driveway.

"What's she like?"

"She's incredibly smart and kind, and she takes in sick and hurt animals when people can't get them to the shelter."

Iris's betrayal hits me all over again, the crease in her forehead as she read that life-altering email in the cafeteria while I talked about costumes with Maisie.

"That's nice that she lives so close," says my mother.

"It is. But I just found out she got accepted to a school that's like two hundred miles away. I should be happy for her, but I'm so afraid this is the beginning of the end and I'm going to be all alone."

My mother's shoulder bumps against mine. "You're not alone."

I want that to be true so badly that I let her take my gloved hand in hers. The whole world shimmers like I'm seeing it all brand-new, like I'm using her eyes and ears and nose. The trees stretching their bony fingers toward the moon. The loamy scent of their bark and the dirt on the path. The singing of waves on the wind, growing louder as we walk. It's so easy, this slipping back into her. But I can't sink all the way—I keep hold of the edges of myself as we walk in silence, our footsteps synchronized and silent.

Finally, we reach a parking lot flanked by low dunes, and even though I grew up on this beach, a thrill of brand-newness flares through me. My mother drops my hand and runs, my unbuttoned coat flapping behind her like a cape. Stunned, I crash to a stop, watching her fly toward the dunes, growing smaller.

Leaving again.

I'm a bundle of feathers, about to be blown apart by the wind.

"Come on," she shouts over her shoulder, and with a broken laugh, I take off after her. We flounder into the deep sand, through a gap in the long, waving grass and down to the beach. It's the highest tide I've seen in years, the moonlit water wild and foamy and hurling itself at the sliver of sand. I catch up with my mother at the edge and we stop, arms wheeling to keep from falling in. The wind roars across the sea, trying to shove us back, but we push into it, leaning forward with tears streaming from our eyes. Nothing can control us, not the wind or the sky or the stars. Nothing. Not us.

I scoop up a fistful of pebbles from the tideline and hurl them at the starlit sky. My mother gathers a handful too, and soon we're both throwing as fast as we can, scooping and tossing in a manic, desperate loop until we're gasping.

"I hate you," I scream at the sky. At those lights who stole her away. At her.

A wave comes thundering in, and I leap backward, slip, and land on my tailbone. My chest aches too much to stand. She pulls me up, and I shove away with every piece of strength I have, but it's not enough. I'm melting into her, defenseless as this beach is to the tides.

"I was a happy girl who lived in a green house at the top of the world," I say into the front of her coat—my coat. "I was Norwegian—I spoke Norwegian, not English; I was strong and fierce. Now I'm a bunch of broken pieces all glued back together. I wasn't supposed to be like this."

"I'm sorry, I'm sorry," she murmurs into my hair. Her body has lost all its softness, and it's the exact temperature as the air whirling around us. There's something strange about her scent too: a faint hint of charcoal, like the end of a burnt match.

"Look at this place." I gesture at the swirling sea and the rolling dunes. "This isn't where I was supposed to live. None of this has ever fit right."

I want to pound her chest, shove her away and run and run and run, but my knees are shaking, my head is wobbling, my nose is leaking, and all I truly want is for her to keep holding me.

"Let's sit down," she says, and I can't do anything but nod. We find a hollow in the dunes, out of the wind, where it's quieter. I shouldn't let her be this close—it's draining away my indignation, my sense of self—but it's so easy to slip.

"Your stories were beautiful," says my mother. "They cracked my ribs open and broke my heart."

Out on the water, a blast of water shoots skyward and a hump appears. A spike pokes out of the water, twisted and gnarled like a unicorn's horn, getting longer and longer until I'm not sure it's real anymore. Finally, at the bottom of the horn, a whale's rounded head appears.

"A *narhval*," says my mother. "Look, that's its tusk."

"But we don't have narwhals here."

Kids on Cape Cod start learning about marine ecology in preschool. We have humpback whales, finbacks and right whales, occasionally minkes. Great white sharks, even. But not narwhals. I gawk as more tusks appear, poking up at the stars. There must be thirty of them breathing and diving in turns.

My mother grinds her heels, digging two small holes in the sand.

"That old woman lied about the wishing ring," I say.

Her feet are half-buried now, and the sand is creeping up over her jeans, like she's slowly disappearing into the dune.

"What ring?" she says absently.

I resist the impulse to tug her disappearing legs out of the sand. "That woman who ate all of my cookies. She said it would grant me two wishes, but it only gave me one. I wished the lights away, but I wasn't fast enough, and then you were gone with them."

"I read that in your story." Her voice is distant, distracted.

"But I was supposed to have another wish. I should have been able to save you. I spent ten years wondering if this was all my fault, but that old lady shouldn't have lied to me if there was only one wish."

Slowly, her feet sink into the sand until only her toes are visible.

"Can you please stop doing that?" I say. "You're scaring me."

She glances down like she's forgotten she had feet. Her boots emerge, sand streaming off them. "You used both of your wishes. Don't you remember?"

Another whale blows its breath at the stars, and a fishy, decomposing smell wafts toward us.

"No." But something foggy and terrible is bumping in the depths of my memory.

She tips her head up and sighs like the whales. "You crossed it out of your story."

I know the story she means. Though I've tried for years to read what's underneath those heavy black marker lines, I've never managed it, and my brain refuses to remember.

"What did I wish for?"

"Don't worry about it. It made no difference in the end, and there's no sense in blaming yourself."

Her legs are sinking again, and I want to pull them out. "But I just wonder—"

"Tell me about your father," she says. "How is he?"

"He works a lot," I say. "He stays busy all the time. He goes on dates sometimes, but it usually doesn't last more than a few months."

"Oh, Peter," she whispers.

"Why did you get in his bed?" I say. "I thought you didn't want him to know you were back."

There's only one narwhal left, huffing and diving, and I wonder where the rest of its pod has gone, if it will be able to find them in this dark, strange bay so far from its home.

"I couldn't help it," says my mother. "I needed to see him, just for a minute." She picks at the frayed cuff of her sweater sticking out of her coat sleeve. "His hair's all gone now. He used to have the most beautiful dark curls."

"He saw you," I say.

She tucks her sleeve back inside her coat. "But he didn't want to. He rolled over and went back to sleep."

"I don't think he didn't want to see you," I say. "I think he couldn't let himself see you."

She makes a soft *hmm* sound. "I think you're right."

"He needs things to make sense, and making sense of *that* would mean he had to re-understand everything," I say. "So he told himself it was a dream. But what if you showed up at the door in broad daylight? Then he'd have to believe it."

Her heels are grinding, scraping, sinking lower.

"Mamma?"

"Yes."

"Will you try to see him again soon? In a more obvious way?"

I shouldn't keep this from him, not after every night he's sat up with me while I sobbed from nightmares. Every school play and dance recital he's endured, every stomach bug he's nursed me through without complaining, even the time I threw up on his pillow. This is a massive black hole of a secret, considering how much he loved her too.

"I will," she says. "But I need a little more time. He's not going to react well."

She's probably right. The water is still now, the last whale is gone, and a line of gray smudges the horizon.

"He'll be awake any minute now," I say. "I need to go."

My mother pulls herself out of the sand, and we hurry through the dunes and the woods, dawn lighting our way now instead of moonlight. She stops at the perimeter between the woods and my yard and catches my hand. Her fingers are ice.

"Good night, my heart," she whispers.

It's everything I wanted, but it's nothing like I expected it to be. I let go of her hand and tiptoe through the yard. There's a small crater beside the brick walkway, sand and scraps of grass scattered in a ring around it. At the bottom of the hole lies a dimpled black stone. I stoop to pick it up. It's the temperature of a fresh cup of tea.

"What are you doing?"

My dad's voice. The front door is open. Hissing in my breath, I glance back at the woods, where my mother just was, but she's gone.

"I . . . heard a crash," I stammer, holding up the meteorite. "So I went outside to see what it was and found this hole."

I wonder if she's hiding behind a tree again, if she's watching us. I wonder how long my dad has been standing there. Mutter-swearing, he stomps down the broken steps in his slippers and peers into the crater. "Another one."

The sky is falling, Chicken Little. I choke down a hysterical peep of a laugh. It's not remotely funny. "Did you just wake up?"

"Yeah. No. Sort of." He rubs his eyes. "I couldn't shut my brain off, and then some jerk of an owl was hooting around the house all night."

So he *is* worrying. Maybe he *is* starting to see.

"What do you think this means?" I hold out the meteorite.

He starts to reach for the stone, then waves it away. "I don't want you wandering around by yourself in the dark. This is two nights in a row."

"It's barely night." I gesture at the gray-pink sky, and he grimaces.

"You know what I mean." He dusts off his hands, though he hasn't touched anything. "Come on inside. If we're both up early, I may as well make pancakes."

As I head up the steps, I scan the holly bush for notes, but there's nothing there.

CHAPTER 17

Once upon a time, in a stark white hotel at the top of the world, a girl sat alone in a half-clean bathroom. She had just finished scrubbing the grout around the sink and toilet with a toothbrush. Now she had a rag and a bucket of disinfectant, and her cracked knuckles oozed blood into the tub she was meant to be scouring.

Out in the hall, the grandmother's broom scritch-scritch-scritched in an even, deliberate rhythm. Everything her grand-mother did was economical and precise. Even the quantities of bleach were exactly measured for each bathroom, so as not to waste a drop. The girl hated her grandmother with every electron in her body. She turned on the bathtub's tap, stuck her hands underneath, and gasped as the cold water slid into the cracks in her skin.

The hallway sweeping stopped, and the bathroom door opened. The grandmother peered down at the kneeling, gasping girl. Her gray eyebrow twitched.

"Leave the tub for now," she said. "You may dust my apartment instead."

The girl refused to meet her grandmother's eye, would not thank her for this act of pity. It had been seventeen days since her father had left her at this hotel, and though he had come to visit her every day, she hadn't said a single word to him or her grandmother. The grandmother didn't seem bothered; she was perfectly happy to issue commands and then work in silence. The girl was afraid if she didn't obey, the grandmother would tell her mother what an ill-tempered, naughty girl she was and then her mother wouldn't want her back.

Sometimes the girl would touch the frigid gold ring tied in her hair and think about wishing to go home. But she wasn't sure that was what her mother wanted. After all, she had let her father take her away and she hadn't come to visit, not once. The girl wondered if she should wish for her mother to love her, to want her back. But she wasn't sure if wishes worked that way, and the old woman had said to be very careful about how she used them.

The girl took a dusting cloth and a spray bottle that smelled of vinegar, and she wiped all the woodwork in her grandmother's sitting and dining rooms. She climbed up onto a chair and ran the cloth over the old cuckoo clock, hoping that when she wiped the round little door, the bird would come out and tell her what to do. It didn't.

The girl drifted into her grandmother's bedroom, which she had only glimpsed through its doorway. She rubbed vinegar spray all over the immaculate bedside table and wondered if her grandmother ever read. There wasn't a single book or magazine in the hotel.

At the foot of the bed sat a wide cedar chest. As the girl wiped its glossy surface, the urge to open the lid sprouted in her heart and grew until it was unbearable. She listened carefully for her grandmother, then eased the trunk open. Inside were blankets knitted in the softest yarns the girl had ever touched. She looked at her grandmother's bed, which was covered in a scratchy wool coverlet, and wondered why she'd kept these gorgeous blankets tucked away.

The girl pulled the blankets out, one by one, and buried her face in each. It was the closest thing to love she'd felt in seventeen days. The blanket at the bottom of the trunk was soft as the belly of a kitten, knitted in an ornate pattern of peacock blue and white. The girl spread it out so she could look at the design. Three beautiful young women stood in front of a snowy mountain range. They wore long gowns and crowns on their heads and graceful smiles on their faces, and their arms were linked together. *Sisters*, the girl thought, and she wished she had a sister to link arms with and she missed her mother all the more.

"What do you think you are doing?" Somehow, the grandmother was standing inches behind the girl. She snatched the blanket away, and the girl noticed that her hands shook as she folded it into a neat rectangle. The girl almost apologized, but remembered just in time that she wasn't speaking.

The grandmother sent her to bed that night without supper. The girl lay on her narrow cot, shivering and dreaming of how warm those knitted blankets would be. The woodstove had long since gone out, but from deep inside its belly came a rattle and a groan. The girl sat up, trembling. The window on the stove door glowed green, then gold. It swung open and a folded scrap of paper fell out.

The girl waited until the rattling and groaning stopped. She eased out of bed and unfolded the paper. It was a page torn from a book; she recognized the story. A king and queen locked their three young daughters up in the castle because an old beggar woman had warned they must stay inside until they were all fifteen years old. On the day before the youngest princess's fifteenth birthday, they snuck out and were kidnapped by trolls and taken to a world deep underneath a blue mountain. A soldier rescued them, but then he became trapped underground, so he blew on an old whistle and an eagle came and carried him to safety. The soldier returned to the castle and chose the youngest princess to be his bride (for it was always the youngest who was chosen), but the end of the story had been crossed out with heavy black lines. Below it, someone had written in rounded, childish printing:

The three princesses decided they were tired of everyone telling them what to do, so they ran away and were fierce and free and beholden to no one for the rest of their days.

CHAPTER 18

I'm halfway to third period, dragging along in an underslept daze, when Maisie emerges from the rushing mob, wearing a pair of pin-striped trousers, suspenders, and a bowler hat.

"Have you seen Iris?" I say. Her truck wasn't in the driveway this morning, and there's been no sign of her all morning.

"Probably at Indian Neck," says Maisie. "It's horrid, isn't it?"

"What is?" I have no idea why Iris would be at a beach right now. She never misses school, not even when she had bronchitis and had to keep going out in the hall to cough out pieces of her lungs.

"Those whales." Maisie waves to someone on the other side of the hall. "Have you been under a rock all morning?"

"Sort of." I've been so lost in thoughts about my mother and that strange girl by the side of the road, I don't think I've spoken to a single person since I left the house.

"A pod of whales got stranded near Indian Neck," says Maisie, scrolling through her phone. "Look." She holds up a blurry photo of a gray lump lying in a tide pool. "Iris literally ran out of here between first and second period."

Iris volunteers for the Cape-wide marine animal rescue team.

Even though she can't be an official member until she turns eighteen, she gets all of their alerts and they let her help with rescues. She's not supposed to go anywhere during school hours, though.

"How many?" I say.

"Eight or nine." Maisie stuffs her phone into her bag and waves to somebody else. "The tide's still going out, and it's not looking good."

Those poor animals must be terrified. Iris must be panicking too. The last time a dolphin got stranded and died, she cried for days. As furious as I am at her for lying to me, I can't leave her to face that alone.

"I have to go," I say, veering back toward my locker. "Tell Ms. Cohen I went home sick."

The beach parking lot is swarming with people, some wearing wet suits, others in street clothes, everyone confused and yelling into the wind. I skirt through the crowd, edge around a police officer talking to a man with a walkie-talkie, and dash onto the beach. It's low tide, and massive banks of fog are billowing into the harbor. Eight black-and-white-speckled whales lie in the shallows among the sandbars.

"They look like unicorns!" somebody shouts.

I'm going to be sick. I'm going to be sick right here on the beach. They're narwhals.

"Iris!" I yell. "Iris Pells, where are you?"

One of the figures beside the whale closest to shore looks up, gives a distracted wave, and then goes back to scooping water over the animal, which is covered in wet towels. She's not wearing a coat, just her thin green hoodie, and it can't be warmer than forty degrees.

"They're not supposed to be here," I say to no one. None of this is supposed to be here. Not the whales, not the meteorites. Not my mother. Zipping up my coat and pulling on my hood, I let the wind shove me toward the whales. At the tide line, I kick off my shoes.

"Stay away from that thing," yells a man on the shore. "Watch out for its horn." But nobody stops me from plunging into the water, so frigid it sends knifing pangs through my feet and calves. The whale must be fifteen feet long. Small waves lap around its body, and its stillness is far scarier than if it had been thrashing around, fighting for survival. I can feel the waves of terror radiating off the poor creature. Its tusk slowly sinks into the murky sand, an echo of my mother's heels last night.

"What should I do?" I say. "What can I do?"

"Nothing." Iris sloshes a bucket of water over the whale's back. "We need the truck to come so we can get them out of here before they die."

I sink down to my haunches and lay my palm on the bulbous top of the whale's head. Its skin is rubbery and smooth, coursing with frantic energy underneath. Above its left eye, the white spots form a shape that looks like a bird with outstretched wings.

"It's okay, it's okay," I whisper to the whale. "You're going to swim back into that big blue sea. You'll go way up north, where it's nice and cold and deep."

Behind my hand, the blowhole gusts. A tremor goes through the whale, then through me.

"Shh, shh." I pat some water onto its side and start to hum, an aimless tune that becomes the lullaby the blue lights sang when I was trapped under the ice. The waterline drops lower, lower, and I wish I could apologize to this whale for starting the chain of events that brought him here. But I don't know his songs, and he doesn't understand my words.

"We need more towels." Iris's lips are purple. "Do you have any in your car? Or a blanket?"

It takes a couple of tries to make my frozen legs stand, and then I dash to the parking lot, stumbling on feet that feel like bricks. I find an old army blanket and a ratty towel in the trunk of my car and am hobble-running back across the sand when a whisper sizzles deep inside my ear.

Eline.

A red-haired girl in a cloak glides, unnoticed, through the crowd of people yelling into their phones, taking photos, shooting videos. She speaks a long string of Norwegian, and I shake my head.

"What do you want?" I bunch the blanket and the towel against my chest as if that will somehow ward her off.

She gives a sharp little laugh. "Can't even speak Norwegian anymore? You've forgotten everything, haven't you?"

The smoky fog is thickening. Soon the whales won't be visible from the shore. They wouldn't be here if I hadn't whistled at those lights and brought my mother back.

"I don't want to talk to you," I say. "Please go away."

The girl inclines her head toward Iris. "I thought you hated her."

"I never hated Iris. She's my best friend. I'm just upset with her for lying."

The girl snaps her hand up and catches something out of the wind. A scrap of paper.

"Your *best friend* has been planning to leave you for a long time." Her emerald eyes flash as she unfolds the paper and hands it to me.

The scrap has been torn from a notebook, the blue lines covered in Iris's impeccable handwriting.

> *going to send the application soon but Eli will lose*
> *her mind when she finds out. I know she has massive*
> *abandonment issues, but I wish I knew how to tell her*
> *she needs to let me breathe sometimes.*

Blinking back tears, I crumple the paper into a tiny ball and stuff it into my pocket. "Why are you showing me this?"

"My sisters and I are trying to help you." The girl runs her tongue over sharp white teeth. "The sooner you know everything, the sooner you'll be free of all that weight."

Something about the flatness of her voice, the serpentine shine of her eyes, makes me certain I don't want her help.

She has massive abandonment issues. Even when I squeeze my eyes shut, I still see those horrible words. Shaking my head, I start toward the whales, but new people are crashing through the surf now: men and women wearing dry suits and matching red vests.

"Step around the tusk. Be careful."

"Check its heart rate."

"Narwhals in Wellfleet Harbor. Wildest thing I've ever seen."

It's far from the wildest thing I've ever seen.

"Eli! Why aren't you at school?" My dad comes barging across the sand, clad in the heavyweight dry suit he used to wear in the Arctic. He stares, aghast, at my soaked-through jeans. "You're going to get hypothermia."

He spots Iris, who is shaking so hard she misses the whale entirely with her bucketful of water, and charges into the tide pool. "You. Out of the water now. What were you two thinking? You shouldn't be out here without a suit, and you know better." He physically lifts her away from the whale and carries her to the tide line.

"Everything is . . . f-fine . . . I mean, it's not, but I'm . . . okay." Iris's words slip and crash into one another as he sets her down. She's still clinging to her empty bucket.

. . . *she needs to let me breathe* . . .

Humming quietly, the red-haired girl slips away through a knot of reporters and photographers.

"You're not fine," says my dad. "Eli, take her home right now, and I want you both to put on dry clothes, drink something warm, and stay inside. Iris, I'm calling your mother."

"But—"

"But nothing. Go." There's more than just worry in my dad's voice—there's fear too. He calls out to a woman wearing a red vest, barely visible through the ghosting fog, and I pry the bucket from Iris's stiff fingers. As soon as the weight leaves her hands, she sags and I grab her waist to keep her from falling. She leans in the whales' direction like they're her gravity. They're dying, and it's all my fault.

We ride in silence for several miles, the heat roaring as high as it'll go and Iris's teeth chattering so hard I'm worried they'll shatter.

"I'm sorry I didn't tell you about Dickinson," she mumbles, unfolding her mottled pink fingers next to the heating vent and hissing in pain.

"Well, *I'm* sorry I'm suffocating you." I pull the scrap of notebook paper from my pocket and toss it into her lap.

She can barely make her hands work to unfold it. "This is from my Moleskine," she says. "How did you get it?"

A girl in a cloak plucked it out of thin air? There's no way to explain how I got it without sounding absurd. "I just . . . sort of . . . found it," I say. "But you did write that, didn't you?"

She's silent as we turn onto the dirt road. The fog has crept all the way into our neighborhood. It shrouds the lower halves of the houses and trees in white nothingness, like the world is slowly erasing itself.

"I'm sorry I hurt you," says Iris finally. "You know I love you to death, Eli, and I never meant for you to read that. But I'm allowed to write things down that I'd never share with you in a million years. I'm allowed to process my feelings and work stuff out and rant and complain and do whatever I want, as long as I keep it to myself. You were never supposed to look at it. That's my private diary."

"You think I have massive abandonment issues." The words sting just as badly as they did the first time I read them.

Iris makes a choking sound. "How could you not? Your mom literally *abandoned* you. It's the worst thing that could happen to a kid. Of course you're going to have issues. But that doesn't make it okay for you to go through my stuff. I don't know how you found my hiding spot. Did you go in my room when I wasn't home?"

"I told you, I didn't steal it."

She scoffs, and I hit the brakes in the middle of the road between our two houses. The kind thing would be to pull up Iris's driveway, considering how frozen and shaky she still is. But another kind thing is not writing spiteful things about your best friend. I wonder how many other pages of her diary are filled with deeply cruel analysis of my emotional problems. Cutting the wheel hard, I swing into my own driveway.

"You said you didn't know how to ask me, but don't worry about it," I say, shutting off the engine and opening my door. "Here's your space to breathe."

"Eli, come on," she calls, but I'm already halfway to the house. Leaving her shivering in my car, I slam the front door and lock it.

CHAPTER 19

Once upon a time, in a stark white hotel at the top of the world, a girl lay on a narrow cot, thinking of her mother. It had been nineteen days now that she had not come to visit, had not called, had not sent a letter or a note. The girl wondered if her mother had found another little girl to read her stories to. One who always went to bed when she was supposed to, who never talked back or broke things or was noisy when she was supposed to be quiet. These past nineteen days, the girl had gotten very good at being quiet. She wondered if it would make her mother love her again.

As the girl lay wondering, a shadow whispered across the hotel's lobby, though there was nothing there to cast it. It slipped underneath the apartment door, rustling and crackling and snickering as it crawled. Then it began to grow and grow and grow until it was a scaly serpent with twisted horns and glowing yellow eyes set in a face that looked almost like a man's. With a gasp, the girl threw her thin blanket over her head and tucked herself into a tight ball.

The lindworm slithered to the cot and snuck its head under the blanket. With cold breath that smelled like rotting meat and, somehow, her mother, it whispered.

"She doesn't love you anymore."

"Go away," the girl said in the firmest voice she could muster, praying that if she could just be strong enough, the creature would leave.

"I crawled inside her heart last night." The lindworm's cold tongue slid across the girl's hair. "It was rotten and wretched, and there was nothing in there for you."

"Stop it." The girl's voice began to crack.

The creature rubbed its horrible, slick cheek against hers. "You should have tried harder to behave, little one. Mothers only love their good children. The rest they give to me."

The girl shook so hard the bed wobbled, but she couldn't let herself cry. "I did try."

But maybe she didn't, not hard enough.

"I'll crawl inside your heart too, and I'll turn it black," said the creature. "Soon, little one, soon."

The girl shrieked, the first sound she'd made in nineteen days. But no one came to help, even when she kept on screaming. Once the girl had screamed her voice away, the lindworm let out a poison laugh and curled up at the foot of her bed. It began to snore. All night long, the girl sat watching it, too petrified to move, too frightened to wake this grotesque thing, this awful reminder. Finally, dawn crept in through her little window and the creature faded and disappeared.

But she knew it wasn't really gone.

CHAPTER 20

In my bedroom, I strip off my drenched clothing and pull on a dry pair of sweatpants, a hoodie, and wool socks. I can't stop replaying that horrible conversation with Iris in my head; I keep trying to find the one thing I could say that would make her realize this is her fault, not mine. That it's all been her fault and she shouldn't go away to Amherst.

There's a soft knock on the door. Thinking it's Iris come to tell me how wrong she was, I run through the living room and into the front hall. But on the other side of the door I find my mother, half swallowed in fog.

She takes one look at my blotchy face. "What happened?"

"Those narwhals we saw last night beached themselves," I say, wiping my eye with my sleeve and stepping back to let her inside. She follows me into the living room.

"How awful," she says. "Is your dad out there helping them?"

I nod. "And Iris thinks I'm a horrible person and she can't wait to get away from me."

"I'm sure that's not true," she says, but she's never met Iris, so there's no way she could actually be sure.

"She always knew I was messed up. Sort of broken." My mother starts to contradict me, but I wave her off. "No, it's true, and that's not the point. The thing is, I thought she didn't mind that I was broken. I thought she saw me outside of all of that stuff. Really saw *me*."

My mother nods. "The way you always saw me."

I sigh and slump onto the couch. She hesitates, then sits a hand's width away.

"But I think it's different when it's your mother," I say. "You and I have the same electrons. Iris can walk away from me anytime she wants, and I guess I didn't quite get that."

When I was four or five, I brought home a library book about atoms. My mother told me they were the building blocks for everything on the planet and the sky and the stars. I said the electrons were my favorite, and she told me she'd given me some of hers when she grew me inside her body. Through all the days and years I spent missing her, whenever the ache was too much to bear, I'd remember that her electrons were inside me, whizzing at thousands of kilometers a second, and nothing would stop them. Not death, not the Northern Lights, not my own sorrow or rage.

"I understand," says my mother. "And it really is a terrible thing. But have you considered that her decision isn't about running away from you as much as it is running *toward* something she needs?"

I pick at the hem of my sweatshirt and wish I had my worry scarf to knit. "I read part of her diary, and she said she wished she could tell me she needed to breathe."

"Oh, Eline. I wish I could fix everything for you." My mother gathers me into a hug, my head nestled against her collarbone, and this time it's not forced or awkward, though her body is still colder than mine. As she strokes my hair, something chilly drips onto my scalp, and I wonder if she's crying.

"Iris thinks I stole her diary," I say "but I didn't. These strange girls—"

My mother stiffens, draws in a sharp breath, and I sit up.

"What?"

She stares, dumbstruck, at her hand, then holds it out toward me. Her fingernails are completely gone, the skin underneath pink and smooth.

"They melted," she says, her face raw with fear.

"What's happening to you?" I whisper.

She shuts her eyes for a long while, and when they reopen, there's almost no white left around the irises. "I thought I was . . . normal again when I came down. I hoped it was going to be okay. I hoped so much that I've been ignoring the signs."

Her jaw is set so tight it makes mine ache. My mother was supposed to come back and make everything in my life right again. This is the polar opposite. I want to scream, I want to sob, I want to beg somebody to fix all of this, but there's nobody who can.

"Let's try the freezer." Pulling her up from the couch, I tuck my arm around her waist and lead her into the kitchen. Her shaking frame seems smaller today, lighter, and I'm struck by an irrational fear that she might blow away. I open the freezer and she buries her hands in the ice bin, sending a shower of cubes clattering to the floor.

My own fingertips begin to tingle, and then an itchy sensation crawls over them like a scab forming. The fear in my mother's eyes slowly ebbs, and when she pulls her hands out, they're covered in frosty blue-white again.

"That's better," she says, but her voice wobbles and her laugh is forced and her eyes are still very wrong.

I almost can't say the words, but I need to know. "Is anything else melting?"

Will you melt away into nothing?

"No."

I wish with all my heart for it to be true, but I'm not sure it is.

On the counter, my phone pings three times. A string of messages from my dad appears.

> **Dad:** *Are you okay?*
>
> *Are you warm?*
>
> *Did you drink something hot?*

Yes yes yes, I write back, even though the first and last answers aren't true. At least I'm not shivering anymore.

How are the whales? I write.

There's a long pause.

> **Dad:** *One of them died. But the rest are going to make it. We're loading them into the rescue trailer and will release them at Herring Cove. It's going to take a long time. Don't wait up.*

My knees start to wobble.

> **Me:** *Was it the one with the white spot that looked like a bird?*
>
> **Dad:** *I think so. Sorry, Eli-bug.*

I slump against the counter. "One of the whales died," I say. "The one Iris was trying to save. She's going to be devastated. She stayed with it as long as she could, and I tried to help it too."

"You're a kind person." She says it with such deep certainty, despite the fact that she knows nothing about how kind I've been for the past ten years.

"It's my fault," I say. "When I whistled, I must have done something to call them here, along with the lights. I don't know what else I've messed up. I'm afraid there's more. I'm scared that I . . . that maybe we broke something."

Something bangs onto the roof and clatters down. My mother stares at her ice fingernails and blows out her breath. From several feet away it makes me shiver.

"Can we pretend none of it exists tonight?" Her beautiful face is so ragged and sad, it hurts my stomach to look at her. "Can we just be us, like the old days, for a few hours? I promise we'll talk about everything tomorrow."

"But how do we just pretend?" It doesn't feel right, but I'm so, so tired.

She smooths her sweater down, tugs at its ragged cuffs. Her smile is almost genuine, almost unafraid. "Will you show me your room?"

"I . . . Okay." Before the words are out, she's halfway down the hall. By the time I catch her, she's standing in front of my bookshelf, head tipped to read the spines.

"What happened to my books?" Her voice is almost calm.

"I haven't seen them since we moved. I think maybe Dad got rid of them."

"Or your grandmother did," she says, then presses her lips together like she's holding in something bitter. "Would you like me to tell you a story instead?"

The threads of her are pulling at me, and I'm so tired. I'm tired of sneaking, of lying, of hiding. I'm tired of today and its landslide of disasters. I'm tired of feeling like I've broken the universe, of carrying this guilt, even though all I wanted was my mother back. I just want to let it all go for a few hours and pretend she's mine.

"Okay."

My mother lies down and pats the bed, and even though I'm too old for this, I curl up beside her, just like we used to lie, with my knees tucked up against her hip. Instead of her body warming mine like it used to, a chill seeps into my bones, but I don't shift away. I'm not going to break the spell. She tucks the blanket around me and nestles the pillow until it's just right.

"Close your eyes."

We could almost be home, back in Longyearbyen, back in time. If I pretend hard enough, I can almost smell the floorboards of our old house, feel my body shrinking to child size. My eyelids float shut, and colored lights swim in the darkness. Green swirls with crimson, spirals into purple and gold.

"I'm ready," I whisper, and my mother begins.

CHAPTER 21

Once upon a time, in a stark white hotel at the top of the world, there lived a girl who would one day become a mother. Her father had just gotten a job in a coal mine, and her family had moved to a small cluster of islands lost in a frigid sea. Not long after they arrived, the old woman who ran their guesthouse was sent back to the mainland to die, and the girl's mother decided to take over the place and turn it into a proper hotel. It was hard, never-ending work, day and night, and the girl and her younger sister were forced to help, though the pine-scented cleaning liquid left them with itchy, bleeding knuckles.

One beautiful spring day, the girl and her mother put on their snowshoes and set out walking in the wilderness, just as they always did when the weather was nice and they'd finished their work for the day.

They climbed up the faces of bright, white hills and slid down their backs. After an hour or two, the little girl was sweating inside her coat even though her nose was numb with cold. "I'm hungry," she said to her mother, sinking down to her heels at the foot of a lumpy hill.

"We'll eat when we reach the next peak," said her mother.

The girl pushed out her lower lip and knitted her eyebrows. "I want to eat now."

The mother tugged the straps on her backpack tighter and set off again. The girl watched her grow smaller and smaller. She found a rock that jutted out from the snow, brushed it off, and sat. Today, her mother would be the one to turn back and come to her.

Soon, the mother was a tiny speck moving up the next hill, and the girl's heart began to flutter. But as she sat awhile, she began to feel lighter. The girl tucked her knees up, rested her chin on them, and closed her eyes.

When she snapped awake, the sky was pink and gold, and only a sliver of sun was visible above the mountains. A set of footprints ran all the way through the valley and up the hill, and another set ran back, ending at her mother, who loomed over her with a face twisted in anger.

"Look at what you're sitting on," said the mother.

Groggily, the girl peered at the gray stone. She didn't understand what her mother wanted her to see. The mother lifted her daughter off the rock and began to brush away snow. A toe took shape, with a cracked, stubby nail on it, then another.

"One night in Trondheim when I was a little girl, I snuck out of my house and went walking in some hills just like these," said the mother. "It was dark, but I'd brought a lantern and I knew the place as well as my own garden."

The girl burrowed her hands into her pockets and shivered. She didn't know this place nearly as well as her own garden. And now that the sun was sinking low, the shadows twisted and crept and danced.

"Suddenly, a giant, meaty hand snatched me off the ground," said the mother. "A troll had been following me, a huge, foul creature with peeling skin and breath that smelled like weeks-dead fish."

The girl wanted to bury her face in her mother's chest, but her mother's face sparked with malice. "He opened a mouth full of rotten, brown teeth and tried to put me inside."

The girl let out a squeak as her mother bent down and brushed off more toes, then a great, gnarly foot.

"I had to think quickly," said the mother. "So I planted my foot on his festering lip and I said, 'Troll, don't you think I'd taste better if you cooked me first? With some mushrooms and lingonberries, perhaps?'"

The thought of her mother stewing in a pot of hot broth, her skin pinkening and her flesh slowly cooking, made sweat bead on the girl's forehead.

"The troll laughed," said the mother. "'That is a good idea,' he said.

"'Do you have any lingonberries?' I asked him. He thought for a moment, then shook his head.

"'I know where they grow,' I told him. 'Follow me, and we'll pick some to put in your pot.'

"I led him over hills and through valleys, all the while watching the sky. He began to huff and pant and grumble about his hunger." The mother cast a pointed look at her daughter, whose traitorous stomach chose that moment to growl loudly.

"'We're almost there,' I told him. 'Don't get discouraged. Think about how delicious I'll taste.' The troll smacked his lips and followed me up a hill just like this one. On the other side, the sky was lightening. I kept him distracted by reciting all of my mother's recipes, with people for ingredients instead of meat."

Again, the girl's stomach grumbled, though the thought of cooked human flesh made her want to be sick.

"At the bottom of a hill, the troll stopped," said the mother. "He sat down in the snow just like you did and told me he was too hungry and didn't want to be bothered with cooking me anymore. He tried to snatch me again, but I ran. By some miracle, we reached the top of the hill just as the sun burst into the sky. The troll screamed as its light hit him. He fell down and turned to stone."

The mother pointed to the lumpy hill behind the girl. It was connected to the foot. And it was the exact outline of a troll's body, bigger than the house she lived in.

"He looked just like this," said the mother. "Perhaps this is his brother?"

The girl clapped her mittened hands over her mouth and moaned. Still, her mother made no move to hold her or pick her up. "This one is probably turned to stone forever," said the mother. "But you can't be sure of something like that. I'm grown-up now, not quite so tasty anymore, but little girls are their favorite snack."

"I want to go home," whispered the girl. "I'm sorry."

A smile crept over the mother's narrow mouth. "Let's go."

The girl nearly cried as her mother's safe hand closed around hers. With an empty, sour stomach and without slowing once, she followed her down the hill and all the way their house.

CHAPTER 22

My eyes float open as my mother's voice trails off. Night has filled my room. "Was that Mormor?" I say.

"It was."

"So she was cruel to everybody, not just to me?"

My mother's laugh is quiet. "No, not just to you, though I don't think she ever thought she was being cruel."

"Why was she like that?"

She winds a strand of my hair around her finger, and a tiny flake of ice falls onto my pillow. "A lot of people your grandmother's age think you have to scare children or punish them to get them to behave. I'm sure she thought she was doing the best for us."

"It must have been awful, having a mother like that."

In her long silence, I start to worry that I've hurt her feelings. It's not like she can help what Mormor is like.

"It wasn't easy," she says finally. "Sometimes I felt like I'd split into two pieces, like your grandmother had threatened and scared and punished my real self out of my body."

With a shudder, I tuck my cheek against her chilly shoulder. "That sounds horrible. I'm so glad you're my mother instead of her."

Her body tenses. "I was a far worse mother than Mormor could ever dream of being."

"You weren't." I prop myself up on one elbow so she can see how much I mean this. But she just shakes her head and sighs.

"Let's not talk about that now, okay? It's very, very late and you should try to sleep."

As she strokes my hair, a yawn leaks out of my mouth. If I can just ignore how cold she is, I can go back to pretending we're still in Longyearbyen, that nothing ever changed. I tuck the blanket tighter around myself and try not to shiver.

"This isn't fair."

It's not fair that a single wish from an insignificant person, one of billions on a little blue planet, could cause such an epic mess. I don't understand why the universe can't just let me have my mother.

"It isn't," she says. "I just wanted us to have a little bit of time together that wasn't sad."

"But that's just it," I say. "We can't, can we?"

She says something quietly in Norwegian, something I can't understand because I was ripped away from the life where it was my language.

"The longer you stay, the more things are breaking." My tongue stumbles around the words because I don't want them to be true. "You're not supposed to be here."

My mother closes her black-button eyes. "What if I could fix this?"

"How?"

"I don't know exactly. But I can't let you carry the weight of this. It's my fault, not yours."

I know that's not entirely true, even if I can't quite remember why. A shadowy, guilty thing is bumping around the back of my mind, still unformed.

"Let me try," my mother says, and there's so much sadness and regret in her face that I can barely stand to look at her. "Just let me try."

"Okay," I say, and she kisses the tip of my nose with her frosty lips. "But we'll talk about everything tomorrow, right?"

"Yes," she murmurs. "Go to sleep now. Forget about everything for a little while. Let go. I love you, Eline."

"I love you too."

"Goodbye."

I open an eye. "You mean good night."

She smiles. "My English is a little rusty. Yes, good night."

"Good night, Mamma."

Knees tucked up tight against her side, I nestle into my pillow and let go.

CHAPTER 23

I dream I'm drifting someplace up higher than the sky. The earth is a foggy blue-and-white thing, round and inconsequential. It holds no draw to me; nothing does. There's not a word for the disconnectedness. I'm not aware of having a body, but it doesn't matter. There's nothing outside of this exact moment, no past or future, and it's clear and pure and devoid of emotion or even thought.

A sharp sound shoots up from the mass of blue and white. A whistle pierces through what shreds of me still exist, and suddenly I remember it all. A child. My child. Down in that frigid, shimmering night, she's calling me, and I need to go. I need to disconnect from this place, this state, whatever it is.

At first it's floating. Then it's falling.

I fall and fall and fall and I'm burning up as I tear through the atmosphere. Then everything's freezing as I plummet into sky and crystallized air. It's too fast. I can't slow down. There's a hook of land jutting out into the ocean, but I'm shooting farther away from it by the second. Mountains and ice loom closer and closer, and I can't stop. I have a body again, and it's filled with adrenaline and terror and regret.

I can't stop.

I wake with a gasp, pulse pounding. My bed is empty; my mother is gone. We were supposed to talk about everything, but instead she snuck away. It still feels like I'm falling, falling, falling. Queasy and sore, I creak out of bed and peer out my window. Yesterday's fog is gone, the sunlight bright and cold. Iris's truck isn't in her driveway, and my dad's car is gone too.

Are you still at Herring Cove? I text him.

> **Dad:** *At Indian Neck now. Dealing with a weird situation. Home soon, I promise.*

I'm still wearing my clothes from yesterday, so I pull on a coat and shoes and step outside. The wind carries splinters of ice, and my car is diamond-crusted with frost, just like my mother's fingernails. There's nothing in the holly bush, and I still can't shake that sickening sensation of falling.

As I wind through the neighborhood streets, heading for the main road that leads to Indian Neck, I wonder what the weird situation at the beach could be. I wonder if it has anything to do with my mother disappearing or her plan to fix things, however impossible that seems.

Down, down, down I tumble every time I blink. Opening the window, I suck in icy air and try to focus on what's here and real. My hands clenching the steering wheel, the backs of my legs pressing against the seat. I'm not falling. I'm here.

A tired-looking cop stands in the middle of the road just before the beach parking lot, gesturing for me to turn around. Beside him, a sign says ROAD CLOSED. I poke my head out the window.

"Is everything okay?"

"The parking lot is flooded," he says. "Tide came way up, and the beach is closed."

"My dad is there. He's a scientist," I add, as if this somehow makes it okay for me to be there too.

"You have to turn around," says the officer.

"Can I walk?"

He looks over his shoulder, grumbles, and shrugs. "Fine, but you can't park here."

I turn around and find a quiet street full of summer houses to leave my car on, then jog back down the road, past the officer, and into the parking lot. The gray ocean has come swirling up around the low dunes, gushing through the footpaths and crawling across the pavement. The waterline cuts the parking lot exactly in half. Overhead, gulls float in the roaring wind, which whips my clothing and stings my cheeks.

My dad's car sits in the dry back corner, his trunk wide open. He stands beside it, gesticulating wildly at a bearded man I recognize from the oceanographic institute.

"Dad!" I call, and he beckons me over. His colleague waves and heads off to his own car.

"What's going on?" I say. "Where are the whales?"

"Seven of them were released at Herring Cove. And one disappeared into thin air." He lets out a funny, frantic little laugh. "Or thin water."

"What?"

"Some volunteers carried the dead whale up to the parking lot. Joseph and I took a few quick tissue samples and were waiting for the truck so we could take it to the lab for a full necropsy. We wanted to figure out if it was sick, find some explanation for why the pod came all the way down here."

Some explanation, like a sad, motherless girl who wished the universe upside-down.

"Could be any number of things," he continues. "Global warming, higher ocean temperatures, or unusual currents." He pinches the bridge of his chapped nose with his fingers. "It might have something to do with the Northern Lights."

Sour nausea fills the back of my throat.

"If the solar storms were strong enough, they could disrupt the earth's magnetic field, maybe throw off a whale's internal compass." My dad's eyes have taken on a manic sort of gleam. "It's entirely possible, combined with an old or sick leader who led the pod astray."

I want to scream at him that it's irresponsible to ignore what's happening to us. I want to fill his shoes with meteorites so he can't keep walking away. I want to grab him by the front of his dry suit and drag him to my mother and force him to see her. If only I knew where she was.

"Anyway, we were tired and freezing after spending the night in the water," he says. "So we left the whale here and went to grab a coffee. It was five in the morning, and we figured nobody would touch it. The tide was out, and we can't have been gone more than twenty minutes." He rakes his fingers over his bald scalp. "But the water must have come up as soon as we left, and the whale just . . . vanished. At first I thought Dave came back with the truck and took it, but when I called, everybody was still at Herring Cove."

"Do you think it managed to swim away?" I say, wondering if my mother somehow resuscitated the animal and brought it into deeper water.

He scoffs. "That thing was deader than a doornail."

I flinch. That beautiful creature is now *that thing*.

"Somebody must have stolen it." His left eye is twitching visibly. "But I can't figure out how. They must have had a boat."

"But why would anybody steal a whale?" I say.

He ponders this for a moment. "Probably for the tusk. It's not legal to sell them, but you could make good money on the black market."

"So they *made* the tide come up, brought their boat over, and dragged the whale away?" I want to scream. It used to be like a game, hiding everything from him. Now I wonder how much of his not knowing was sheer willfulness.

He squints at the swirling, sandy water. "They could have brought a truck in right before the cops closed the parking lot."

"But you were here twenty minutes before and the tide was still out," I say. "Have you ever heard of it coming up that fast? With no storm or tsunami or anything?"

He rubs the back of his neck and mutters something about moon phases and spring equinoxes.

"Dad, seriously?"

"I need to go home and take a shower," he says, backing away from the lapping water. "And sleep for a couple of hours . . . or days."

A flutter of movement from across the beach catches my eye. On the top of a nearly submerged dune, a girl in a cloak stands facing the ocean, her black hair swirling like smoke.

"Where's your car?" says my dad.

I point vaguely behind me. "Down on one of the side roads."

"Want a ride?"

"No, thanks." Water laps against the toes of my shoes, and I can't drag my eyes away from that girl. "I think I'll hang out here for a little while. Maybe I'll look for some clues for you."

He lets out a roar of a yawn. "I really need to eat something and go to bed."

"That's fine. I'll be okay by myself."

"You sure?" He's already in the car, buckling his seat belt. "You're going to stay out of the water this time, right?"

"Yeah," I say. "You should shut your trunk before you go."

Sheepishly, he gets out and closes his trunk.

"I'll leave some pancakes in the oven for you," he promises. "Don't stay too long."

As his car leaves the parking lot, I skirt along the waterline toward the girl. She turns, and her mouth slithers into a grin.

"You're not supposed to climb on the dunes," I say. "It makes the sand erode and destroys them."

She tosses her wild hair. "This tide will wash away far more sand than my feet ever will."

"Did you do this?" I say.

"No." Her sapphire eyes gleam. "Your mother did. What's left of her, anyway."

I hate this girl with every electron in my body. "Have you found any more secret things to ruin my life with?"

Her mouth turns up, a wry slash. "We're not ruining anything. We're setting you free. Like your mother did for us."

"I don't want you to set me free." Frigid water sloshes around my ankles. Somehow I've stepped into the sea, or it's risen up over my feet. "I want you to leave me alone."

She bends low and whispers. "You don't get to tell us what to do. Nobody does."

Her words buzz inside my ear, and I take a splashing step backward. There's some kind of promise in the girl's stare; I don't understand it but it fills me with ice.

She straightens, brushing the sand from her cloak. "Anyway, your mother's gone, and your boring little friend is leaving, so you're much closer to freedom. Do you feel any lighter?"

"My mother isn't gone," I say. "I just saw her a few hours ago."

The look she gives me is somewhere between pity and amusement.

"She wouldn't leave me again." I feel like a petulant child, insisting things are true because I want them to be.

She raises her eyebrows in mock innocence. "Didn't you ask her to fix everything?"

I jolt, wondering how she heard our conversation, but these are girls who steal secret scraps of people's diaries out of the wind. "That's none of your business."

She shrugs. "Well, it's your fault she's gone. Or maybe it's her fault. It doesn't really matter now that it's done. One day you'll see it all clearly."

Turning away, the girl pulls up her hood. She steps off the dune and disappears into the water without making a single ripple.

CHAPTER 24

My mother can't be gone. She can't, she can't, she can't.

I mutter the words as I speed back up the main road, cursing every slow driver and red light in my way. The thermometer on my dashboard drops, ticking down the numbers, as I stomp on the gas and swing around turns. Thirty-four degrees. Thirty-three. Thirty-two. Falling, falling, falling.

It's twenty-six degrees by the time I pull into the driveway behind my dad's car.

She can't be gone.

A white feather flutters in the holly bush; I pluck it out and leap up the front steps.

In the living room, my knitted afghan is neatly folded across the back of the couch. The throw pillow sits back in its usual spot, clean and unrumpled and looking like it never spent a night in a tree house. As I head down the hall, my dad's voice floats out of his office. He's on the phone with somebody from work.

In my room, the blue book of my stories is back on its shelf. My legs start to wobble as I open my closet and shuffle through the clothes, stubbornly thinking that maybe this is hide-and-seek and she'll be crouching behind them. But she isn't there, and my wool coat hangs neat and smooth on its hanger. I press it to my face and inhale; it smells of ocean and wind. Not of her, not even that wrong, burnt-match scent.

I check every inch of my house, even the attic and the basement, but the longer I search, the more my sense of her dissipates. The electric hum in the air is fading so fast I can barely remember what it felt like. The threads aren't pulling anymore.

Forget about everything, she said. *Let go.*

Pulling on my—her—wool coat, I let myself outside.

Gone, gone, she's gone, trill the birds as my feet snap brittle pine needles. For the first time in years, I climb the tree-house ladder. As I ease the shack's door open, trails of gauzy cobwebs pull away and float on the breeze. The dust covering everything inside is undisturbed.

Like she was never here.

Curling up on the tree-house floor with my cheek in the dust, I let myself fall. I break apart and sob. Even when the universe gives me my mother back from the sky, I ruin it. She told me she'd fix this, and I let her. I let her go.

I cry until there's no sound left, until I'm unwound, unraveled. Then I roll on my back and stare up through a hole in the ceiling, at the little circle of faraway sky. The same sky that stole her. Wind gusts through the gaps in the tree-house walls, and I might be shaking from sorrow or I might be shivering, or it might be both.

Something white drops through the hole and lands on my chest. A scrap of paper with a single line of spidery handwriting across the middle. My mother's writing.

Find me where I left you.

CHAPTER 25

Once upon a time, in a green house at the top of the world, a little girl returned home with her mother after twenty-three days spent as a prisoner in a hotel. Once inside, her mother gave her a distracted kiss on the forehead, went into the living room, and turned on the television. The mother hated television; she said it was for people who lacked imagination. The girl didn't know how to look at her, didn't know what to say. She expected an apology or an explanation, but there was none.

After a morning spent awkwardly bumping into each other, the mother announced it was time go to the store.

"I don't want to go," said the girl. She wasn't entirely sure her mother wasn't bringing her back to that horrible, chilly hotel that reeked of pine. Without a word, the mother pulled their coats from the closet. The girl dithered and dawdled and did everything she could to avoid putting on her outdoor clothes, and finally her mother began to shout.

"Fine! Stay home by yourself." She banged the closet door shut and stuffed her fists into mittens. "Just make sure not to answer the door if trolls come knocking."

Shivers broke out on the girl's skin, and she hurried her feet into her boots and followed her mother outside without a word.

The grocery store was fluorescent-neon overload. The girl trailed behind her mother like a reluctant shadow, irritated each time she put another item in her basket. The lights buzzed through her scalp, making her brain jiggle in the bowl of her skull. As her mother picked up a third loaf of bread and squeezed it to check for freshness, the girl began to suspect she was wasting time on purpose.

"Mamma," she wheedled, tugging on the basket. "I need to pee."

"Can't you wait until we get home?" The look on her mother's face was undisguised irritation. Perhaps she was annoyed that the girl had come home. Perhaps she preferred her life without any difficult, whining children.

"No," said the girl, crossing one ankle over the other.

The mother sighed and picked up another loaf of bread. "I'll be done in a minute."

The girl uncrossed her legs and let go. Liquid streamed down her leg, out the cuff of her pants; it pooled on the eggshell tile and puddled inside her boot. She'd thought it would feel like triumph, but instead shame flooded through her, hotter than the urine on her skin. She hadn't done this in years.

"Eline," the mother hissed, dropping her basket and snatching the girl's arm.

The girl stared at the yellow puddle, which was shaped like a heart.

The mother didn't say a word as they rushed home without any groceries. The girl's pants froze solid, and when they reached their house, her mother had to put her under a hot shower until they thawed.

"You are much too old for this nonsense," she said as she left the bathroom.

The girl stayed under the shower until it ran cold and her fingertips shriveled. Then she got out and pulled pajamas over her clammy skin. She crept through the living room, where her mother was watching television again.

If she says anything, I'll stop. If she notices me, if she looks at me for even one second, it'll be my sign to stop.

But her mother's eyes stayed locked on the screen, and the girl kept walking until she reached the foot of the couch. She found the ring that was tangled in her hair. ████████████████████ ███████████████████████████████████████ ████████████████████████████

The girl hugged her arms around her middle and wondered what would happen now.

CHAPTER 26

I've gone to Indian Neck every morning and every afternoon for five days now, looking for another sign from her. The tide is back to normal, though huge chunks of dune have been carved away, eroded beyond repair.

My fault.

I've sat in the tree house, knitting in the fog and the rain and the sun and the wind, but she hasn't appeared. It's unimaginable that she's gone again, that she left without warning just like the last time.

Find me where I left you.

But I don't know where she left me. The last time I saw her was in my bed, and she's clearly not there now. I haven't seen a trace of magic since that day the whale disappeared. No snow in lockers, no owls or meteorites or narwhals. No girls in cloaks. My mother promised she'd fix everything, and maybe she has, but I feel more broken than ever.

It's five thirty, and I'm driving home from the beach, my joints stiff from sitting in cold sand. I can't keep doing this, can't keep up this painful hope. I'm starting to lose the sharpness of what she looked like, felt like, sounded like, and it's terrifying. Maybe

I'll fake an illness and spend the next week in bed. My dad's been so busy investigating his whale mystery that I doubt he'd even notice. And Iris and I still aren't speaking.

His car sits in the driveway with its engine off but the headlights still on. With a sigh, I lean inside and turn them off before his battery dies. The house is dark except for his office window, and I contemplate getting back in my car because I can't bear another night of rattling around by myself, useless and untethered.

The meteorite holes have been filled in with dirt. The crack in the front steps is repaired, though the concrete isn't quite the right color and there's a little ridge that I keep tripping over. The one thing that isn't fixed is the stupid, sticky door latch, and as I wedge my shoulder against the frame, my phone tumbles out of my coat pocket. Into the gap between steps and bush it falls, and I drop to my knees to fish it out.

Under a thin layer of dirt, a glimpse of white. I leap down from the steps and dig the envelope out. My name is printed on the front, once again, in M's dashed-off handwriting. Heart slamming, I tear it open.

Hvor er du? Skynd deg!

Sitting in the dirt with the holly scraping my cheek, I type the words into my phone.

Where are you? Hurry up!

"Hurry up where?" I say, gathering my things in a daze. The door springs open before my fingers touch the knob.

"That you?" calls my dad from his office. It's barely six o'clock and his words are muddled. He's been drinking a lot this week.

"Yeah." I drift down the hall to my room, muttering my mother's words like a mantra. *Find me where I left you. Find me where I left you. Find me where I left you.*

The *first time* she left me.

I open my desk drawer and rummage through papers and long-forgotten forms until I find the card. "Happy Birthday to a Wonderful Daughter," it says in elaborate script over a glittery vase of flowers. Clutching the card to my chest, I tap on my dad's half-open office door.

"Listen to this," he says, eyes locked on his laptop screen. "A juvenile male narwhal with unusual markings was spotted off Svalbard three days ago. It looks like the same one." He points to the screen, where a grainy photo shows a whale with a white spot over its eye in the shape of a bird in flight.

Elation flares in my chest. She brought it back. This is *right*. I set the open card down beside his computer and point to his note inside about the plane ticket.

"I'm ready," I say.

He's got an email window open, and words are soaring across the screen as he types. "Sorry, what?"

"I want to go to Svalbard. Next week."

"You're kidding." The words on the screen stop flying. "Right?"

I shake my head. "It's school vacation, and I have nothing else to do. Can I go?"

My dad leans back in his chair and squints up at me. "Why do you want to go to Svalbard all of a sudden?"

My hand strays to my pocket, where her note lies hidden. I want to tell him the truth, that his wife is back and if he goes to Svalbard, he might see her again. But I know he still resents what she did. He won't be happy that I hid her from him all this time, and he's already uneasy about the strange things that have been happening. If he snaps, if he says no to this trip, I might never see her again.

"What if it *is* the same whale?" I say. "We could go up there together and you could find out."

He clicks back to the photo of the whale, and his cursor dances around the bird-shaped spot. "But why do *you* want to go?"

"I've been wanting to for a long time." The words tumble out fast, and I'm painfully aware of the nervous insincerity behind them. "But I keep chickening out right before I ask you, and I was thinking that I need to just do it fast, make the decision. Like ripping off a Band-Aid."

My dad gives me a long look, his expression unreadable. "You don't just pop up to the Arctic on a whim. You need time to plan and pack. Organize things. Talk to people."

"I have all my ski stuff. And you just got me those new boots for Christmas, and Mormor is there. She'd probably love to see us."

This is probably the biggest lie I've told so far, and I can tell by his dubious expression that I'm losing him. I cannot let that happen.

"If it really is the same whale, this could answer all your questions," I say. "You could find it, do some more tests, maybe put a tracker on it and see where it goes next. Think about all the possibilities, Dad. You could figure out this whole mystery." My voice is about an octave too high, but I catch the hungry flash in his eyes. "Could you just check if we can get flights for next week? If not, it's fine."

It's the furthest thing from fine, technically, but I can't let that stop me.

My dad's hand strays to his mouse. "I'll think about it."

An excited squeak slips out of my mouth, and he holds up his three-fingered hand. "I said *think*. No promises. And I'll need to call your grandmother."

If only this didn't have to involve my grandmother. Leaving him the card and the ticket, I head for my room on wobbling legs. This has to be the right choice. She wouldn't have just left me, not again, and M's note seems to confirm it. But the idea of going to Svalbard is terrifying.

I crash to a stop on the threshold of my room. My window is wide open, and a book lies on my desk, its pages fluttering and whipping in the wind. The book is handmade; its covers are two mismatched squares of cardboard stitched together with yarn. Its pages are random scraps: half a sheet of notebook paper, a pizza delivery menu, the back of an electricity bill, a paper towel. Each sheet is covered in my mother's spidery cursive.

The first story begins, as all the stories do:

Once upon a time . . .

PART
TWO

CHAPTER 27

Once upon a time, in a green house at the top of the world, a mother waited for her child to be born. She had bought her plane ticket, packed and repacked her suitcase: books, pajamas, toothbrush, diapers, more books. She was supposed to be sleeping, but an ache in her lower back kept nudging her awake, irritating pain in a body that was stretched too tight and no longer hers. She left her husband snoring in bed and quietly let herself outside.

Even at midnight, the low sun was bright, the air scented with cold sea and wind over stone. On an improvised clothesline behind the house, the mother had hung three pairs of tiny footed pajamas that she'd recently bought. She wanted them to absorb that night-sun smell so her daughter would know it as soon as she came into the world. She knew this child already, had borne her weight, felt her tiny hiccups against her ribs. She understood the soft calmness of her daughter's personality, so different from her own whirring nervousness. Already, she loved her more than her own self.

As the mother reached up to unpin the first sleeve, a fist clenched her heart and she let go of the clothespin with a gasp. The pajamas fell in the mud and the mother bent low, hands on knees, and tried to pull together the whirling pieces of herself. Soon she and this baby would be separate entities; soon she would be responsible for a fragile creature who depended on no one but her. There were so many things out of her control, so many wild, unpredictable dangers. Her husband always told her to stop worrying about these things, that they were all in her imagination, but she knew they weren't. She wished she could keep the child inside her body, keep her safe forever, but that simply wasn't possible.

"I can't do it," she whispered. "Please, I can't."

The whispering of wings filled the air. Claws grasped the shoulders of her bathrobe, her hair, her wrists and fingers. White feathers flew like snow as the birds flapped and pulled and rose. The mother wanted to scream, but if her husband heard her scream, he might pull her down, and she wasn't sure if she wanted him to. So up the mother flew, over the little town of Longyearbyen, its rows of candy-colored houses cradled by flat-topped mountains. Down through a fjord with water like blue stained glass. Over a craggy glacier with waterfalls pouring into the sea, then up, up again to the top of a snow-covered peak.

The birds' claws pierced the mother's skin as she flew, sent droplets of blood raining down to Earth. The inevitable pain in her back grew deeper, fiercer, until it felt like she might turn inside out. The birds set her down in a nest made of down feathers, softer than clouds, and with a great, gasping shudder, the mother realized she hadn't escaped a thing. She pushed her child out into the world, wet and steaming in the cold.

The mother pulled off her bathrobe and wrapped the child in it. She looked and looked and looked at her somber-eyed daughter, who radiated calm and was made with her own electrons.

Wild elation and terror sang through her veins, made her feel she could rocket into space. She could have walked home naked and not shivered once.

When the birds picked her up again, she didn't feel the sting of their claws, for she was concentrating too hard on not dropping her baby. The mother and child flew back across the fjord and into the town that was now slowly waking up, though it had been light all night long. She pointed to her house at the end of the row, and as the birds set her down, her feet slid right into her slippers where she'd left them.

The mother looked at the tiny yellow pajamas lying in the mud, and the fist closed around her heart again. The door had latched shut behind her, and she hadn't brought her key. She didn't know what she was doing, the baby was less than an hour old, and she had already taken her on a reckless flight over fjords and mountains that could have killed her. If anyone found out about this, she'd lose her child.

Cold, stone-scented wind blustered in from the sea, and the baby began to cry.

"Come back, birds," whispered the mother.

The door swung open, and her husband appeared, bleary and tousled. The mother stood there, holding the child he hadn't been expecting to see for weeks, not knowing what to say or how to explain. The confusion in his face faded to love as he drank the child in.

It didn't matter how or why, he said. She was back. They were home. They were safe.

CHAPTER 28

Over the tip of our airplane's wing, Svalbard's mountains sprawl, covered in snow that is blue instead of white. At this time of year, the sun hovers just under the horizon during the brightest part of the days, still not visible. The days are lightening from the black polar night, but they'll remain shrouded in twilight for a while still.

The pilot announces in Norwegian and English that we'll soon be making our descent, and it's too late to change my mind, too late to beg my dad to take me home. A cluster of taller mountains drifts past, fleecy clouds like blankets pulled up to just below their peaks. I feel as if I could leap out of this plane and run across the soft blue.

This is the last leg of our trip, the second in Norway. After an overnight flight to Oslo, then a layover and a two-hour delay in Tromsø, we were up again, heading northeast over snowy peaks and yawning fjords and then the wide, flat sea. By then I could barely fight the exhaustion of eighteen hours of traveling, and finally, the gentle bouncing and the engine's hum lulled me to sleep.

A Norwegian phrase book lies open in my lap. Even with the

phonetic guides, I know my accent is utterly wrong as I mutter quietly to myself. I should have swallowed my pride and asked my mother to speak Norwegian with me, even if it was awkward and embarrassing to start all over again like a baby.

I've read her story at least a hundred times now, this new version that isn't the same as the one she told me when I was little. Or it isn't the same as what I remembered. I hadn't realized that she was so afraid of having me, that she'd wanted to escape even all those years ago. I hope she isn't trying to escape again now. But she can't be if she sent me that note.

"Don't be nervous," says my dad, though he's the one who's bitten all his nails off on this flight, a habit he supposedly kicked years ago.

I don't want to be nervous either—I want to believe that what I'm doing is right—but it's impossible to ignore the worry gnawing at my stomach. I try to focus on the landscape outside, but it's so unreal, so overwhelmingly blue, that it's just making things worse. This feels like another planet. There are no towns, not a single house. No sign of humanity anywhere.

The plane bumps down through clouds like spun sugar, and a wide fjord appears, frozen in some places and rippling in others.

"Didn't there use to be more ice in the winter?" I press my forehead against the window, straining for a glimpse of Ekmanfjorden, which is a smaller branch off the larger channel of Isfjorden, on the opposite side from Longyearbyen. I don't know how I'll get out there if the ice isn't solid. It'd take forever to go all the way around on land.

"That's right." My dad leans over me to peer out the window. "But everything's been warming since we left. Most of the fjords aren't freezing solid in the winter anymore. The sea ice has been decreasing by staggeringly large amounts in the last few years. The snow's been slushy too, and they've had avalanches in town. A few years ago, houses got destroyed and a man died."

His breath is sour after two days of traveling, and I shift, trying to find an inch or two more of space. "Did you know him?"

My dad shakes his head and gives me back my precious window view and air. "People have had to move out of their houses in the danger zones, and they've had to condemn entire buildings."

"Was our house in the danger zone?" I say.

"No."

Even though it's selfish relief, the knot in my chest eases a little. The low mountains look softer under the clouds, their edges rounded by snow that glows purple now in the fading light. We bank hard, and a flat-bottomed valley opens up between the mountains. At its base, a smattering of block structures slide into view, growing denser and organizing themselves into rows on either sides of a handful of roads. The plane drops into an air pocket, and everybody gasps. To the right of the town, a peninsula stretches out toward us, with a runway that begins and ends at the sea. This place hovers just on the brink of familiarity, not quite new to my eyes, but not old or comfortable either.

"Ten years," says my dad, rubbing the stubble on his jaw. "Could be a hundred years, could be a day." He bumps his shoulder against mine, and we watch Longyearbyen unfold, both of us lost in thought. We bank again, dipping lower and lower until I wonder if we're going to land on the fjord. Then, with a lurch and a skidding bounce, we're tearing across the runway, reverse thrusters screaming. My dad's eyes are clenched shut, but all I can think is that I'm back, I'm back to this place at the top of the world I thought I'd never see again. My heart echoes the rocketing engines, and my ribs are the brakes pulling against it, reining it in.

I'm here, I want to scream. *I flew to the top of the world to find you.* But I've heard nothing from her since finding her book last week. I did get two more letters from M, though. Both the same: *Hurry up.*

The seat belt light goes off, and the pilot starts talking, but I can't process anything he's saying. Cold seeps into the plane as the flight attendants open the door. Everybody's standing, pulling coats and bags down from overhead, but my dad is cemented in place, staring at the in-flight magazine poking out of the seat pocket.

"Dad?" I nudge his arm, and for a second, he looks like a lost little boy.

What I mean to say is *Are you all right?* but what comes out is "Can we get off the plane?"

He jumps up, narrowly missing the overhead bin with the top of his head. "Got your hat and mittens?" he says, but it sounds like he means to say *Are you all right?* too.

I'm not, but hopefully I will be soon. My dad pulls on the double-knit wool cap I made him, and I follow him down the aisle.

There's no jet bridge, just a set of stairs going down to the runway. The moment I step out of the plane, glacial wind shears through all my layers of clothing. I don't recall the air hurting like this. I thought my body would automatically remember how to cope with this Arctic climate, but the cold is a punch to the chest.

"Try to breathe through your nose," says my dad, but when I

do, it feels like wooden spears being shoved up my nostrils. He laughs. "You'll get used to it again."

I wonder how that's possible as we head toward the airport. The daylight is almost gone now, the sky an inky blue. A thin crust of snow covers everything, and it's still not quite how I remember. Everything's stark and rocky and huge on a scale I can't quite get my brain around. It's so beautiful and so impossibly cold.

A crowd of people mill around the single baggage carousel, weary and anxious for their belongings. In the center of the carousel stands a taxidermied polar bear, its massive head slung low and its dead face arranged into a grim attempt at a smile. Iris would have a heart attack if she saw this poor creature. My stomach aches at the thought of her, and I wonder if she still hates me.

"Isbjørn," says my father, like he's testing the word to see if it still works. He mutters a few more words, and his pronunciation is better than mine, which is unfair considering I'm the actual Norwegian. Half-Norwegian.

As the carousel clanks to life and begins to trundle out bags, I stare into the bear's glass eyes, wondering if it's the one that saved me from freezing to death all those years ago. But there's nothing remarkable about its features, nothing that sparks memory, and for that I'm relieved.

"There it is." My dad hefts his enormous pack from the carousel, then my red wheeled suitcase a few seconds later. I scan the crowd for my grandmother. Among the jumble of passengers, there's a dark swish that might be a cloak. I shrink closer to my dad, who is fiddling with his phone.

"Mormor said she'd meet us out in the parking lot," he says, frowning at the screen.

She couldn't even be bothered to come into the airport. I don't know why this surprises me. I scan the crowd, searching for one of those sinister girls in cloaks, or all of them, but everyone's wearing woolen sweaters or bright outdoor gear. Maybe I imagined it.

"I specifically turned on roaming before we left," mutters my dad. "Remind me to cancel this contract when we get home."

After a few more minutes of swearing and swiping, my dad shoves his phone in his pocket and moves toward the exit. As soon as we step into the parking area, the wind snatches my breath away again. My dad points to a battered SUV behind a shuttle bus, headlights flashing. Inside the vehicle, the shadowy form of my grandmother doesn't move, doesn't wave. As we skirt around the bus, snow squeaking under our boots, the SUV's window lowers and a woman with short gray hair peers out.

Mormor's face looks just as I remember it: paper-thin skin stretched over sharp cheekbones, a narrow, unsmiling mouth. Her flinty eyes flick up and down the length of me, and I wonder what she makes of me now that I'm no longer a child, whether the difference registers at all, whether she cares.

"You can put your things in the back." She doesn't even attempt to speak Norwegian, and hot shame washes over me. The tailgate of the SUV opens. My dad takes my suitcase and loads it in, but I wait in the searing cold until he climbs into the front seat before opening my own door.

"Welcome." Mormor's tone is anything but welcoming. Her eyes find mine in the rearview mirror, and I have a sudden sense of what a fly feels like when it realizes it's stuck in a web. I cough, rub my nose, and mutter my thanks.

"It's good to see you again, Astrid," says my dad, and Mormor makes a noncommittal *hmm* sound, not unlike the one my mother makes. "Seat belts," she orders, and my dad clicks his on and tosses me a sheepish look. She cares if we die in a car accident. That's something, at least.

It's fully dark now as we rattle along the road that runs along the sometimes frozen, sometimes watery expanse of Isfjorden. The light spilling from our headlights gives occasional glimpses of chunky ice, of snow, of surprisingly well-maintained road. After a few minutes, we round a bend, and my heart soars as the lights of town come into view. This feels almost like it could be home. More buildings, more signs of humanity appear: some warehouses, a marina with big, shadowy boats. Snowmobiles everywhere, everywhere. A large building that looks like it belongs in a sci-fi movie, obtuse angles and jutting corners and glowing windows. My father cranes his neck as we pass; it's UNIS, the university center where he worked on his PhD.

Memory-pieces of this place are slowly sweeping in, fitting back together. The boxy shapes of the buildings, the spaces between them. The brown-gray ice along the sides of the street. The looming mountains turned to shadows in the dark. We pass more shops and businesses, a road that I'm nearly certain is the one I used to live on, but nothing looks quite like I remember.

And then we're turning into a driveway beside a stark, white hotel and my bones are turning to ice. I haven't been here since I was carried, unwilling, by my father. Mormor pulls her car up tight against the building and shuts off the engine. Her steel eyes find mine in the rearview mirror again.

"Your aunt and her family are here for dinner."

My mother's sister, Grete, moved to Oslo as soon as she

finished school and never came back. I have no memory of her whatsoever, and I didn't realize she had a family.

"Hopefully they haven't managed to burn anything while I was gone." Mormor climbs out of the SUV, leaving us to gather our things and follow her around the side of the building.

My dad pulls on his backpack and tries to take my suitcase too.

"I can do it," I insist, wanting a little more time before I have to walk into that building. Moving at a sloth's pace, I drag my bag across the packed snow and stop at the foot of the stairs. HOTEL LUND, says the sign in tight black font. A faint whiff of pine-scented cleaning liquid tickles my nostrils, and the urge to throw up is overwhelming.

I can't do it.

My dad's mitten closes over mine on the handle of my suitcase. "It's going to be okay, Eli-bug."

I'm afraid if I open my mouth, vomit will come out, so I give him a quick nod.

He pulls me into an awkward, one-armed hug. "You have no idea how many times I wished I'd never brought you here."

I want to tell him it's all right, but it really isn't. A sliver of moon appears behind the hotel. I can taste its light, cold and metallic like the back of a spoon.

"I thought it was the only way to make your mother get help," he says.

Extricating my shoulder, I squint at him. "So you used me as a bargaining chip?"

He shakes his head. "It wasn't safe for her to be alone with you anymore. Don't you remember her burning our carpet with that film projector?"

My hand snaps open in shock; my suitcase tips back into the snow. "The fireplace made those shadows. We didn't even own a film projector."

"Of course we did," says my dad with such utter conviction that I almost believe him.

Almost.

I turn around to pick up my suitcase, and a flash of silver catches my eye. From across the street comes the rustle of heavy fabric. Three girl-shaped shadows shift and murmur.

"Why are you here?" I whisper, stepping into the road.

"Eli!" My dad yanks my coat, and I trip backward over my bag. A snowmobile roars past, and by the time I've wiped the stinging snow off my face, the girl-shaped shadows are gone. My dad shouts something in Norwegian, but the snowmobile driver careens around a corner without slowing. A hunting rifle is slung across their back.

"You okay?" says my dad, helping me brush the rest of the snow off my coat.

I'm nowhere near okay, but it's too late now. I've flown to the top of the world to find my mother, and so have those girls. Which means she hasn't fixed everything, but it must also mean I'm on the right track to finding her. I just have to keep moving. Cotton-mouthed and shaking, I drag my suitcase up the hotel steps and pull open the heavy door.

CHAPTER 29

As I step into the hotel, the harsh scent of wood polish and pine stings my eyes. Nothing has changed since I was last here, not the wooden chairs or the straight-backed sofa that no one ever sits on. There's no fire in the fireplace, and the room is barely warmer than the outside.

"You can put your things in room twelve, at the top of the stairs," calls my grandmother. "Leave your boots on the rack."

The walls on either side of the door are lined with long metal shoe racks. I remember them being crammed so full that Mormor was constantly picking stray boots up off the floor and complaining about all the mud. Tonight there are only two pairs of brand-new hiking boots on one end and four pairs of scuffed-up snow boots on the other. None of them are my mother's, though I wasn't exactly expecting her to show up for dinner. After pulling off my own boots, I peer up the spotless steps and shiver.

"Give me that." My dad shifts his backpack and takes the handle of my suitcase. "You go first. Know where it is?"

I nod and gulp, wondering if I can make it through a night here without running out into the snow. My dad follows me up the stairs, thumping and grunting. "Couldn't have put us on the ground floor," he mutters.

"Maybe the other rooms are full?"

"Doubt it," he says.

At the top, the polished floor radiates cold through my socks, and I wish I'd brought slippers. Our room's door has a burnished brass number twelve on it, and as it swings open, the cloying scent of roses wafts out. My throat goes tight. This room is exactly the same as it was the last time I cleaned it: a metal set of bunk beds and a single twin bed with a narrow desk between them. Same pale blue curtains, same green striped blankets. This place is a time capsule.

My dad wheels my suitcase in and flops down on the lower bunk. The metal frame grates and groans in protest. "Not exactly the Ritz," he says, staring up at a crack that runs across the ceiling. "Your mother always hated it here."

I'm back on that cot in Mormor's apartment, shivering as the woodstove grows cold and the massive weight of the hotel creaks overhead. Wondering if my mother will ever come and take me home. Wondering if she's forgotten about me, if she's decided it's better this way.

My dad's foot taps against the bed frame. "I feel like I'm drowning in memories," he says.

Drowning is a good word for it. I haven't drawn a full breath since we walked in the door. Setting my backpack on the single bed by the window, I check for the hundredth time that both of our books are still in there. "How could you possibly have thought taking me away from her would fix everything?" I say.

He makes a sound like someone just elbowed his stomach. "I didn't think it would fix *everything*."

"So why did you do it?"

"Because I was out of options," he says. "You remember what she was like. Beaming one minute, flat as cement the next. I knew she had a rough childhood and a lot of lingering issues, but I didn't realize how deep it all went. And it got worse after you were born."

"She wasn't that bad," I insist.

"You were a child," he says. "There was a lot you missed."

I bristle at the insinuation. "There was a lot you missed too."

"I just wanted her to get some help," he says. "I was crazy in love with her, but sometimes I didn't know her at all. Sometimes she scared me. But then I'd look at the two of you without me, and it seemed like everything was fine. You were happy, you were loved, and maybe it didn't matter if your mom wasn't always the way I wanted her to be. If accepting that meant you were happy, I could deal with it."

"So you started ignoring things," I say. This is all starting to make sense.

"Living with her was like walking on ice," he says. "It was like carrying the whole family over a frozen lake. I thought if I didn't talk about her . . . emotional stuff, if we all pretended it was fine, I could keep us all safe. If I could just make sure nobody looked down and saw how thin the ice was, we could make it across."

Memory floods my senses: my mother carrying me across Ekmanfjorden under the ghosting, green sky. There was so much more than the stuff my dad worried about, so many things beyond her and me in our sad, unbelievable story.

My dad sighs heavily. "But then one day, the house was on fire and you could have been killed. So I did the only thing I could think of. I took you away, and I broke everything. We all fell."

Now I'm under the ice, numb and screaming for breath.

Sinking under the weight of my winter clothes and my sorrow.

No.

I'm here, in a rose-reeking room in a hotel at the top of the world. Here to find her. Here to fix this.

"I need to brush my teeth." Pulling my toiletry bag from my suitcase, I escape into the hall, where the shared bathroom is. The one I scrubbed until my knuckles bled. It looks like Mormor has managed to find somebody else to scrub the grout: the white on everything is pristine, though the fixtures are old and the folded bath mat is threadbare. At least the floral stench is fainter in here. I shut the door and slide the lock into place.

"Mamma?" I whisper. "Can you hear me?" I lean in close to the mirror over the sink, closer until I can see the pores in my forehead, the stray eyebrow hairs I can never manage to pluck. I used to spend hours staring at myself in the mirror, wondering when I'd start to look like her, if I'd ever start to look like her. If I'd grow into these long features and lose the round cheeks I got from my father. Half closing my eyes, I let my vision go foggy, tip my chin so that the angles of my face narrow. I could almost be her like this.

The door crashes open, and I slam my elbow against the sink. The slide-bolt lock has been ripped from the wall, dusty screws poking out. A wash of cold air floods the bathroom. There's no one in the hall.

"Dinner is ready," calls Mormor from downstairs.

CHAPTER 30

Once upon a time, in a stark white hotel at the top of the world, a girl who would one day become a mother lay in her bed, cradling a flashlight and a book. It was well past midnight, and she knew she'd be exhausted in the morning, but she couldn't bring herself to close the book, a collection of stories from all over the world about the Northern Lights. As the girl read, tendrils of silvery moonlight slipped in through the cracks around her window shade. She wiggled her foot under the blanket, and the light darted and danced around it. It wanted to play.

The girl cast a glance at the narrow bed beside hers, where her sister lay sleeping. The girl could never, ever fall asleep when she was supposed to. There were too many things hiding at the edges, on the undersides of the ordinary world, things no one else seemed to notice. The moonlight flicked up to her face and tickled the tip of the girl's nose. She sneezed, then sprang out of bed.

The slow breathing and snores of the hotel guests slipped out from under their doors as the girl crept to the lobby. She slid her feet into the boots she'd left on the rack, pulled her coat over her nightgown, and escaped.

There wasn't a sound in the streets, not a light in any house.

The moon had hidden, and the sky was filled with green, slow-swirling like smoke. In a whisper, the girl called out to the North Wind, and it swept her along the deserted street, the toes of her boots trailing lines in the snow. Down to Isfjorden she flew, and the wind set her down right in the center of the frozen fjord. Up in the sky, the thousand shades of green whispered in a thousand hushing languages. The light seeped through her clothes and skin and filled her heart with a softness she never felt anymore when she was with her mother.

The girl stretched her hand up, and a thread of light began to unspool, swirling lower and lower. The multitudes of whispering became a single word, repeating over and over. Her name. She closed her eyes and reached.

Suddenly, she was airborne. Pain crushed around her middle, and she slammed down. Something heavy landed on top of her; it grunted as they hit the ice. The girl opened her eyes to her mother's looming face, her eyes blazing like two comets.

"What on earth were you thinking?" hissed the mother.

The girl could barely speak with her mother's weight crushing her lungs. "The lights. They only . . . wanted to . . . play."

"Play?" The mother set her hands on both sides of the girl's face and leaned in so close that she blocked out the entire sky. "They'd snatch you up and throw you away as soon as they got bored. You're nothing to them."

"I'm not nothing," the girl whispered. Her mother rolled off her, but there was no relief in being able to breathe again.

"You will not leave the hotel for the rest of the week except to go to school," said the mother, stomping back toward the lights of their tiny town.

"But, Mamma, Marit's Christmas party is tomorrow," wailed the girl.

Her mother scoffed. "Marit will be celebrating without you."

The lights danced and spun as if they were laughing at the girl as she trailed behind her mother. When they reached the outskirts of town, the aurora winked out and the moon reemerged, luminous and serene. As she climbed the steps of the pine-scented hotel, the girl wished her mother had been just a second too slow.

CHAPTER 31

As I head downstairs with my dad, for some reason all I can think of is the lingonberry-and-people stew from the troll story Mormor told my mother when she was little. But as we enter the apartment behind the hotel's front desk, a real smell takes over from the ghastly one in my imagination; it's brothy and rich and scented with onions. Definitely not made from people. The flopping in my stomach eases.

In a perfectly white kitchen, Mormor stands at the stove, poking a spoon into a large stockpot and frowning. "Your aunt has been fiddling with the spices," she says, jabbing her spoon at the dining room. The tall woman standing beside the table looks like my mother, but her hair is thinner, and she's got tiny lines around her eyes and mouth. My mother doesn't have any lines, though she's four years older than her sister.

"Eline," she says, drawing me into a hug. Her body is soft like my mother's used to be.

"Sorry," I say. "My Norwegian is rusty. And by *rusty*, I mean nonexistent."

Her smile reaches all the way up to her eyebrows, and the similarity to my mother's expression stabs me in the gut. It's so unlike what she looks like now. "Your father told Mormor. Don't worry, we all speak English."

Over her shoulder, a grinning, curly-haired man catches my eye. Beside him is a teenage girl who looks around my age. Her dark hair is cut in a bob with ruler-straight bangs, and she's almost as small as Iris. It feels like missing a limb, not having Iris around anymore.

"This is your uncle Álvaro and your cousin Kaja," says Grete, letting go of me with what feels like reluctance.

A tiny stud glints in the side of Kaja's nose. "Love your sweater," she says.

I finger the gray wool hem. "Thanks, I made it."

"Maybe Eline can teach you how to knit," says Aunt Grete. "Since you don't seem to be interested in learning from your grandmother." There's an edge in her tone, not unlike the way Mormor speaks. My mother gets that edge sometimes too.

"I didn't know Mormor knitted." I peer into the kitchen, where my grandmother is wiping down counters with a cloth. The room is full of the yeasty aroma of fresh-baked bread, and my stomach gurgles.

"Are you kidding?" says Uncle Álvaro, whose accent is different from everyone else's, smoother with rounder vowels. "She knits, sews, weaves, macramés, you name it. Genetics are a beautiful thing, eh?"

"I do not make *macramé*." Mormor says the word like it's some kind of pornography as she nudges past us, carrying a steaming tureen of stew. "Now, will you all sit down before everything gets cold?"

On the wall above the table, a hand-painted cuckoo clock ticks and clinks. In all the days I spent here, I never saw it strike the hour, though I often heard the bird's eerie call echoing through the hotel. It's three minutes to six now. I wonder where my mother is.

"How long have you all been back on Svalbard?" says my dad.

"Nine years." My aunt's eyes slide to Mormor, who is steadfastly doling out bowls of thick, meaty stew and giving no indication of listening. "Álvaro, Kaja, and I were living in Oslo, but we came up to give Mamma a hand with the hotel and ended up never leaving."

I can't imagine Mormor ever needing a hand with anything. Forcing small underlings to help her scrub toilets, yes, but not asking for help.

"Grete's still helping with the hotel bookkeeping and the website, and I run an expedition company," says Uncle Álvaro.

"He guides people up mountains and makes sure they don't fall into glaciers," says Kaja, passing me a bowl.

"These are hills compared to what we have in Argentina," says Uncle Álvaro with a wink.

"Do you ever go out to Ekmanfjorden?" I say.

"Be careful of my tablecloth," barks Mormor at my aunt.

Uncle Álvaro tilts his head so Mormor can't see him rolling his eyes. "We do some longer trips in the summertime with boats, but the fjords are a mess of ice and water right now. Can't take a small boat, can't take a snowmobile without going all the way around."

It is utterly impossible that I've come thousands of miles, only to be trapped less than fifty away from where she left me. I refuse to even consider it. There must be a way. With my spoon, I nudge a chunk of meat in my bowl. "Is this . . . beef?"

"Of course it is," says Mormor. "I wanted to get reindeer, but they were all out at the market."

With a twinge of relief for the sweet, goat-size reindeer who live in this area, I scoop up a mouthful of the stew. Instantly, I'm thrown back to my old kitchen table, my mother sitting across from me, both of us leaning over bowls and laughing as steam billowed up over our faces. She must have used Mormor's recipe.

"What are your plans while you're here?" asks Aunt Grete, handing the bread basket to my dad.

"I'm meeting up with some marine biologists at UNIS in the morning," says my dad. "Eli was saying she'd like to have a look around town, maybe climb a mountain or two?" He waggles his eyebrows.

"Actually, I was wondering . . ." I drag myself away from my stew and my memories. "Do any of you know somebody named Marit who used to be friends with my mother?"

Mormor stabs her spoon into a potato. "Grete, what did you do to this stew while I was out?"

Aunt Grete laughs. "It's just a bit of paprika, Mamma."

"It's delicious," I say, wondering if anyone heard my question.

"It tastes like you ground up an entire pepper plant, roots and all," says Mormor. "Oof, I can't trust anyone to do anything around here."

As Mormor and Aunt Grete bicker about spicing, Kaja nudges my foot under the table. "I know Marit," she says.

"Oh, is she still here?" There's a sour undertone to my dad's words, though his expression is politely interested.

"Of course," says Kaja. "I can't imagine her ever leaving."

"Do you know where she lives?" I say.

"Sure. Want me to take you there tomorrow?"

"I would love that." Glancing at the window, I wish we could go this very second, but it's pitch-dark outside. The minute hand of the clock hits the number twelve, and it lets out a creak and a pop, but no bird appears. A door slams in the lobby, and I'm out of my seat before I realize. Everyone looks up, still chewing.

"It's those awful newlyweds," says Mormor, sopping up stew with her bread and grimacing. "They clogged the bathtub with flower petals last night. And who do you think had to scrape them all out?"

"Mamma, keep your voice down," says Grete. "You can't afford for your online reviews to get any worse."

"Massage oil all over the pillowcases." Mormor does not keep her voice down. "Disgusting."

I peer out through the sitting room. A giggling man and woman are tiptoeing through the lobby. She's clutching a bottle of wine.

"Is anybody else staying here tonight?" I say, easing down onto my chair again.

"Just you and the newlyweds." Mormor rubs at a spot on the table with her napkin. "Don't worry, they're on the ground floor, so you won't hear their . . . noise." She wrinkles her nose, and Kaja chokes on a mouthful of bread.

"So, tell us about this whale," says Uncle Álvaro to my dad.

"You mean the zombie narwhal?" says my dad. "The one that somehow swam two thousand miles with no heartbeat?"

I gulp and press a hand over my mouth. The stew is threatening to make its way back up.

Kaja starts gathering plates and bowls. "Want to give me a hand with dessert, Eline?"

"Sure. And you can call me Eli. Everyone at home . . . I mean, in the US . . . does."

Mormor's thin lips purse, and I grab a handful of plates and follow my cousin into the kitchen.

Kaja cranks a window open and fans her face. "It was getting so stuffy in there," she says, motioning to a chair by the window. Then she rummages in her bag, pulls out a ginger candy, and hands it to me.

"Thanks." I tuck the candy into my mouth, and sharp spice floods my tongue.

"I always feel queasy after long plane trips." Kaja starts piling dishes beside the sink. "So, what year are you in school?"

"Eleventh. You?"

"VG2." Kaja squirts soap into a basin in the sink and turns on the tap. "I think that's like a year above you?"

"That's high school . . . secondary school here, right?" The ginger heat spreads through my stomach, tempering the bitter nausea.

"Upper secondary. But it's all the same building here: primary, secondary." Kaja waves a hand and bubbles splat onto the counter. "How many kids are in your class?"

"Around two hundred and fifty."

Her eyes go wide.

"It's a regional school, though, so that includes a bunch of towns," I say. "It must be nice to have the same small group of people."

"It's really hard, actually," says Kaja. "Most people's parents only have job postings here for a couple of years, so it's like there's a revolving door at the school. My best friend just moved back to

Madrid last month. Every time I get close to anybody, they leave."

"My best friend is probably leaving too." I gather up the dirty silverware and pass it to Kaja. "She just got accepted to a school that's two hundred miles away."

"Sorry to hear it," says Kaja. "There's nothing worse than missing someone you love. But two hundred miles doesn't seem so bad."

I laugh. "Maybe for you it's not."

Kaja piles the rest of the plates in the basin and turns off the tap. "At least you can drive that distance. I have to fly literally everywhere."

"I know, I know." I wipe a fleck of broth off the counter with my thumb. "Still, it doesn't always seem fair that she's leaving me behind."

"Ah well, Mormor always says life isn't supposed to be fair." Kaja turns to the fridge. "But you're here now, and that's pretty great. I've always wanted to meet you."

I wish I could say the same—I wish I'd known Kaja even existed. "Did your mother ever tell you about my mother?"

Kaja's hand pauses on the refrigerator door. "A little."

"What happened to that dessert?" calls Uncle Álvaro from the dining room.

"Coming!" Kaja pulls a cake covered in cream and berries from the refrigerator shelf. "We'll talk more tomorrow. I can pick you up around nine if you're not too jet-lagged?"

"Sure, that'd be perfect."

Still a little nauseous, I spend the rest of the meal building whipped-cream mountains on my plate and balancing berries on top, but then the juice starts leaking out, dripping blood-like stains down the mountains.

At seven o'clock, the little doors on the cuckoo clock bulge again, but don't open. The bird is hiding. Just like my mother.

At five past seven, Mormor gets up and starts clearing away plates and unfinished drinks. "I've got an early day tomorrow," she says. "Thank you for coming over, Grete. Next time you won't ruin my stew, I hope."

Grete pulls a face. "Next time I'll make it even better."

"See you at nine!" sings Kaja as she pulls on her coat and follows her parents out into the moonlight.

Once they're gone, my dad does an exaggerated shivery dance. "Need any help cleaning up, Astrid?" he calls.

"No," she says. "Good night."

I follow him up the creaking stairs to our depressing, rose-scented room.

"Why were you asking about Ekmanfjorden earlier?" he asks, digging through his backpack and fishing out his toiletry bag.

Turning my back, I open my own suitcase and start to rummage even though there's nothing I need. "I just thought . . . I don't know, that it would be good to go back there."

"Why?" He sits on my bed so I have to look at him.

Because Mamma might be there. The words are on the tip of my tongue, but they're so ridiculous. How could she possibly be out there with no food or gear or shelter?

"I just want to." I feel like a petulant, deluded child.

My dad's mouth thins. "You heard your uncle. There's no way to get there at this time of year."

There has to be a way.

"I agreed to take you to Longyearbyen." There's a microscopic

wobble in his voice. "Not to Ekmanfjorden. It's way too dangerous, and I don't want to hear another word about it. Do you
understand?"

I grit my teeth and stare at my folded clothing. "Yes."

Without another word, he heads for the bathroom, and I
slump onto my bed. A tiny ping sounds in my backpack—my
phone has finally found a signal.

> *Iris: I just went to bring in your mail and I found a letter in
> the bush with your name on it.*

I almost drop the phone. Rocket fast, I write back:

> *Me: Can you open it and send me a pic?*

An eternity of about a minute passes before my phone pings
again. It's a grainy photo of a sheet of white paper, with the
shadow of Iris's phone blurring the bottom. Two words sit in
the center of the page.

> Skynd deg!

Hurry up.

I tap out a reply:

> *Me: Can you write "she's there, she'll see you tomor-
> row" on it?*
> *Can you also put it back in the envelope and stick it
> back in the bush?*
>
> *I know this is super weird, sorry*

Another long pause.

> *Iris: That comma should be a semicolon.*

Me: *Oh my god use whatever punctuation you want*

Iris: *So I'm just putting it in the bush? Underneath? In the branches?*
You're right, this is super weird. Even for you.

Me: *Yes wherever you found it. Please!*

Two minutes later.

Iris: *OK, done. Why did I just do that?*

Me: *I can't explain right now but I might be able to when I get back*

If you don't still hate me

No answer, which means she might still hate me. I wish I knew how to neatly explain any of this in a text message. I wish I knew how to apologize to her, and also to make her understand that I didn't steal her diary. But maybe proving I'm right isn't as important as telling her I'm sorry for how horribly I've been acting. I type and delete a hundred different messages before realizing my phone signal has vanished again.

Too drained to wash my face or brush my teeth, I nestle down on the creaky old bed. My dad is already snoring on top of his covers, and as I reach over to switch off the light, a cuckoo's looping song floats through the still hotel.

CHAPTER 32

Once upon a time, in a stark white hotel at the top of the world, a girl who would one day become a mother woke on her birthday. Keeping her eyes closed, she savored the delicious anticipation that this day would be more special than all the others. It was unusually cozy in her bed; her blankets felt warmer than normal. She opened her eyes and found her mother sitting on a stool beside her bed, wearing something almost like a smile.

"Do you like it?" she said.

The girl looked down. Spread over her bed was the most beautiful blanket she'd ever seen. Finely knit in peacock blue and white, the design was of three beautiful girls in long dresses and crowns, standing before a mountain range. Her mother had placed it upside down on her bed so that she could admire the details, the curls of their hair, their tiny earrings, the snowflakes and stars filling the sky over their heads.

"It's 'The Three Princesses in the Blue Mountain,'" said the mother. "Would you like me to read it to you?"

The girl shifted uncomfortably. The blanket was becoming a little too warm. "You don't have to, Mamma."

"It's your birthday," said the mother, pulling out an illustrated storybook—the girl's favorite one—and opening it. "I insist." She began to read a tale that the girl had heard a hundred times. The poor, infertile queen, the old crone who promised she could help her to have three beautiful daughters, but she must keep them locked in the castle until they all turned fifteen.

"But they didn't listen to their parents, those naughty girls," said the mother, looking up from her book. "And you know what happened next."

The girl nodded. She knew what was written on the page, and she knew that her mother was embellishing the details of their kidnapping. She gave the troll dripping, jagged fangs as long as carving knives, fingers like rancid sausages that he used to squeeze the poor princesses' cheeks.

"A greedy captain, a foolish lieutenant, and a clever soldier happened to be passing through their kingdom," said the mother, returning her eyes to the book. The girl squirmed and wished she could roll under her bed or climb out the window. She listened as the brave, wonderful soldier outsmarted a bear, then a lion, then a little old man who beat him with his crutches. Finally, after catching the little old man by his beard, the soldier forced him to show him where the princesses were. Then the soldier, the lieutenant, and the captain climbed into a basket and descended deep inside the blue mountain.

As the mother turned the page, the girl wished she had a basket that would take her into a mountain before her mother saw what she'd done to the book.

"Of course, all of this trouble could have been easily avoided if those foolish girls had just listened to their parents," said the mother. She resumed the story: the soldier killed three trolls, each more horrid than the last, and the princesses could barely express the depths of their gratitude. The mother embellished their guilty groveling and deep regret. As a token of her thanks, the youngest princess knotted a gold ring in the soldier's hair.

"You can stop reading now, Mamma," said the girl. "I'm so hungry for my birthday breakfast, and Marit will be here any minute." In truth, she was far from hungry, but she needed to keep her mother from turning to the next page.

"Nonsense," said the mother. "Marit isn't coming until ten, and we're nearly finished." She tucked her chin low and read the next passage. "The captain, the lieutenant, and the princesses went back up in the basket, but when it was the soldier's turn, the captain and the lieutenant cut the rope. He was trapped inside the mountain!"

And the girl was trapped in her room, nearly suffocating under a blanket her mother had spent months making to remind her that she must behave.

"The soldier found a whistle, and when he blew it a great eagle swooped down. It took him in its claws and flew him to the aboveground world. He ran to the castle and arrived moments before the two eldest princesses were to be married to the greedy captain and the foolish lieutenant."

The mother peered over the edge of the book.

"They would never have had to marry those awful men if they'd just listened in the first place. They might have married handsome princes and lived in enormous castles." With a smug grunt, she turned to the last page.

The girl dove underneath her blankets and heard her mother's breath hiss in. After the youngest princess found her ring in the soldier's hair, thus proving that he had rescued them, the rest of the story had been blacked out of the book. The girl had written in her own ending. In the stuffy under-blanket darkness, she trembled and sweated.

" 'They ran away and were fierce and free and *beholden to no one* for the rest of their days'?" The mother's voice was barely a whisper. "I think there was a troll waiting outside the castle's gates, and he crunched their bones as he ate them whole."

Everything went dazzling bright as the mother pulled the blanket off the shaking girl. "I'm sorry," wailed the girl, but her mother folded up the blanket without a word and left the room.

CHAPTER 33

Mormor isn't in her apartment when my dad and I stumble downstairs the next morning, jet-lagged and off-kilter, but there's a steaming loaf of fresh bread on her kitchen table beside a plate of brown cheese. Tucked under the plate is a note:

Help yourselves. Don't share with the newlyweds.

Already, I'm sweating in my long underwear, sweater, and snow pants, but Kaja will be here soon and I don't want to waste a second. I am going to find my mother today. Even if I can't make it out to Ekmanfjorden right away, maybe she can feel that I'm here and will find me. Those threads go both ways between us.

And maybe Marit will have some answers—if she's M, that is.

I'm suspicious of the brown cheese, but it's surprisingly delicious, and I scarf down three slices of crusty, cheese-draped bread before a snowmobile roars outside. Kaja's bright pink parka appears in the driveway outside the window; she pushes her helmet visor up and waves.

"Gotta run," I say, dropping my plate in the sink.

"Hang on a minute." My dad holds out his arm to block me. "I want to talk about a couple of things before you leave."

I peer around his big, concerned head at the window, where Kaja is adjusting bags on the back of her snowmobile. "Okay, tell me."

The clock hits nine o'clock, pops, and pings, but no bird comes out.

"The Arctic is a dangerous place," says my dad. "I want you to be very, very careful. Do *not* go out on any ice unless you're sure it's solid. In fact, don't go out on any ice at all. Watch out for bears. Listen to your cousin at all times, and keep your mittens on." He waggles his three-fingered hand at me, and I groan.

"I will."

"Marit is a little . . . unconventional," he says. "Don't let her put any weird ideas in your head, okay?"

As if my head were filled with anything *but* weird ideas. "I won't. Can I please—"

"If you need me, call my cell. If I don't answer, call Mormor at the hotel. Call Uncle Álvaro. I want you back here by one o'clock."

"Got it, I promise." I slip around his arm. "Kaja's waiting."

"Be careful!" he yells.

Halfway to the door, I spin around on a slippery wool sock and dash back into the kitchen to plant a kiss on the top of his bald head. "Love you, Dad. Have fun doing science."

His face cracks into a smile. "Love you too, Eli-bug."

February morning in Longyearbyen feels like evening in the rest of the world. The sky casts the snow in waves of blue and purple, and deep shadows are tucked into the corners of the little glowing shops and businesses along the road. There's no wind, but the cold is deep and seeping. As I tuck my scarf up over my mouth, Kaja coasts around the side of the building.

"Hi!" She hands me a helmet, then scoots forward to make room for me. "Feeling better today?"

"Yeah, thanks." It's mostly true, aside from the anxiety clanging around inside me.

"Want to go straight to Marit's?"

"Sure." I bang my knee as I climb onto the snowmobile, and I'm not sure where to hold on. As we lurch off down the street, I yelp and clutch Kaja around the waist. Her stomach shakes as she laughs.

We glide past a larger, much fancier hotel, then along a row of candy-colored houses, their hues muted in the twilight. Then we turn away toward the mountains, and the buildings slowly disappear, replaced by rock and deep blue snow. Kaja pulls into a gap between two hills and cuts the engine.

"Before we go any farther, I want you to take this." She hands me an orange pistol. As my hand slides around its grip, my stomach fills with lead.

"I'm not really used to guns," I say.

"It's just a flare," she says. "If we see a bear, this is what we shoot first to scare it off." She shows me how to fit a cartridge into the pistol, how to cock the hammer and pull the trigger. It looks simple enough, but when it's my turn, my arm wobbles so hard I can barely hold the pistol up. I don't know why the sight of guns is making me so queasy. This is normal for Svalbard. It's the law that nobody can leave the settlement without a firearm, in case they run into a polar bear.

"Sorry," I mutter, using my other hand to steady it. I squeeze my eyes into slits, pull the trigger, and as the pistol kicks back, it springs out of my hands. A sizzling gold flare blasts into a nearby hill, kicking up a cloud of snow.

Kaja's mouth twitches. "You'll get the hang of it." She pulls a rifle from a holder on the side of the snowmobile and begins to load it with smooth, practiced movements. I've never seen a girl my own age look so comfortable with a firearm.

"If the flares don't work and the bear gets within thirty meters, this is what we use," she says. "But of course, we *really* hope that never happens."

Snick goes the bullet. *Snick, snick* go its sisters. The snow starts to swim. Whispering fills my head. My mother's voice. *Please, Eline, please*, she's saying.

"Hey," says Kaja. "Are you all right?"

I press my cold hands over my ears, and the whispering fades. "More jet lag, I guess. I don't have to shoot that big gun, do I?"

Kaja cocks an eyebrow in a gesture that's surprisingly like my mother. "Definitely not. You need a firearms permit."

"Oh, thank God."

She trudges off to collect the used-up flare and then picks up the pistol and hands it to me. "Do you think you can manage this? You do need to have something."

"Yep." I gulp down the bitterness in my throat and put the pistol into one coat pocket and the flares into another. It's just a dangerous-looking noisemaker, not technically a weapon. "Pretty stupid that I'm more afraid of guns than deadly predators, isn't it?"

Kaja gives me a funny look as she puts her rifle back into the case. "We probably won't see any polar bears, but you need to know how to be safe."

The pressure in my chest eases slightly as we set off into a stunning landscape that feels like the moon, cobalt and purple and gray. "Have you ever shot a polar bear?" I yell as we stop at the end of a narrow pass that leads onto a flat trail crisscrossed with hundreds of snowmobile tracks.

"Of course not." Kaja laughs. "They're protected, and you're only allowed to shoot them if it's a life-or-death situation. If you do end up killing one, they launch an investigation, sort of like if you murdered a person."

Iris would approve of that rule. She'd want mandatory jail time. I wonder what she's doing right now, if she'll ever forgive me.

The wind whistles up the rocky mountains as we set off again, and I tuck my chin low, grateful for my helmet visor and my cousin who knows all these things I was supposed to learn in the life I never got to have. I don't remember this trail or these exact mountains, but there's an underlying sense of familiarity. Nothing I can pinpoint.

Gold flashes high to our left. Three silhouettes stride along the top of a ridge. Three swirling cloaks moving in the same direction as us. My hand strays to the flare gun in my pocket, though I'm fairly sure those girls would laugh in my face if I pointed it at them.

"Can we go faster?" I yell. A whoop is my answer as I'm jolted backward, barely catching hold of Kaja as we shoot forward. The engine's whine turns to a scream. Across the flat, empty valley we fly, the wind roaring around us, snatching at anything loose on our clothing. Halfway across the expanse, Kaja cuts left and we angle up through a series of progressively steeper hills, then down again. The faint sound of barking grows louder.

In a gulley, a chain-link-fenced dog yard appears, with a tiny hut huddled beside it, and every electron in my body fizzles with memory. Half covered in snow, the hut looks like something a child might have made with strips of wood and glue. My heart is singing with memories of this place. The dogs yip and howl, each one chained beside a little wooden house with its name printed over the doorway.

We pull up between the dog yard and the hut and park beside several barrels resting on platforms above the ground.

"God morgen!" sings a woman's voice. We skirt around to the back of the hut and find her sitting on a camping chair, hacking at a piece of white stone with a tool that's somewhere between an ax and a chisel. It can't be above ten degrees, but she's not wearing a hat, and her limp blond-and-gray hair straggles around her face. A cigarette dangles from the corner of her mouth.

"Marit?" I say.

She glances up from her hacking but doesn't stop, which makes me nervous for her fingers. Her gloves aren't thick, and one slip with that ax would probably lop off a digit or two. She speaks so fast I don't catch a word of her Norwegian.

"This is Eline," says Kaja pointedly in English. "Silje's daughter. She's come all the way from America."

"Well, of course she has." Marit's English is accented but smooth. I wait for her to say more, but she doesn't.

"What are you making?" I ask.

"Maybe a whale, maybe a bird. It hasn't figured out yet what it wants to be." Marit sets the rock down, takes a long drag of her cigarette, and exhales it in a swirling stream over our heads. She takes me in with watery blue eyes smudged with black eyeliner, then gives a little nod. "Come inside."

We pick our way through her yard, which is littered with rocks in various stages of being carved, and then she pushes the hut's door open to reveal a single-room space. A couch and table sit beside a camp stove and a sink without any taps. The other side of the room is a jumble of canvases, brushes, tubs and tubes, palettes and pencils. In an alcove sits a low bed.

A lantern hangs from the ceiling in the center of the main space. The walls are covered in paintings of myriad shapes and sizes. Underneath are rows and rows of carvings arranged on shelves made from rough, unpainted boards.

I remember sitting on this floor, laying those wood and stone sculptures out in two straight lines. Reindeer and birds and girls in long dresses with flower crowns. My mother and Marit were sitting on the couch, talking about grown-up things I wasn't interested in. It was almost time to go, but I didn't want to leave one of the carvings, a little bearded man with a funny face, so I slipped him into my coat pocket. As we got to the door, he started wiggling, then thrashing around, beating his fists against my ribs. My mother asked me why I was squirming, but I couldn't tell her. The little man sank his teeth into my side, and I screamed and threw him on the floor. He landed with a thud, unmoving stone again.

I curl my hands into fists and tuck them under my thighs. Marit. *This* is Marit. How could I have forgotten her name? I'd always just thought of her as the strange artist with the sealskin slippers. There are so many holes in my memories, so many pieces I'm missing even though I thought I'd recorded everything perfectly. And then there are the parts I've scratched out, forced myself to forget. Now I desperately wish I hadn't, because I need those pieces to make sense of this all.

"Coffee?" Marit gestures to the couch and sets a kettle on the stove. Kaja and I take our boots off, and the stale scent of cigarettes wafts out of the sofa cushions as we sit. On the opposite wall hangs a large, square painting of a woman holding a little girl. Her head is tipped so she can kiss the girl's laughing cheek, and her long, dark hair streams over her shoulder. Above them stretches a black sky filled with blurring green lights.

I clench the cushions under my legs, waiting for Marit to speak, but she just stands there like one of her statues, waiting as the kettle heats up.

"Was it you who sent that letter?" I finally blurt out.

Marit un-statues herself and spoons instant coffee and sugar into chipped mugs. A cryptic almost-smile flits around her mouth as she pours the water, stirs, and hands the mugs to Kaja and me.

"How did you know she was up there?" I say.

"I heard her singing." Marit's plaid shirt gapes open to reveal a dirty thermal undershirt as she tugs open a window. "One hears all sorts of things out here."

We're all quiet, breath held. The breeze that slips through the window carries whispers, snatches of songs, the crunching of boots on snow, rustling cloth. A girl's laugh, sharp as an icicle. I tug my sweater tighter around me. "Would you mind closing that? I'm not used to this cold yet."

Marit gives me another amused half smile as she slides the window shut.

"How did the Northern Lights come to Cape Cod?" I say.

Marit pulls a bottle of aquavit liquor from a cupboard and pours a long draught into her own mug. "I asked the North Wind to blow them over so you could call her."

The couch lets out another huff of tobacco as Kaja shifts beside me. I can't read the expression on her face—it's a mix of confusion and curiosity—and I wonder if this is a conversation better had without her, but then her hand sneaks out and her pinky finger crooks around mine and I feel that somehow, possibly, she knows parts of this.

"But why did you think it would work if I called her?" I say. "Why could she only hear me?"

Marit takes a slow slurp of coffee. "You're the only one she ever listened to."

I let out a barbed-wire laugh, and my gaze returns to the painting of us under the ghosting lights. "Not when it mattered."

Marit gives a sad tut of agreement. "I dreamed about her the other night. Something was wrong with her eyes."

Something *is* wrong with her eyes. Something's wrong with her everything. The paintings on the wall start to swim, and I concentrate on one at the bottom to steady my focus. It's a portrait of a young woman with blond braids coiled on top of her head. Swooping eyebrows and silver eyes.

Marit drains half her coffee in a gulp. "Sometime around midnight the night you both disappeared, my dogs started barking. I was in the middle of painting—a reindeer for your mother—and I didn't go out to see what it was. So many times, I've wondered what would have happened if I'd just looked out my window." She stares into her mug.

Two canvases over and three up, there's a painting of a girl on horseback, long red curls cascading down her back and a thin circle of gold on her head. I stand to inspect the rest of the paintings. Mountains, castles, and caves. Soft-eyed polar bears, little girls with rings tied in their hair, swirling green lights above frozen fjords. All of the stories, every single one.

There.

Tucked in the corner between two walls and the ceiling. A tiny painting of a sapphire-eyed girl, her black hair curling in the wind, her lips curved in a knowing smile.

"Who are those three girls?" I say. "The ones in the long dresses and cloaks."

"So you've met them." Marit leans her elbows back onto the counter, crosses one furry slipper over the other. "That is a rather unfortunate story. I'm surprised your mother never told you, but perhaps she felt too guilty."

"Why?" I can't imagine any reason for my mother to feel guilty about those malicious girls.

"Listen and you'll find out," says Marit.

CHAPTER 34

Once upon a time, outside a snowy school at the top of the world, two little girls sat in the playground reading a book of stories together. The first girl read faster than the second girl, but she always stopped to wait for her friend to catch up before turning the page.

"It's rubbish how these princesses get locked up all the time," said the second girl. "By their parents, by trolls, even by their husbands. Look at this." She pointed to an illustration of three beautiful young girls buried up to their necks in the ground, while a dashing young man stood gawking at them. "Why doesn't he go and find a shovel?"

"They're not always locked up," said the first girl. "Sometimes they go on adventures."

The second girl huffed. "Not the princesses. Whenever there are three of those in a story, they're always locked up and in trouble. And once the hero rescues them, he marries the youngest one. What happens to the older sisters? Do they have to stay at home with their horrible parents forever?"

The first girl considered the possibility of staying forever in the hotel where she lived with her own horrible mother and shuddered. "You're right, it isn't fair at all. Even if they are rich and have castles to live in."

"We should write new stories for them," said the second girl, whose own mother was nearly as horrible as the first girl's.

"Even better, we should fix the stories they're already in." The first girl pulled a black marker from her pocket and flipped to the last page of "The Three Princesses in the Blue Mountain." As the tip of her marker kissed the page, the second girl gasped.

"That's permanent ink. Your mother will be furious."

"This is my book. I can do what I like with it." The first girl spoke the words loudly to make herself brave.

Starting from the moment when the prince asked for the youngest daughter's hand in marriage, she drew a thick black line through the rest of the story. Then she went back and drew another line over it, then another.

"That's enough," whispered her friend, horror-struck at the destruction of this beautiful illustrated tome.

"What shall we write instead?" said the first girl.

The second girl swallowed her horror and thought of what she wished for herself. "The three princesses decided they were tired of everyone telling them what to do, so they ran away."

"Yes, that's perfect," said the first girl, carefully printing the words. "And they were fierce and free and beholden to no one for the rest of their days."

"Children!" called the teacher. "It's time to come inside."

The first girl stowed the book in her bag, and they ran inside with the other children. Later, as they sat in their classroom learning to multiply and the light outside began to wane, three shadowy figures darted past the window, gold gleaming in their hair.

CHAPTER 35

"So my mother is the one who let those princesses out of their story?" I say.

"Not exactly. Every time we read a story . . ." Marit flashes a glance at Kaja. "Well, every time *some of us* read a story, we let the characters out. But Silje changed them as she let them out. We both changed them, though she always blamed herself for having the idea in the first place and writing the words."

"You were only trying to help," says Kaja.

"But there were things we didn't understand," says Marit. "We'd given them freedom, yes, but nothing more. They were blank slates—pretty dolls for trolls to hoard and princes to win. So when we gave them fierceness and freedom and no attachments to anyone, that was all they got. And that grew and warped into what they are now."

I shiver, wishing I still had my coat on. "My grandmother knitted them into a blanket too."

"Silje mentioned something about that," says Marit. "For her birthday? But then she didn't get to keep it?"

"That's right. I wonder if it's linked to them too, if it also changed something about them?"

Marit scratches the back of her head, staring at the floor. "It's certainly possible."

"Anyway, they seem more meddling than actually dangerous," I say. "They stole my best friend's diary and showed me something cruel she'd written."

Marit's eyes flash. "Let's hope that meddling is the worst you ever see of them. They seem to have some sort of fixation with you, Eline. Probably because you're Silje's daughter. You need to be careful."

I understand that—those girls make my insides crawl. But they keep saying they want to help me, and my options are dwindling.

"Come over here." Marit's slippers shuffle across the dusty floor to the alcove where her bed is. Its walls are covered with paintings of my mother. They start when she's a child standing in the snow with too-big mittens and a pom-pom hat. The early paintings are crafted with much clumsier brushstrokes and less perspective than the ones out in the main room. As my mother ages, the technique improves, and the last few—of her at the age when she disappeared—are breathtaking. Each individual eyelash, each tiny line in her face is rendered in an impeccable, nearly photo-realistic way. I could almost reach into them and feel her skin.

In the last painting, my mother has black holes for eyes. There's a fist inside my chest, crushing my heart.

"Is this how she looked in your dream?" I say.

"Yes." Marit's voice drops to a whisper. "She looks like she's falling apart, doesn't she?"

Speechless, I stare at the painting. Those hole-like eyes, the hollow cheeks, the painful sharpness of all of her bones. It's worse than the last time I saw her.

"I did tell you to hurry." Marit returns to the kitchen area and pours more aquavit into her mug, but leaves it sitting on the counter. She wraps her arms around her middle, and for a speck of a moment, she looks like a frightened child.

Underneath the painting of the third princess, there's a narrow canvas covered with a scaly, twisting lindworm. Its mouth gapes open, and a little girl cowers under one huge fang.

"What am I supposed to do now?" I say.

Marit lets out a phlegmy, crackling cough. "Find her while you still can."

The smell of paint fumes and cigarettes and aquavit is making me dizzy. "Will you help me? Everybody keeps saying you can't get to Ekmanfjorden at this time of year, but can we try?"

She starts to reach for her pack of cigarettes, then catches herself. "You can still get to Ekmanfjorden if you know what you're doing. It might take a couple of days, depending on the ice conditions on the fjords and the weather. There's not much daylight still for traveling."

"Can we go?" I'm practically yelling, and I don't care.

Marit takes a long swill from her mug, wincing as she swallows. "My friend has a cabin near Pyramiden. We could sleep there if we needed to . . ."

"Yes," I gasp, but she holds up a yellow-stained finger.

"If your father says it's okay."

He'll never agree to that. It doesn't matter, though.

"I'll ask him as soon as we get back," I say. Kaja lifts an eyebrow, and I pretend not to notice. "Can we go tomorrow if he says yes?"

Marit contemplates the inside of her mug, then nods. "This is too important to waste any more time. Let me give you my phone number so you can text me as soon as you talk to your father, and I'll start packing this afternoon. We'll need to leave as soon as it's light."

"Sounds good." I tap Marit's number into my phone, and Kaja shoots me an incredulous look as we pull on our boots and coats. "I'll text you as soon as I can."

"Good luck," says Marit. "And tell Peter I said hello."

Just as we're stepping outside, Marit holds up her hand. "Watch out for those princesses. They might offer to help you too, but they'll want some kind of payment."

"Okay."

She sets her empty mug on the counter and burps quietly into her sleeve. "It might be more than you can afford."

CHAPTER 36

Kaja's eyes are full of worry and questions as we pick our way through the stones and barrels in the shadowy snow.

"Can we go somewhere to talk for a minute?" I say. "Someplace quiet where nobody will overhear us." I peer into the slopes again, but there's no sign of life, no swishing of cloaks.

"I know the perfect spot." Kaja starts the snowmobile's engine, and I clamber on behind her.

We skirt through hills that eventually open up onto the wide Isfjorden. So much of the ice that should be here is gone, and it's only going to get worse. I curse global warming under my breath. All the cars I've ridden in when I could have walked, all the electricity I wasted, all the times I was too lazy to recycle. Climate change is breaking far more things than my mother or I could ever dream of, and it's sickening to think what will happen to this beautiful, fragile place if it continues.

With a rattle, we veer to the right, lurching and grinding along a trail that climbs diagonally up a slope. It gets steeper and steeper, then flattens before continuing up to become a mountain. In the middle of the plateau, Kaja shuts off the engine. Spread below us is the whole wide ice-edged fjord. To our left,

Longyearbyen is a glowing speck of humanity in a sea of purple-blue mountains stretching as far as I can see. I didn't give this scenery much thought when I lived here, but now that I'm looking at it as an outsider, its beauty stuns me.

A crinkling sound brings me back to reality. Kaja stuffs a wad of black licorice into her mouth and hands me the bag.

"Do you honestly think your dad's going to let you go to Ekmanfjorden with Marit?" she says.

The licorice is unexpectedly salty. I force myself to chew. "No. But I'm going to do it anyway. Any punishment he could possibly give me would never be as bad as not seeing my mother again. Will you come too?"

Kaja shakes her head. "I have school tomorrow. They'll know something's up if I don't go, and I'd hate to ruin your plan."

My eyes start to water as my mouth fills with a harsh ammonia-like flavor. "You won't tell on me, will you?"

"Of course not," she says, stuffing another wad of licorice in her mouth. "Marit's lived here since she was a kid. She knows the terrain better than anybody else. As long as she's not drunk, you'll be safe with her."

"Hopefully she won't be drunk."

We both let out a nervous laugh.

"You should let people know where you've gone, though," says Kaja. "Otherwise they'll send out a whole rescue operation and it'll be a big mess."

"I'm going to leave my dad a note," I say. "Somewhere he won't find it right away."

"If he hasn't found it by tomorrow evening, I'll tell him," says Kaja. "That will give you a solid head start."

"And it'll get you in huge trouble," I say.

She shrugs. "Like you said, any punishment is worth it if you find your mother." She bites her lip. "Will you tell me what's happening with her? It's totally fine if you don't want to."

"No, I do. It's just . . . a strange and complicated story." I gulp again, trying to rid my mouth of that ammonia-salt taste, and contemplate eating a mouthful of snow. "God, that licorice was really intense."

With a grin, Kaja hands me her water bottle, and I gulp its nearly frozen contents gratefully. "I'm not surprised it's strange, considering it involves our family," she says.

I've never spoken a word of this story to anyone, but it needs to come out, and there's only a handful people in this world who'd understand. Kaja is one of them.

"Do you promise not to share this with a soul if I tell you?" My palms are damp, even as the wind freezes my fingers.

Kaja sets down the bag of licorice and gives me a solemn nod. "I promise and swear."

"Okay." I rub my sweaty hands on my snow pants and pull my mittens on like I promised my dad I would. "It all started here, ten years ago."

Once the final word of the story has been told, I let out a cloud of breath between Kaja and me. The telling was difficult, but my bones feel lighter and the fist around my heart has loosened, and I realize how much easier everything would have been if I'd just told Iris too. Instead I made a giant mess of our friendship.

Kaja is quiet for a long while, but it's a comfortable silence. A processing silence.

"I'm glad you're going to Ekmanfjorden," she says. "Marit's right that you can't waste any more time."

I drag the heel of my boot through the snow, making parallel lines. "Did your mom ever tell you stories like my mother's?"

"No, she only reads magazines. She never even read picture books to me when I was a kid. My dad always did it."

I scuff another line with my boot. "Do you know why?"

"My mother said stories were Silje's thing," says Kaja. "She said she was always reading books and then strange and scary things would happen."

"It's true," I mutter, and Kaja scoots a little closer.

"Mormor never gave up on your mother either," she says. "My mom's been trying to get her to retire and move to Oslo for years now, but she won't. We all know it's because she's still holding on to this thread of hope that Silje will come back. My mom says she was always her favorite."

I laugh. "Mormor actually liked somebody? How could she tell?"

My cousin breaks into a huge grin. "I know, right?"

"My mother didn't think she did." Through all of this, I've never doubted that my own mother loved me fiercely, even when we were furious with each other, and I can't imagine how difficult it must have been for her as a child. Thinking about the way Mormor made her feel like nothing makes me ache.

"Mormor had a breakdown after your mom disappeared and you left for America," says Kaja. "She kicked all the guests out of the hotel and sat in her apartment for weeks and weeks, until my parents and I came." She leans in close like she's about to whisper a secret. "She didn't cry or anything, but the hotel was filthy."

"She didn't clean?" I open my mouth in fake horror, but my

chest hurts for Mormor too, buttoned up so tight she can't breathe, with no way to ever let go.

"We recently found out she's got a heart condition," says Kaja. "It's not getting better, and she's worried they're going to send her back to the mainland. Honestly, that's what my mom wants anyway."

"She could get treatment in Norway and then come back, though, right?" I say.

Kaja shrugs. "One of our elderly neighbors was having trouble walking, and we started picking up groceries for her. She went to her doctor last month and he presented her with a plane ticket and told her it was time to leave Svalbard. No negotiation, no warning. She had two weeks to go."

I scuff out all the lines in the snow. "Where would Mormor go if they sent her away?"

"We'd all move back to Oslo," says Kaja. "We'd sell the hotel. But Mormor is fighting it as hard as she can. And hiding it. They've given her a lot of leniency so far because she's lived here so long and contributed so much to the town, but it won't last forever."

"Wow." Even though I hate that hotel with every particle of my being, I can't imagine it no longer belonging to Mormor, to my family.

"Anyway," says Kaja. "You're going to be late if we don't head back. Thank you for telling me everything. I'm sad for your mother, and I'm really, really sad for what you had to go through. But it's also quite a beautiful story. Even the sky couldn't take her away from you."

There's no word for how I feel. I might scream my lungs out of my body or I might fly up into the clouds or I might fling myself off this mountain and roll down into the fjord. Or I might curl up and cry forever about my mother, who left me nothing but a cardboard book of scraps and a note delivered by the wind. Who might be there if we make it to Ekmanfjorden or might not be.

I shut my eyes tight as we scream down the side of the mountain. By the time we arrive at the stark white hotel, my fingers and toes are numb.

"Thanks for taking me out today," I say, climbing off the snowmobile and stumbling on wood-block feet. "And thanks for keeping my secret."

"Of course," says Kaja. "Good luck with Marit tomorrow. Be safe."

My stomach churns at the thought of what I'm going to have to pull off, both the lying and the journey. I hate how terrified my dad will be when he finds out I'm gone. I hate who I've become over these past few weeks, a person who hurts her father and her best friend and pushes them away. Maybe those princesses are getting inside my head after all. But if I ask my dad if I can go to Ekmanfjorden with Marit and he says no—because of course he will say no—he'll watch me like a hawk for the rest of the trip. I can't let that happen. I have to keep moving until I find her.

CHAPTER 37

Once upon a time, in a stark white hotel at the top of the world, a girl who would one day become a mother was alone. Her sister was visiting a friend, her father was at work, and her mother had gone to the store. It felt like the world had forgotten about the girl, but she didn't mind. On days like these, she liked to roam the hotel and pretend it was her castle.

Up to the top of the stairs she swept, a blanket cape draped around her shoulders. If her mother were home, she'd have yelled at her for dirtying the blanket, and the girl relished her secret transgression. She visited each of the guest rooms and bestowed a gift upon each pillow as a token of her generosity and kindness. A scrap of paper with *hallo* written beside a drawing of a tree. A little purple paper umbrella that came from a fancy drink. A free bookmark from the library. The head of a fake pink carnation she'd stolen from a vase.

Having reached the top floor and given out all of her gifts, the girl swept her glorious cape all the way down the hall to the last door. It had no number on it. Her mother had told her many times never to open this door, and though she had often tried when no one was looking, it was always locked.

The girl tested the doorknob, just in case, but it didn't turn. She returned to the room where she'd left the drawing of the tree and retrieved her pencil. She turned the scrap of paper over and wrote a single word.

Open.

She swept back down the hall and pressed the scrap of paper to the door. The handle clicked and turned. The girl pushed.

There was a *whoosh*, a great sucking sound, and the girl's hair streamed forward, pulled into the narrow gap in the door. She pushed harder—she couldn't stop now—and a roaring filled her ears; her eyeballs felt like they might pop out of their sockets. The girl wedged her knee against the door, braced her shoulder against the wood, and heaved with all of her strength.

The door crashed open. Inside was black, a vast nothingness. No floor, no walls. The girl teetered on the threshold, clutching the door frame. Then a massive, luminous orb shot up through the darkness. The girl managed to duck out of its way as it flew through the open door, a perfect white sphere covered in craters and shadows. It bounced down the hall, growing larger, cracking floorboards, and knocking chunks of plaster out of the walls, and then it thundered down the stairs.

The girl caught her breath and ran after it. All the way down to the hotel lobby, where her mother was just coming in, laden with shopping bags. The mother's mouth fell open as the moon bowled toward her; she tried to shut the door, but had to dive away before it crushed her. With a bone-shaking crash, the moon punched a hole in the place where the door had been, and it flew up, away into the sky.

The mother lay stunned in a jumble of bags and bread and broken eggs.

"You never, ever listen," she said, and her voice was ice.

CHAPTER 38

"Why are you crying?" Mormor's pinched face pokes out the hotel's doorway. With a start, I swipe at my face with my sleeve.

"It's just the cold making my eyes water."

Her thin lips purse. "Come inside. You're letting all the heat out."

I want to tell her that she's actually the one letting the heat out, standing there with the door wide open, but thinking of my mother has left me feeling like a gutted fish.

"Your father isn't coming back until later," says Mormor as we step inside. "You will spend the afternoon with me."

I pull my whole sock off with my boot, lose my balance, and set my bare foot down in a clump of snow. He made me promise to be home by one, and now he's not even here.

"I'm not cleaning, for the record," I say. If Mormor thinks she's getting free labor out of this arrangement, she's severely mistaken. She seems healthy enough, as grumpy and full of vinegar as she ever was. No wheezing or sickly complexion, though I have no idea what somebody with a heart condition looks like. Maybe she's got more time left here than Kaja thinks.

My grandmother watches me hop out of my other boot, arms

folded across her narrow chest. Her mouth twitches in an expression I'd think was hidden amusement if it were anyone but her.

"I thought we could knit after lunch," she says.

I plant my other foot in a puddle. "Really? That would be . . . nice."

This time she really does smile, and I'm not sure I've ever seen this actual expression on her face. It's unnerving. Before hanging up my coat, I take my phone from the pocket, leaving Kaja's flare gun. The screen flashes with texts from Iris.

> *Iris: A ton of meteorites fell in our neighborhood last night.*
>
> *People's windshields got smashed and there are little rocks everywhere.*
>
> *A few windows in your house are broken.*

I nearly drop my phone.

> *Iris: But don't worry, my mom and I went over and taped trash bags over them.*
>
> *She tried calling your dad but he didn't answer, so she found a place to fix them.*
>
> *We have your spare key and they'll send you a bill.*

My mouth is cotton-dry. Everything is still breaking.
Thank you for doing that, I write. *I hope you guys are ok.*

> *Iris: I saw the wind blow that letter out of your bush. It hovered in the air like somebody was reading it and then it zoomed up into the air.*

Hundreds of feet straight up, higher than the trees.

Something strange is happening, isn't it?

A thousand different responses flood into my head.

Me: *Yes*

Iris: *Are you OK?*

"Eline, are you coming?" calls Mormor.

Me: *I will be, don't worry.*

And I'm sorry for literally everything.

In her kitchen, Mormor is putting together a platter of sliced bread and toppings to make open-faced sandwiches. The word for them—*smørbrød*—pops, unexpected, into my head, and maybe if I stayed here long enough, all of my Norwegian would come back.

"You didn't wash your plate from breakfast," says Mormor as she slices hard-boiled egg beside a little pile of smoked salmon. "I left it for you to clean."

With a twinge of annoyance, I notice that my dad's plate has been carefully washed and left to dry in the rack.

A morning spent in the Arctic cold has given me a ravenous appetite. I polish off three sandwiches, and Mormor eats two just as quickly. She wipes her mouth and gathers up the tray before I can reach for another slice of bread. "We'll save the rest for your father," she says. "I expect he'll be hungry when he gets back."

I wash the dishes, making sure to clean every square milli-meter of plate. If the meteorites are still falling, my mother must still be out there somewhere. She *has* to be. I just hope she's not broken too.

Mormor wipes down the table and the already-spotless counters, dries her hands on a starched tea towel, and nods curtly. "Shall we?"

Before I can answer, she turns into her sparse bedroom, and I follow. Sensible gray blankets cover the bed, and beside it is the same polished nightstand, still with nothing on it. She opens a door I'd always assumed was a closet, but on the other side is a bright space even larger than her bedroom. As we step through the doorway, the cuckoo in the dining room begins to hoot.

Even though the light outside has deepened to charcoal, Mormor's sewing room has a bright, airy feel. Shelves line three of its walls, and wide windows take up most of the fourth. A rocking chair and a sewing table sit beside the windows, and a bulky antique radio huddles between them. One wall of shelves is full of fabrics in every color and texture imaginable; the opposite wall is stacked with skein upon skein of yarn. I run my fingers over the soft wool and cotton and cashmere.

"I didn't know this was even here," I breathe.

"There are many things right under your nose if you know where to look." Mormor settles herself in the rocking chair and pulls a knitting project from a basket beside it. It's a shawl, undyed natural brown with a pattern of angled stitches and holes that form a complicated design of feathers. I move to the shelves beside the door, which are full of folded, handmade garments: corduroy trousers and cotton blouses, alpaca scarves and felted hats.

"You made all of these?" It's not really a question; I can tell from the proud set of Mormor's mouth that she did. I inspect the embroidery on the hem of a wool skirt. "You do beautiful work."

"I should hope so." Mormor's silver needles dip and flash through the shawl. "I've been working at it for sixty years." She slips a tiny, round stitch marker onto her right needle. "From what I saw of your sweater yesterday, you work hard too."

It's almost a compliment, and I'll take it. I shift through the stacks of clothing, careful not to rumple anything. On the lowest shelf, there's a pair of mittens, knitted in red-and-white color work, snowflakes dancing around reindeer and stars scattered over them. They've been worked on very small needles, and the details are breathtakingly fine. The cuffs are a slightly paler, rougher yarn than the rest of the mittens.

"I used to have some like these." I can't resist slipping one onto my hand—it fits. "The design was a little different, though."

Mormor makes an annoyed *tsk*ing sound. "Who do you think made them for you?"

"Oh, right. Thank you." Warmth radiates all the way up my arm and into my shoulder. Within seconds, I'm sweating. "I wonder whatever happened to them."

"They washed up on the shore the summer after you left." Mormor frowns at her work and recounts the stitches on her needle. "I expect you left them out on Ekmanfjorden."

"What?" It's all whispering back, that night on the fjord, the sky awash in green and purple. Ripping the child-size version of these mittens off to grab the wishing ring that burned cold in my hair.

Mormor counts her stitches once more, then sighs. "They were filthy and shredded from being underwater so long. I managed to salvage some of the wool, though, and I reknit them into a larger size for when you came back."

I slide the other mitten onto my left hand, and my entire body flushes with warmth. "These are for me?"

"If you want them," says Mormor offhandedly. "Otherwise I will donate them to charity."

"Thank you." The words come out stiff and starched like one of Mormor's tea towels, but she doesn't seem to notice. She inclines her head toward the other wall.

"Why don't you choose some yarn? There are patterns in the drawer if you need one."

I settle on a skein of wool that's exactly the blue of a fjord in sunlit summer. Mormor points to a carved wooden rack full of needles, and I pull out the chair by the sewing machine. I don't need a pattern—fingerless gloves are simple. These will keep my mother's hands warm without melting her fingernails.

Before I cast the yarn onto the double-pointed needles, I peer at the shawl spread across Mormor's lap. As she shifts her legs, the feathers flutter.

"What was my mother like when she was little?" I say.

Mormor's silent for a long while, and I wonder if this means we're supposed to pretend I never asked the question. She knits to the end of her row, fingers working so fast they're a blur. The rustling sound of wings fills the room as she turns her work around.

"She was an obstinate child," she says. "Never listened to anything I told her, always had to figure things out the hard way. Once I told her a story about a troll who'd turned to stone on top of a mountain near our house. A few days later, I sent her to her room without supper. She climbed out her window and walked up the mountain by herself. Seven years old, she was."

Mormor slips a stitch marker off her needle, holds it in her mouth, and continues to talk around it. "I followed her footprints and found her in the dark with a shovel, digging snow off the stone and begging the troll to wake up so he could come to our house and eat me." She snorts. "She's lucky the polar bears didn't catch her before I did."

I know what my mother did was wrong, but it's also lucky that I never knew about the troll all those years ago when Mormor sent *me* to bed without supper.

She flips the shawl again, and the downy scent of feathers wafts out.

"You loved her, though," I say. "Didn't you?"

"Of course I did," huffs Mormor. "What kind of monster do you think I am?"

I divide my cast-on stitches among the four short needles. "She never brought me to see you, she never talked about you. I was so afraid of you, and then when I had to stay here, you were angry all the time."

Mormor frowns at her shawl. "Your mother and I have very different opinions on certain things that are best left hidden."

Have. Not *had.*

"You're still waiting for her to come back," I say.

Mormor tuts. "Nonsense. Your mother is gone."

The words should crush me, but they don't because I know they're wrong.

Mormor sets her shawl down suddenly and peers out the window. "Those filthy wretches," she mutters.

"Who, the newlyweds?"

She stares at me like I've said something strange. "No."

"Who, then?"

Mormor's glaring out the window again, but I can't see anything in the dim, narrow alley. "Three horrible young women. Full of lies and cruelty. Waltzing around thinking they can fix everything." Her glare snaps to me. "Keep well away from them."

"Are you afraid of them too?" I say.

Mormor looks like she's swallowed a rock.

"Of course I'm not. What an absurd thing to say." The color seeps back into her thin cheeks as she stuffs her knitting into its basket. She hadn't even finished the row she was working on. With trembling fingers she pulls a pill bottle from her pocket and shakes two white tablets into her palm, then swallows them dry. My own chest catches painfully.

"Are you all right?" I say.

Mormor blinks at me like I'm an idiot. "That's enough knitting for now. Your father should be back any minute."

I set my barely started glove on the sewing table, and Mormor stands, wincing as she straightens her back.

"Keep them while you're here." She waves at the needles and yarn and disappears through the door into her apartment.

CHAPTER 39

My father isn't in the lobby or the street outside, and I'm irked that he gave me a curfew and then didn't come back himself. And I still haven't forgiven him for foisting me on Mormor all those years ago, even if she is much less scary now than she used to be. With a sigh, I flop down on the uncomfortable couch by the fireless fireplace and resume my knitting. It must be ten degrees cooler out here than it is in Mormor's sewing room; my fingers are cold and clumsy. Marit's words loop through my head along with the rhythm of my fingers.

Fall-ing a-part. Fall-ing a-part.

Heavy boots thump up the front steps and my dad's tuneless whistle floats through the cracks around the door. He gusts in, stamping off the snow and making a big show of how cold he is.

"You missed lunch," I say, finishing a row and switching out the needle.

"Sorry about that." He leans against the wall and unties his bootlace. "I got caught up in whale DNA."

"Sounds messy," I mutter.

"Guess what?" Before I can answer, he continues. "It's definitely the same whale. The samples match."

Even though I already knew this, goose bumps still whisper across my skin. I stare hard at my knitting, at the cuff that's going to fit around my mother's wrist. "Oh?"

"It was spotted again here two days ago." My dad plops down beside me, wincing at the thump his body makes on the hard surface. "It came back, and Karl said it was perfectly healthy. But I *saw* it die. I stayed with it for hours afterward and it never breathed. I just don't get it, Eli-bug. Maybe there's an explanation, but I can't begin to think what it is."

Of course there's an explanation: my mother brought the whale here and she healed it. But she can't heal herself.

. . . fall-ing a-part, fall-ing a-part . . .

A stitch slips off my needle, and I watch it unravel down through the cuff.

"You all right?" My dad's face dips into view. Specks of ice are stuck in his nose hair.

"Yeah." I catch the fallen stitch and start weaving it back through the cuff. I'm afraid if I look up, he'll somehow see inside my pupils, all the way to the retinas and into my brain, where all these secrets are swirling around. "Iris is going to be so happy to hear that."

"How was Marit?" he asks.

"There you are, Peter." Mormor's voice cuts through the chilly air.

. . . fall-ing a-part . . .

Maybe even more of my mother has melted away. Maybe she's lying somewhere all alone, with great big pieces of herself gone. Setting my knitting down, I duck into the bathroom beside the staircase.

My dad says yes, I text to Marit.

Excellent, she replies. *I'll pick you up at 08.00.*

But if she shows up at the hotel with a snowmobile full of supplies, my dad will know something's going on.

Can you meet me in front of the café instead? I write. *The hotel coffee is terrible.*

Marit: *Sure*

I turn the cold water tap on full blast.

"Mamma, can you hear me?" I whisper at my reflection, which never looks as much like her as I wish. "I came all the way here, and I thought this would be easier. I'm going to try to get to Ekmanfjorden, but I don't know if that's right. Where are you?" But the worried face in the mirror is me, not her, and I have no answers, only a reckless plan.

"You're wasting water!" calls Mormor from the lobby.

With a groan, I turn off the tap.

"You sure you don't want to come?" my dad is saying as I emerge from the bathroom.

Behind the front desk, Mormor bangs open a drawer and pulls out a ledger. "I've got two more guests arriving this evening, so I can't leave the hotel."

"Can we bring you anything back?" he says.

"Back from where?" Thankfully, my voice doesn't sound nearly as unsteady as the rest of me.

"I thought we'd go out for dinner." My dad leans against the gleaming counter, and Mormor looks like she'd like to shove his elbow off. "Give your grandmother a break from cooking."

"How very kind," says Mormor.

"What are you in the mood for?" He flips through a stack of brochures, then sets them back in a crooked pile. Half of Mormor's face twitches.

"Is Elins Hus still here?" I say. My mother used to take me to the little blue restaurant whenever my dad had to work late.

"Yes." Mormor rolls her eyes. "Though I can't understand why. They use far too much flour to thicken their sauces. Everything tastes like cement."

"Want us to bring some back to fix the walkway out front?" says my dad, winking at me.

"No, thank you," says Mormor. "I'll reheat the stew. Wouldn't want it going to waste. Hopefully these new guests will arrive at a sensible hour so I can get some sleep."

My dad checks his watch. "You ready to go now?"

"Yeah." I glance up the stairs. "Just need to get something."

The front door bangs open, shoving an empty gust inside. Tendrils of cold slither around my ankles as I dash up the steps. Our room has been tidied up, though it still reeks of roses. I pull a sheet of paper from a notepad on the desk and dash a single line across its middle.

I'm coming to Ekmanfjorden tomorrow, Mamma. I hope you're there.

Sliding the window open, I let the wind snatch the paper from my fingers. "North Wind, please bring this to Silje," I whisper, though I have no idea if the wind hears or cares. My pulse skitters as the tiny scrap of paper flicks away into the night. Tomorrow I will trek through the snow and ice, cross mountains and valleys and fjords, until I find her.

My dad's voice floats up the stairs—he's telling Mormor about narwhal genes in the overexcited way people talk about football playoffs. I pull out my phone to text Iris.

> **Me:** *That narwhal you tried to save isn't dead after all.*

> *It's here. It swam all the way to Svalbard.*

As I'm heading out of my room, a tiny object blows past my foot, caught in some imperceptible breeze, and tumbles down the hall, stopping in front of the broom closet. It's a purple paper umbrella, the kind that comes in tropical cocktails. The kind my mother used to leave on the guests' pillows. It *snick*s shut and slides closer to the closet. I dash after it, but the umbrella slips into the black gap beneath the door.

"Eli, are you ready?" calls my dad.

The closet's handle turns easily, but the door sticks in its frame like it hasn't been opened in decades.

"Eli?" There's a note of worry in Mormor's voice. I jam my shoulder against the wood and heave.

The door swings open. The closet is empty, aside from the paper umbrella and a cardboard box in the corner. I slip inside, leaving the door partially open for light. The walls are solid; no trapdoors lie hidden in the floor. There's nothing extraordinary about this space or the things in it, no sign of the bottomless cavern that my mother found. No moon.

I pocket the umbrella, then lift the flap of the cardboard box. It's full of photo albums and scrapbooks. Crouching, I prop a faded album on my knees and open it to the first page.

SPITSBERGENPOSTEN

LONGYEARBYEN-KVINNE SAVNET, DATTER FUNNET PÅ FJORDISEN

Tidlig fredag morgen fant en ekspedisjonsgruppe en sek-
sårig jente på isen på Ekmanfjorden, nesten 50 kilometer
fra Longyearbyen . . .

The photo of my mother beside the headline is the same as the
first page of my scrapbook at home. This is the same article, in
Norwegian instead of English. I flip through the pages—they're
all printouts of articles about my mother: in English, in Norwegian, in Swedish and German and Dutch. Mormor has collected
far more articles than I ever did, and she's still going. One article
is from this week, a sober commemoration of the upcoming ten-
year anniversary of the tragic event.

Setting the scrapbook down, I pull a manila envelope from the
box. It's crammed full of maps. Maps of Svalbard's islands, of the
fjords, of the decreasing sea ice charted by year, all the way up to
last winter. On each map, a small black X has been marked in the
center of Ekmanfjorden, and on several of them, arrows and lines
lead off in different directions from the X.

My grandmother lied. She's still looking for my mother too.

The door snaps open.

"What are you doing?" Mormor pulls a ring of keys from her
pocket and jingles them with an irritated air.

"I . . . was just wondering what was in here." I stammer. "Are
these yours?"

She flicks through the keys, as if she can't bring herself to look at me, then shakes her head. "Just some junk I found. It needs to be recycled."

"It's okay if you're still looking for her," I say. "I'm the last person who'd judge you. Maybe we could search together."

Mormor finds the correct key and brandishes it at the open door. "Out of the closet now. This isn't a playground."

And I'm not a six-year-old child to be ordered around anymore. But Mormor won't even look at me as I edge around her, and I know I've hit a nerve. As I head down the stairs, I hear the *crick* of her key in the lock.

CHAPTER 40

Once upon a time, in a stark white hotel at the top of the world, a girl who would one day become a mother stood in the lobby, mopping up mud. The door burst open, and three beautiful young women swept inside. They wore floor-length cloaks, but underneath them the girl saw flashes of brocade and silk.

"We would like a room for one night," said the tallest, whose hair was gold and her eyes silver.

The girl's mother grumbled about the waste of taking a room for only one night, all the extra cleaning it involved, but it had been a slow season and she needed the money. She gave the three young women a single key and pointed them to the room all the way at the top of the stairs.

"May I bring up your bags?" the girl asked the young women, and they handed her a silver box the size of a loaf of bread. As they swept up the stairs, a cloud of rose-scented perfume wafted down. The mother sneezed and waved her hand in front of her face. "I wish it were tomorrow already," she said loudly.

Something heavy slid around inside the silver box as the girl raced up the stairs. When she reached the room at the top of the hotel, the princesses—for that is what they were—had taken off their cloaks and were smoothing out their shimmering dresses. Awestruck, the girl stopped in the doorway, but they waved her inside, sat her down on one of the beds, and fussed over her.

"What is your name?" said the eldest princess, a tall woman with golden hair and silver eyes. Pearl droplets hung from her earlobes.

"Silje," said the girl.

"Are you a good girl?" said the second-eldest princess, who was rounder and softer, with hair the color of fire and eyes like emeralds.

The girl thought about this for a moment. "Not always."

The youngest princess tossed her gleaming black hair and clapped her hands. "Neither are we. We've run away from our castle."

The girl froze, wondering if these were the same three princesses from her storybook. It couldn't be possible, but how many trios of princesses had ever come wandering into her tiny town at the top of the world? The girl didn't know whether to feel thrilled or terrified.

The eldest princess gathered the girl's hair at the nape of her neck and began to braid it. "Our mother thinks she can control us, tell us how to speak and walk and think. But we won't be her marionettes anymore. We can help you cut your strings too."

The girl looked down at her scabbed, sore knuckles. "How did you get away?"

"We stole her heart," said the second princess, pointing to the silver box.

The girl's breath caught. "How did you get it?"

"For a long time, we'd suspected it wasn't in her chest," said the third princess. "After months of searching, we finally found it in a cupboard."

"What will you do with it?" said the girl.

The third princess's sapphire eyes danced. "We'll keep it until she promises to let us do as we please. And if she refuses, we'll throw it into a fjord." She picked up the box and gave it a hard shake. Inside, the heart thumped.

The girl winced. "Doesn't that hurt your mother?"

"Yes," all three princesses said.

The girl rubbed the tail of her braid along her upper lip, worry gnawing at her stomach like a rat. "I have to go back downstairs."

"That's fine," said the eldest princess. "If you ever need us, ring this." She held out a golden bell that looked like it had been cut from a horse's harness. The girl took the bell, thinking it should probably be the other way around, that they should ring for her since they were the guests.

"Can I bring you anything?" said the girl.

"Some wine, please," said the first princess.

The girl nodded and went down the stairs. In the kitchen, her mother was banging pots and muttering. The girl fetched a stool and stood on tiptoe to reach the shelf where they kept their nicest wines, but as she stretched, the stool began to wobble. Down she crashed, and the green glass bottle bounced off the counter and shattered.

Dead silence. Blood-red liquid everywhere, puddling on the floor, splashed across her mother's trousers. The girl pressed her face to the tile.

"Clumsy girl," hissed her mother. "That bottle cost more than those awful young women are paying us. You will clean this up immediately, and you will scrub every floor in this hotel before you go to bed tonight."

As the girl picked up a shard of glass, it sliced her thumb open. Droplets of blood fell into the puddle of wine, and the girl wondered where her mother might be keeping her own heart.

CHAPTER 41

A full moon glows overhead as my dad and I step into the snow and streetlight. Even though it's barely dinnertime, it feels like midnight. A surprising number of people are milling around the central area of town, their breath making clouds. The shops and bars and restaurants are all open, windows glowing bright, and in the center of the brick street stands the miners' memorial statue, a bearded man carrying pickaxes and looking tired but determined. Like me.

Tomorrow I will leave this tiny settlement behind and become a speck in the vast, white wilderness. I hope I'm right to trust Marit. I hope she won't get drunk or get us eaten by polar bears. I hope we don't have to sleep in her friend's cabin for too many nights. What I'm about to do is absurd and dangerous, but if there's ever been a time for recklessness, this is it.

A woman swerves around us, and there's something magnetic about the rifle slung over her shoulder, something hypnotic, something my brain wants me to remember.

"Did we have a gun?" I ask my dad.

"Of course." He laughs. "Otherwise we'd have been stuck in this tiny town all the time."

"But we don't have it anymore. What happened to it?"

He steers me around a patch of glistening ice. "It, uh, disappeared that night with your mother."

A high-pitched whine begins in my left ear. "But it's normal that she brought it with us, right?"

He coughs. "I can't say it was the responsible thing to do, because look at all the other choices she made, but yes, it—"

I stop in my tracks and grab his arm. "Dad, look!"

About fifty yards ahead, a woman walks, heading away from us. Her dark hair cascades down the back of her light blue parka. Her shoulders hunch, like she's carrying a heavy, invisible backpack. And she's wearing those boots. The ones that make diamond shapes.

"Mamma!" I yell.

Showing no sign of having heard me, she keeps walking. I break into a jog, then realize my dad is standing frozen in the middle of the road. I dash back and grab his sleeve. He shakes his head, mutters something, rubs his eyes.

"Come on, I know you can see her too." I grab his other sleeve. He shakes his head again, and then something in him snaps and we're both running, crunching and sliding through the crystal snow.

She turns a corner. Beyond the scattered lights of town, above the tip of a mountaintop, the black sky is beginning to glow green.

"Mamma!" I yell again. I don't understand why she's not stopping, why she's not turning around and running for me. Maybe her ears are breaking too.

"Silje!" calls my dad, and his actual, out-loud acknowledgment of her makes my heart leap, even as she turns another corner and slips onto the road heading away from town.

Our boots pound the snow, our breath comes in short gasps, but we won't stop for anything. The golden streetlight begins to fade as the buildings grow sparser. The moon is gone now too, the sky filling with whispery emerald strands.

My mother stops in the middle of the road, keeping her back to us, and as I run toward her, a flame of worry flickers in my chest. Maybe her face is falling apart too, and she's afraid to show us. My dad must sense something as well, because he takes my hand and we both slow to a walk. He pulls out his phone and turns on the flashlight.

"Silje?" he calls into the frigid night.

She turns slowly, and acid swims up my throat. In the bright flashlight glare, it's not my mother's face on this body that looks just like hers. It's a pale girl with eyes that flash sapphire in the darkness.

My dad swears and pulls me close. We're much farther outside town than I thought, emptiness whispering around us. And we haven't brought a gun. Slowly, we back away from the girl, who is now laughing.

"Why would you do that?" I say. "What is wrong with you?"

The princess strips off her jacket, and a long dress spills out as she bends to pull off her boots and snowpants. Then she gathers a clump of snow and presses it between her bare hands. As she opens them, a black cloak unfurls; she clasps it around her neck and lifts the hood.

"I asked you a question!" I shout, ignoring the bite of apprehension in my lungs and lunging toward her. My dad catches my coat and hauls me backward. The princess smirks, and from the hills behind her comes a rasping hiss. An ache takes root in my chest and begins to twist and worm.

"Let's go, Eli," says my dad. "We shouldn't be out here un-armed. We shouldn't be out here at all."

"Hello, Peter," says the princess, but my dad looks away, and I can't tell if it's because he refuses to see her or he's afraid. Probably both.

"No. I've had it with this cryptic bullshit," I say, straining against his grasp, but this time he tugs hard enough to send me stumbling.

"Now." His angry voice shakes.

Behind the girl, a shadow creeps. A long, scaly body, slithering and rasping along the snow.

I'll crawl inside your heart. I remember that creature's slick cheek against mine, its rotten breath and sickening promises. I can almost feel the edges of my heart blackening. Withering.

"You don't have to go with your father, Eline." The girl's expression is feral, hungry. "You don't have to let anybody tell you what to do."

I step closer to my dad. "You're right. But I choose to. You and your sisters are truly horrible creatures."

With a shrug, she lifts her skirts, steps off the road, and disappears into the snow. I can't see the lindworm anymore, but I hear its hissing breath. Pressing both hands over my chest, I tell myself the withering sensation is just my imagination, but still it aches.

"Soon," whispers the lindworm. "Ssssoon."

Wordless, my dad and I back away, like we'd do with a snarling, unleashed dog. Once we're far enough, he grabs my hand and we run down the icy, dark road, slipping and stumbling. It takes a hundred times longer to get back than it did to leave, and my head spins with fury and fear and devastating disappointment.

It's not until we're bathed in the safe shop-front lights of Longyearbyen that my legs start to shake.

An hour later, we're both in bed, having shared the leftover stew with Mormor and then gone straight to our room. The blackening sensation in my chest is gone, but my pulse still rockets at the thought of tomorrow. Once we're deep in the wilderness, there will be no running back to safety.

"Your mom used to say that people see what they want to see," says my dad, his words slurring with exhaustion. "I guess she's what I wanted to see tonight."

"But what about when we realized it wasn't her?" I say. "You didn't want to see that girl, but you did. Right?"

"It was just someone with hair like your mother's and a similar coat," he says. "We shouldn't have chased after her like that."

"Are you kidding me?" I should be used to this blatant ignoring of things by now, but this is far beyond anything he's ever ignored. "What about the lindworm?"

"You always saw what you wanted to see too," he continues, like I hadn't even spoken. "You only ever saw the beauty of your mother. I was so caught up in the negativity, her problems, all the things I thought she was doing wrong. You saw the opposite."

I saw the beauty of her because I had no choice. My mother created me; she bent and shaped my life, my thoughts, my feelings. I carry her electrons inside me. But I heard the words she used to hurl at him like razor-edged stars. I've seen her fingernails melting away, her pupils widening to holes. There's no beauty in that—at least not one I understand.

"Dad, can I go to Ekmanfjorden with Marit tomorrow?" I whisper, so quietly even I can barely hear it.

He lets out a soft snore.

Checking the window and the cracks around the door one last time to make sure no shadows have slithered in, I burrow under the scratchy blankets and try to punch some shape into my flat pillow. Tomorrow I will find my mother, and those princesses and that disgusting lindworm won't stop me. They're just storybook characters. I am flesh and bone.

As I'm floating in the hazy space between waking and dreaming, my phone pings with a message from Iris.

> **Iris:** *The same whale? Are you serious?*
>
> *Eli, I'm crying.*
>
> *Thank you.*

Too tired to type words, I send her a smiley face and three hearts. A few seconds later, her response comes.

> **Iris:** *In two days I'll find out if I got into the Stanford online program. We can only afford it if I get a scholarship, but it'd mean I don't have to go anywhere.*
>
> *If you'd read the rest of my diary, you'd know about it. I guess you really didn't read the rest of it.*
>
> *I'm sorry I didn't believe you. I'm sorry I ever wrote that about you.*
>
> *I miss you.*

Underneath is a photo of the two of us from last summer, sitting among the tourists on the town pier with melting ice cream cones dripping down to our elbows. My mouth gapes open in a scream-laugh and Iris has a purple raspberry mustache.

I'm not too tired to write back to that.

> **Me:** *No matter how I got it, I shouldn't have read it. And I shouldn't have blown up like that. I'm so sorry too. I love you.*

> **Iris:** *Love you too.*

I tuck the phone full of her words under my pillow and close my eyes.

CHAPTER 42

Once upon a time, on the steps of a red-shingled house, a dark-haired girl sat, trying not to cry. She'd lived in this new place called Cape Cod for three months, and it still felt strange and wrong, like a bad dream she couldn't wake from. The air was too sticky, the people were too loud, and there were trees everywhere. The girl wasn't used to trees. They seemed unstable, unpredictable, with their swaying branches and feathery leaves. She suspected that in the night they uprooted giant, gnarly root-feet and ambled around like trolls while everyone slept.

The screen door of the house across the street opened, and a girl with wispy, white-blond hair stepped out. She started across her lawn, then stopped. Muttering to herself, she clenched her fists and nodded, then crossed the street.

"Hello," she whispered, staring at the dark-haired girl's shoes.

"Hi," said the dark-haired girl.

"We just moved here," said the blond girl.

"I know." The dark-haired girl had watched the yellow truck rumble up and unload all of the other girl's and her mother's things.

The blond girl picked a dandelion and blew its white fluff across the lawn, and the dark-haired girl's heart ached at the memory of her mother in those cotton-grass summers.

"I'll be right back," said the blond girl, dropping the stem and racing back to her house. When she returned, she held out two brownies, one in each hand. The dark-haired girl chose the left brownie, and the blond girl sat beside her as they ate.

"How old are you?" said the dark-haired girl.

"Seven," said the blond girl.

"Me too," said the dark-haired girl, though she wouldn't technically be seven for another week. "Where's your father?"

"He doesn't live with us anymore." The blond girl swiped a pebble off the steps. "He moved to Florida and we have to take a plane if we want to see him."

"My mamma's gone too," said the dark-haired girl.

The blond girl's expression turned somber. "Did she die?"

"No."

The blond girl edged closer until her shoulder bumped the dark-haired girl's. "I'm sad about my dad, but I'd never stop crying if my mom left me."

The dark-haired girl bit her lip and nodded.

The blond girl handed the rest of her brownie to the dark-haired girl, who ate it silently. "You can come to my house whenever you need a mom. Even though I know it's not the same as your own."

The dark-haired girl swallowed the lump of brownie that had turned to paste on her tongue. "Thanks."

The blond girl sprang up and launched into a clumsy cartwheel, almost landing on her head. "Do you know how to play Uno?"

The dark-haired girl's laugh was rusty, but loud. It startled her, this sudden lightness. "What's Uno?"

"It's a card game. Do you want to come over and I'll show you how to play?"

The dark-haired girl attempted a cartwheel and nearly crashed into a tree. With a nervous squeak, she leapt away from its reaching branches. "Okay."

As they crossed the road, the dark-haired girl thought, for the first time since arriving in this strange new place, that it was possible she might survive after all.

CHAPTER 43

I've gone with Marit to Ekmanfjorden. Please don't be mad. I'll be home in a couple of days. I love you.

As soon as my dad leaves for UNIS, I wrap the note around the toothpaste tube in his toilet bag. Then I stuff a granola bar in my pocket, pull on another pair of wool socks, and dash downstairs. I've got fourteen minutes to get to the café and meet Marit.

"Where are you going?" Pushing a mop that looks older than me, Mormor emerges from her apartment.

"I thought I'd explore the town," I say, fighting to keep my voice nonchalant. "Kaja says the museum is really nice?"

Mormor's lips purse. "It's decent, I suppose. Will you be back for lunch?"

"Um, probably not." I struggle to tug my boot on over both layers of socks. "I'll eat at the café and use their Wi-Fi to catch up on emails and stuff."

"We've got Wi-Fi here," says my grandmother, and if I didn't know better I'd think she's actually sad that I'm not coming back. "Those gloves aren't going to knit themselves, you know."

With one boot on, I teeter, steadying myself against the wall. She really does want to spend time with me. "Maybe later this afternoon?" I say, hating myself for getting her hopes up when I've got no intention of being in Longyearbyen this afternoon.

"All right." She pushes the mop beneath the couch and stabs it around like she's trying kill something under there. "See you then."

"Bye." With another twinge of guilt, I push open the door and step into the blue-lit morning.

Outside the café, Marit accepts the black coffee I give her, handing me a blue snowsuit that matches hers in exchange. "Put this on over your coat," she says. "Have you got woolen long underwear on?"

I nod as I tug the snowsuit over my boot. "And a wool sweater. And two pairs of socks." At this rate I'm not going to be able to bend my arms or legs. My dad would approve of all these layers, even though he'll kill me for going on this trip.

Marit gives me a pair of thick, insulated mittens and gestures to the sled attached to the back of her snowmobile. "I've got more clothing if you need it. And camping gear in case we don't make it to the cabin."

The thought of having to sleep in a tent with all those polar bears roaming around is chilling, but hopefully that won't happen. Marit stows my bag with the rest of her supplies and hands me a helmet. "So Peter actually agreed to this adventure."

"Yeah, he definitely did." I fumble the helmet and she rolls her eyes.

"I don't want to hear another word." Marit tosses her cup into a recycle bin, swings her leg over the snowmobile, and checks her rifle in its holster by her knee. "As far as I'm concerned, your father said this trip was fine. I've got it in writing."

"Thank you," I say, climbing on behind her. "I really appreciate—"

My words are lost in the engine's roar as we zoom onto the road, quickly leaving Longyearbyen behind. The gray-blue clouds hang lower in the sky than they did yesterday; they're darker too, and the air smells of ice. As we pass the last few buildings and glide into a wide, flat-bottomed valley, snowflakes begin to fall.

For a while we scream along, gas fumes and cold filling my helmet, and then the valley tapers and we begin a gentle, sloping climb through mountains with snow swept up their sides and black rock cragging out at their tops. Up and up we weave, engine groaning, sled rattling along behind us.

Mamma, we're coming. I'm coming. Please, please be there.

The snowfall thickens and thickens until the mountains fade to shadows. Still our engine roars and strains. *Marit knows what she's doing,* I tell myself as I wipe the snow off my visor. She didn't smell like alcohol. She drank a coffee. Kaja said she knows this terrain better than anyone. I lean closer to her as we weave and climb. Then the slope flattens. On the other side of our hill lies a wide, ice-and-water fjord, barely visible in the swirling white. Marit cuts the engine to an idle and lifts her visor.

"This wasn't in the forecast," she yells, waving her arm in the snow.

"Can we keep going?" We've only been out for less than an hour—I refuse to consider the possibility of giving up this soon.

Marit grunts. "We'll go a bit farther and see. No promises." She shoves her visor down, and we're off again.

We rattle around a rocky bend and the fjord disappears again. The trail narrows and twists, weaving between low mountains with rocks jutting out at irregular intervals. Still, the snow thickens, coming down harder and faster until I can't see anything but whipping flakes in our headlights. I take slow breaths, trying to ignore the desperate crush in my chest. We are safe. I trust Marit. I will find my mother.

We jolt to a stop, and Marit lets out a string of what I assume are swears.

"Is everything okay?" I ask, praying the snowmobile isn't broken, that we're not going to get trapped in this narrow pass, that I'm not going to freeze to death less than an hour outside of Longyearbyen.

"Just wonderful," Marit spits, climbing off the snowmobile and punching her fist into the snowstorm. *"Nordenvinden! Nordenvinden, hvor er du!"*

She speaks in rapid Norwegian that I can't follow, but I know that Nordenvinden is the North Wind. Fascinated, I watch as Marit clambers onto a boulder and waves both arms. She shouts her message again, and a massive gust comes roaring in through the mountain pass, shoving me back in my seat and almost toppling Marit off her rock. She laughs a crooked laugh and shouts again. Then she cocks her head like she's listening. I don't hear any response, but she gives a curt nod and jumps down.

"Let's give it a few minutes," she says, rummaging in a snow-covered bag on the sled and pulling out a thermos.

"What did you do?" I ask as she hands me a steaming drink in a metal mug and pours herself one too. Taking a sip, I'm relieved to taste sugary coffee. No aquavit. Snowflakes patter into the black liquid, instantly melting.

"I asked the North Wind to blow this storm away," she says. "Let's see if he can actually manage it."

"North Wind, please get rid of this storm!" I yell into the whirling sky, and Marit spits out a bit of her coffee.

"I don't think he speaks English," she says, wiping the front of her coat with her mitten.

She might be right. My mother always spoke to him in Norwegian. "How do I ask him to blow me to Ekmanfjorden?" I say.

Her laughing eyes go serious. "That is a horribly dangerous idea."

"I was just joking," I lie.

"Can you even imagine?" says Marit. "Blowing you all that way. He'd rip your clothing and then break your bones when he put you down."

"He didn't break that girl in the story," I say. "The one who went east of the sun and west of the moon." Or me when I was a child, though my mother made sure my feet barely left the ground.

"You are not that girl," says Marit. "And if I'm going to take you to Ekmanfjorden, I don't want to hear any more of that talk."

"Okay, okay," I say. "Sorry."

Marit glances at the sky and her expression brightens. "Looks like he's managing it after all."

She's right: the snow is thinning, and the sky has lightened by a couple of shades.

"Thank you, North Wind!" I pause to remember the right words. *"Takk, Nordenvinden!"*

A tiny gust tickles my cheek.

By the time the coffee cups are put away and we're back on the trail, only a few floating flurries remain. The terrain grows rougher and steeper, but now that we're moving and we've got the North

Wind on our side, I don't mind all the thumps and jolts that are surely leaving bruises up and down my legs.

I'm coming, Mamma, I whisper inside my helmet, wanting to scream to her but also not wanting to startle Marit, who is focused on finding our route. Several times, we have to stop while she assesses the best way through the rock and ice rubble. But I trust her, I trust her, and even if we don't make it to Ekmanfjorden today, we will get there eventually.

As we round a bend, the light turns eerie and greenish, and a rotten smell fills my nostrils. I tap Marit's back, wondering if there's a dead animal ahead. She ignores me, her shoulders hunched as the snowmobile roars and swerves. Maybe a polar bear killed something and left its remains near the trail. But surely it would freeze in this climate, not rot and stink so horribly.

My eyes begin to water.

I don't want to think about things that might be dead. I refuse to even *consider* things that might be dead.

I almost tell Marit to stop, that I'm going to be sick, but I choke the fear down, stuff the thought deep into the back of my brain. I will find my mother. I will.

The front of the snowmobile hits something, and we pitch to the side. I almost tumble off but manage to grab a fistful of Marit's coat.

"Sorry," I yell, but she holds up a hand to silence me.

The rotten stench has become unbearable; it fills my sinuses and my throat, sweet and sickening and sour. The reek of long-dead things, of decomposing flesh.

Falling apart, falling apart.

I yank off my helmet, black stars swimming in my vision, and slide off the snowmobile.

"Eline," hisses Marit. "Get back on. Now."

"I can't," I whisper, dropping to a crouch, pulling off my helmet, and spitting. My saliva is gray against the snow, and everything is whirling and tipping so violently that it feels like my brain has come loose in my skull.

"Right. Now." The fear in Marit's voice is so sharp it pulls me out of my nauseous haze.

From deep in the hills comes a rustle and a hiss. A dark creature slithers out, and every muscle in my body freezes.

"Poor little girl." Its rasping voice sets my teeth on edge. "Ran away to find her mother. Instead I'll crawl inside her sad little heart and turn it black."

"No, you won't." Trying to ignore the ache in my chest, I pick up a chunk of ice and hurl it at the monster, but it darts out of the way, much faster than I'd expect a creature of its size to move.

"I will, I will," croons the lindworm.

As I climb back onto the snowmobile, the dark hurt spreads into my stomach, a sorrow even worse than when my mother flew away. It's like a tide dragging me into a deep sea. I just want to sleep, just want to close my eyes and make it all go away.

Marit revs the engine and tries to speed around the lindworm, but its shadowy body doubles in size, blocking the entire trail.

"Hold on tight," she yells, and I wrap my arms around her as she swerves and tries the other side, but again, the hideous creature swells, its long tail curling like smoke around the side of the snowmobile. The smell of rotting flesh is unbearable; my eyes fill with stinging tears and my breath comes in short, painful gasps.

But I'll be damned if this disgusting *thing* is going to stop me from finding my mother. Working quickly behind Marit's back, I pull the flare gun from my pocket and jam a cartridge inside. Then

I aim it at the hill up ahead, to the left of the trail, and squeeze the trigger. Sparks and snow explode with a crashing bang, and the lindworm rears back. Without hesitating, Marit guns the engine and we roar forward into the empty space.

The lindworm's tail whips out, and Marit swerves up onto the side of the trail. The left ski of our snowmobile crunches over an icy rock, and we tip.

"Watch out!" she yells, but we're already rolling. I tumble into the snow, and the world turns to thundering chaos as the snowmobile rolls over me and lands on the other side. For a long moment I lie there, stunned but unharmed. Snowflakes flutter out of the white sky and land on my visor.

Everything's silent except the lindworm's snarling laugh.

Marit staggers to her feet. Her helmet is somehow not on her head anymore, and a gash above her eyebrow leaks blood down the side of her face.

"Lindworm, you cannot have her heart." Marit's knee buckles, but she catches herself and manages to stay upright. She pulls out a pocket knife and opens its silver blade. "Go away before I skin you and we find out what's underneath."

The lindworm's hiss makes the hair on the back of my neck stand up. "Go back to your father, little one," it whispers. "Get on your airplane. Go home to your safe little life. There's nothing here for you but sorrow."

But it's the one backing away now, keeping its distance from Marit's flashing blade. She lunges and the creature shoots backward, whipping its tail and sending rocks flying.

"Go away!" yells Marit, then repeats herself in Norwegian for good measure, brandishing her knife.

The lindworm looks at our overturned snowmobile and bares its pointy teeth in something like a smile. "I'll find you again," it whispers, and my stomach churns. With a hissing laugh, it slithers away down the trail.

Marit bends low, hands on knees, droplets of her blood falling into the snow. I rush to her side, and all the hope that filled my body like helium this morning gusts out of me. She's shaking harder than I am.

"Are you okay?" I say. "Do you have a first aid kit?"

Marit wipes blood from her eye, smearing it into her hair. "It's in one of the bags on the sled. Help me with the snowmobile."

The vehicle lies on its side, the sled jutting out at a sharp angle and supplies scattered across the snow. Together, Marit and I push the sled back into alignment and then heave the snowmobile upright. A spiderweb of cracks covers the windshield, and a long fracture runs across the hood.

"Where's the first aid kit?" I say, piling things at random onto the sled.

Marit wipes away more blood and inspects a broken headlight. "Inside the big green bag."

I find the kit and pull out a wad of gauze and tape, but her cut gapes so wide I'm not sure what to do. She waves me off and tries the snowmobile's ignition. Miraculously, it starts.

"We have to go to the hospital," I say. "You need stitches."

"Let's give it a few minutes," she insists, pressing the gauze to her head and holding it steady while I tape it down. "Maybe it'll stop bleeding."

"No," I say. "You can't see what it looks like, but I can. It's bad. And we can't take the snowmobile any farther, can we?"

Marit blinks at me for a minute, then stares at the broken windshield. "No. I'm sorry, Eline."

"Don't be sorry."

I'm sorrier than anybody that this didn't work. We're still miles and miles away from where I need to be.

"I'll get some stitches and borrow a snowmobile and we'll come out again tomorrow." Marit tries to put her helmet back on and hisses in pain.

"Sure," I say, but I doubt she'll be in any kind of shape to make this journey tomorrow. An angry lump blooms on the other side of her forehead and her dilated pupils are still struggling to focus. "Let's just concentrate on making it back to Longyearbyen right now, okay? Do you need me to drive? I think you might have a concussion."

Marit fixes her watery gaze on me. "Do you know how to drive a snowmobile? A *broken* snowmobile?"

"Um, no."

She lets out a bark of a laugh. "I'll drive. We'll go slow."

We pack her wound with more gauze and then she puts her goggles on but leaves the helmet off. The snowmobile makes awful scraping sounds as we creep down through the narrow mountain pass, and I pray for her safety, for both of our safety, but mostly for her. I hope she won't have lost too much blood by the time we get to the hospital. I hope the lindworm doesn't come back.

Finally, we reach the flat-bottomed valley and Marit opens up the throttle. We screech and clatter across the blue snow, and my heart sinks lower and lower as we approach the settlement.

I didn't find my mother. I've lost another day. I don't know how

I'll ever make it to Ekmanfjorden without Marit. But there has to be a way. I'll walk over the mountains if I have to. I'll bring my own silver knife and fight a thousand lindworms. I'll put on a dry suit and swim through the ice-crusted fjords. I'll build a boat with a sail and ask the North Wind to blow me there, even if his gusts are too powerful and I capsize or break all my bones.

It's barely past noon as we roar into Longyearbyen, and the crushing defeat hits me all over again. This roller coaster of hoping and failing is slowly killing me. Marit pulls up behind a warehouse and cuts the engine.

"You can walk from here, right?" She eases her goggles up over the bandages, and I'm relieved to see they're still white on the outside. We must have staunched the bleeding.

"I'll come to the hospital with you," I say.

"No. If we're going back out tomorrow, it's better to stick to your cover story for today. Don't let your father or anybody he knows see you with me. Put your snowsuit in the green bag."

It seems impossible that Marit will make it out tomorrow, but I unzip the suit. There's no point in getting in trouble and ruining my options for the rest of the week. "Are you sure you'll be okay by yourself?"

Marit scoffs. "I live alone in a cabin that gets frequently visited by polar bears. I think I will be fine."

My cheeks go hot as I tug the snowsuit down over my legs. "Right. Well, thanks for taking me out today, even though we didn't make it all the way."

She shifts uncomfortably. "Next time we *will* make it all the way."

I'm about to say goodbye to her when something else pops

out of my mouth. "Sorry, this is so random, but do you know how the lindworm's story ends?"

Marit's bleary eyes widen. "Don't you know?"

I shake my head. "I was always too afraid to read it after what happened with the fire."

She tuts. "I don't blame you. How far did you get?"

"Up to when they give him a princess and he eats her."

"Let's see." Marit considers for a moment. "He eats another princess after her, and then all the other kings and queens get wise, so a shepherd's daughter is chosen to be Prince Lindworm's next bride. She sobs and despairs, but a witchy old woman tells her exactly what to do. On her wedding night, the shepherd's daughter asks to be dressed in ten snow-white shifts. Each time the lindworm asks her to remove her shift, she tells him to shed a layer of his skin. Layer after layer until all of the shifts and all of the skins are off."

I gape at her. "Really?"

"Pretty gross, eh?" Marit's grin widens. "Then the shepherd's daughter whips Prince Lindworm with lye and bathes him in a tub full of milk. Finally, she lies down with him in his bed and holds him very tight."

I can't decide if the idea of snuggling naked with a skinless, flayed, milk-covered lindworm is more terrifying or disgusting.

"And then he transforms into a handsome prince," she finishes.

"Wait, what?" I say. "Is that supposed to be a happy ending?"

Marit bursts into raucous laughter, then winces and touches the bandage on her head. "It wouldn't be if I were that girl. I don't care how handsome the prince was. He still *ate* two people."

"Wow, yeah." I don't think the lindworm deserves that ending.

"Still, better than the girl getting eaten, I suppose," says Marit. "Did you have any other questions for me?"

"No," I say, mind still reeling from that gruesome and strange ending. "I hope your head feels better soon."

Marit waves her hand like it's nothing, but her eyes still aren't quite focusing. "I'll text you once I'm out of the hospital. And speaking of fairy tales, remember to stay away from those princesses if you see them."

"I will."

As she zooms away down the snowy street, I think of our conversation yesterday. An idea flickers in my brain, tiny like a candle flame but growing.

They might offer to help you too, but they'll want some kind of payment.

They might offer to help. Yes, the rest of the sentence is important, but not as important as the first part. I've flown to the top of the world. I've tried everything I can think of to find my mother, but nothing is working and I'm running out of time. At this point, I don't care what kind of payment they want as long as they can help me.

Those girls might be my only option left.

CHAPTER 44

Once upon a time, in a little green house at the top of the world, there lived a girl who knew that stories didn't stay in their books. She'd discovered that other people didn't know this, didn't *want* to know this, and so she hid the things she found. Now the girl was a mother, and she had her very own daughter: a clever, sweet creature who filled her life with color and beauty. And the mother began to show her child the secrets that no one else saw.

A few weeks after the mother's twenty-ninth birthday, something began to change. The stories weren't following the words that she read from their books, not even the ones she'd written. The paper birds pecked her hands as she folded them; the moon dropped stones on her head whenever she went outside. The mother didn't understand the betrayal, so she ignored it, buried it, told herself and her daughter lies to make everything feel safe.

One day, the girl woke with a fever that burned the mother's hand when she touched her forehead. It was Saturday and the doctor's office was closed. The mother fought down the swelling panic that she knew wasn't helpful or necessary. She forced a smile onto her mouth and promised the girl that it didn't matter; they would have a nice day together even if they couldn't leave the house. As the girl shivered and begged for more blankets, the mother held her trembling hands behind her back. She built up a fire in the fireplace, stretched a sheet between two chairs, and pulled out her book. The stories would take the girl's mind off her fever and the mother's mind off the girl.

The mother should have paid more heed to the unspooling of things, though, for as she read the story of Prince Lindworm to her feverish child, the story began to spiral, and as she neared the end, it sprang out of her grasp. The dancing shadows burned a trail of black across her carpet and began to lick the chair with their fire tongues. They would have consumed the whole house if her husband hadn't come home.

When he did, it was worse than if the house had burned down.

And then her daughter, her own blood and self, was gone. The mother lay on the floor, curled up like a desiccated bug. Her life was unraveling, and she couldn't weave it back together. Her husband had told her it was better to send the child away, lest she unravel too. The mother knew he was right, but she couldn't forgive him. She told him to leave too.

For a week, the mother tried to stop what was pouring out of her. Kept her mouth shut when she itched to whisper to the clouds. Kept her hands in her pockets when she ached to grab the mountains and pull them crashing down onto the town. For seven days, she held everything in. But one day the wallpaper in the living room began peeling down in great, curling swathes. On the underside of the sheets, words crawled in lines like ants. As soon as the mother looked at the words, the stories leapt to life. Thunderstorms roared and pounded in the bathroom, serpents crawled out of the sink drains, violins wailed, and footsteps that weren't hers pattered up and down the hall all night long.

By the twenty-third day, the mother knew she had to stop this or she would die. She reached down inside herself and found a deep well of strength she was sure had dried up. She ripped the paper from the walls and stuffed it into the fireplace. As she lit the match, she wondered if the whole house would go up in flames, and she wasn't sure if it mattered. Blue flames and green sparks leapt and flickered, and the words screamed as they were eaten, one by one by one.

After it had consumed all of the wallpaper, the fire went out. The words fell silent.

A knock sounded at the door. The mother opened it to find three princesses, the youngest holding a silver box.

"We found your mother's heart," they said.

The mother put on her coat. She thanked them for the silver box. She walked to the hotel and she took her daughter back.

CHAPTER 45

The clock struck midnight three hours ago, and I still haven't found those cloaked princesses or my mother. I spent the rest of the day roaming Longyearbyen, searching between the buildings and in the quiet spaces behind the houses, venturing as far outside the town as I dared. But there was no sign of her or them, and I wanted to scream at the smallness of this place, at the futility of searching in this tiny amount of space I'm allowed to roam by myself.

I stopped at a tourist shop and bought my own knife, not as shiny as Marit's, but sharp nonetheless. Then I came back to the hotel, stole my note out of my father's toilet case, and dragged him out for dinner and another long walk. But nobody looked like my mother or lured us out into the darkness. No lindworms tried to turn our hearts black, though mine still feels gray.

Marit's text message arrived just as we returned to the hotel.

Marit: They're keeping me here overnight. We'll go the day after tomorrow, OK?

The day after tomorrow is not okay.

I waited until Mormor's door was closed and my dad started

snoring, and I searched all through the hotel for some sign of my mother, some clue of what I'm supposed to do, but there isn't a single toothpick out of place, and the closet door is still locked. Even the newlyweds have given up on their romantic fun and gone to sleep. This place is a mausoleum.

With twitchy, impatient fingers, I bind off the last stitch of my mother's fingerless gloves and clip the blue yarn. Despite the sky's hinted promise of green light earlier, it's flat black now. I can't walk over the mountains to Ekmanfjorden, I can't swim through the fjords, I can't build a boat. And I cannot physically stand another minute of waiting.

As my dad's snore rumbles through the dark, I slide my window open a couple of inches and whisper outside.

"Princesses, please come here. It's Eline. I need you."

No answer. Chilly air floods the room, and my dad mutters and shifts. Tearing another sheet from the notepad, I write the same message and hold it out the open window.

"Nordenvinden, please blow this to the princesses," I say quietly before letting go. The paper flutters and hovers for a moment, then falls to the snowy ground.

"Please," I say a little louder, but the note doesn't budge. I want to rip all my hair out, claw my skin off, fling this window all the way open and throw myself out.

From faraway downstairs comes the trilling loop of a cuckoo call. I ease out of bed and slip across the room. My dad's snore breaks off, and I freeze, one hand on the doorknob as he mutters something about reverse transcriptase and stuffs his face into his pillow with a breathy snark. Then I'm out in the hall and flying down the stairs, feet as silent as owl wings.

The cuckoo sings for the second time. I need to move faster because there will only be three. Hair streaming, lungs heaving, I round the front desk and push Mormor's door open.

The sitting room is dim and gray, filled with the sad, simple objects of an old woman. The bird trills for the final time as I burst into the dining room, hands clasped over my mouth to stifle the sound of my breath.

Bathed in shadows, the door at the top of the clock is open. A white bird sits on a perch. It tips its head sideways to looks at me with a beady black eye, and I realize it's the absence of ticking that makes the room so silent. Clasped in the bird's beak, something shimmers. A golden bell tied to a loop of red satin ribbon. Just like the one the princesses gave my mother when they first came to this hotel.

"Don't go back inside, not yet, not yet," I whisper as my socks slide along the cold floorboards. The bird ruffles its feathers, shifts on its perch. Skidding to a stop underneath the clock, I reach up and the bell falls into my palm.

"Thank you," I whisper. The bird jerks backward, the little door snaps shut, and the clock begins to tick again.

Out in the lobby, I sit on the couch, knees tucked up, bell hidden inside my fist.

"Mamma, can you hear me?" I whisper. "I can't wait any longer. I can't waste another day of our time."

The wind heaves and blusters around the hotel. Its moan sounds like a warning.

"Mamma, I'm giving you two more minutes."

The clock ticks off thirty seconds. Sixty. Ninety. One hundred.

"Mamma, please. I'd rather not call them if I don't have to."

Two hundred seconds. Three hundred. My fist unfolds. The bell shines in the darkness with its own gleaming light.

Four hundred.

I crick my finger through the loop of ribbon and let the bell fall. It sings out a sharp tone like ice shattering.

Outside, the wind groans and heaves and sobs.

At the hotel's front door, there comes a knock.

CHAPTER 46

Though some tiny part of me had been hoping to find my mother standing on the other side of the door, I'm not surprised to see the three princesses, their eyes glinting silver, emerald, and sapphire under the hoods of their cloaks.

"Let me get dressed." I know better than to invite them into Mormor's hotel, so I leave the door cracked open while I tug my snowpants over my pajamas and slip into my coat, making sure the flare gun and knife are still in the pocket. The girls wait silently while I pull on my boots and hat, tuck my hair under a scarf. As I let myself out the door, a wall of cold tries to shove me backward, sends a punch of ice searing down my throat. But before the cold has a chance to take my breath away, the sky does. It's streaming with green and fuchsia, the entire space awash with ghosting waves of light a thousand times brighter than that night on the baseball field.

"Bit frosty tonight." The black-haired princess stretches her bare fingers into the night and smiles.

I tuck my face deeper inside my scarf and inhale through the wool. My body is curling in on itself, and I swear the liquid inside my eyeballs is freezing solid. I stuff my hands into my coat pockets and find my new-old mittens. As soon as I slip them on, warmth radiates through my wrists and elbows, up to my shoulders, which begin to ease out of their turtle hunch.

"I need to find my mother," I say. "At Ekmanfjorden. Can you take me there?"

The red-haired princess stares at my mittens as if she'd like to eat them up. "Of course we can."

"But why do you want such a silly thing as a mother?" says the black-haired princess. "They're more trouble than they're worth."

"Maybe so." I grit my teeth and watch the waves of color unfurling overhead. "But I still want her."

"Yours is especially troublesome." The golden-haired princess, the tallest one, leans low to cup my cheek with her frigid fingers. "We've seen the way she treated you. The way you sobbed and suffered."

I tip back, out of her reach. "Then why did you give her my grandmother's heart?"

Her lips curl into a poison smile. "We hated your grandmother even more. It's a vicious cycle, this business of mothers and daughters. Someday, you'll treat your own just as badly as the rest of them."

Inside my mittens, my hands curl into fists. "I won't." But maybe I will. I'm nearly as broken as she was, and there's no guarantee that I won't pass that on to my own child.

"Anyway, your mother had to pay us to help her," says the flame-haired princess.

"What do you want?" I say. "Tell me before we leave, so I can get it."

"We'll sort that out later." The raven-haired princess clicks her tongue, and a low snuffling sound comes from the side of the building. "Don't worry, it's no great hardship for us, so we'll only need something small."

Every instinct in my body is screaming that this is a dangerous, terrible idea, but I can't stand waiting another minute.

"Not my . . . heart, though." My stammering words make tiny clouds.

The laughter of the three sounds like ice cubes tinkling in a glass.

"We've got no use for your heart," says the eldest girl. "A fragile, fluttering thing, yours is. Not worth the trouble."

I clasp both hands over my fierce, thundering heart. A million retorts flood to the tip of my tongue, but none of them will help me find my mother. "Let's go," I say.

The youngest princess snaps her fingers twice, and a massive white bear ambles out from the shadows. I swallow down a shriek as my hand dives into my pocket where Kaja's flare gun and my knife lie hidden. The princess snaps her fingers again, and the huge creature sinks to its haunches. Around its neck, a circle of gold flashes. The bear tips its head and stares at me, and there's something in its face I recognize, unlike the stuffed bear at the airport.

"You'll be too slow on foot," says the eldest princess. "You must ride."

"Ride . . . that?" Even though it might be the bear that saved me, its shoulders are level with my head. Its teeth are easily two inches long.

"He won't hurt you," says the eldest princess. "He knows we'd flog him if he did."

The bear moans and lays its chin on top of one colossal paw. Just a swipe of that paw could end my life, but I'm flooded with pity for the animal, the way it watches the princesses with a mix of devotion and fear.

"Do you want to find your mother or not?" The red-haired princess taps her brocade slipper impatiently in the snow.

"Yes." I edge closer to the bear.

"That's right," says the youngest princess as I ease my leg over the animal's vast body. A shiver races over its skin as I settle onto its back, but the bear remains still, its eyes locked on the youngest princess.

"Good bear." She snaps her fingers twice, and the animal heaves up to standing. I bite down hard on my lip to keep from yelping as I pitch forward, grabbing fistfuls of the bear's fur, which is thicker and softer than I expected it would be. With a whirling swish of their long cloaks, the princesses dash away down the street, and the bear bounds after them.

Clinging desperately with my mittens and knees, I hold my breath as we fly past the low buildings of the town, the snow tinged emerald from the aurora above. Isfjorden stretches ahead, gleaming like a promise. We leave the last building behind and tear down the embankment, and I realize with a start that the fjord is frozen solid, all the way across to the mountains on the other side. Without pausing, the princesses sprint onto the ice and the bear follows.

The fjord was stunning in the twilit daytime, but tonight it's supernatural. Waves of light dart through the sky, fizzling pink and orange at the edges, leaping and dancing like they want to play, urging us on. The air zips with electricity, and my eyes stream tears that instantly freeze on my cheeks. But I can't let go to wipe them; my heart thunders as I begin to find the rhythm of the bear's movements. The collar cuts a deep ridge in its fur, like it was put on when the bear was much smaller. I wonder if there's a way to take it off, but I also wonder if it's the only thing stopping the bear from eating me.

Soon I can't feel the drumming of massive paws on ice anymore. We zoom all the way across vast Isfjorden, the ice reflecting the whirling sky like a mirror. That night with my mother comes flooding back. The reindeer bounding beneath me, my mother's arms around my waist, her chin resting on top of my head. The cracking fear, the slithering, growing awareness that it might be the end of everything.

The wind gusts harder, trying to shove us back to Longyearbyen, and the bear's pace slows. The princesses exchange a sideways glance, then move in front of us, standing shoulder to shoulder in a triangle, the eldest girl the sharp front point. The pressure on my face eases as the princesses' cloaks stream out behind them, their delicate slippers a blur. Furious, the wind roars and whistles around and over, but it can't get through. We're flying again, faster than before.

Even without the wind, I should be shivering, but I'm not. The warmth from my mittens floods every inch of my body. Casting a quick glance at the princesses, I hold tight with my knees and lean closer to inspect the bear's collar. Deep grooves are etched in its design, interlocking circles and diamonds and squares. In the center, there's a clasp with a button shaped like a star. I want to push the star and release the bear from his bondage, but I'm afraid of falling, of being eaten.

We careen up Nordfjorden, past a craggy glacier spilling through a gap between mountains, and I remember all of this, sharp like it happened yesterday. As we veer into the narrower corridor of Ekmanfjorden, the Northern Lights reel and tumble overhead, casting the snow and our skin in an otherworldly glow. Then, just beside a flat-topped line of mountains, the princesses and the polar bear stop. The youngest princess snaps her fingers, and the bear sinks down to the ice.

"Thank you," I whisper as I climb off.

The enormous creature groans and huffs and paws at its collar. The youngest princess steps closer, a warning flashing in her eyes, and the bear cringes away, lowers its chin all the way down to the ice.

I clear my throat. "What happens now?"

The flame-haired princess floats closer, her cloak fluttering silently. "It's time for you to pay us."

"Where's my mother?" I say.

"You have to call her." The golden-haired princess joins her sister, and a bony-fingered chill slithers down the back of my neck.

"How?"

"Just like she called them." The eldest princess inclines her chin toward the swirling colors in the sky. "But you'd better hurry. She's almost gone."

The jolt of panic is an electric shock. "Gone where?"

The youngest princess digs her heel down on the polar bear's foot, and I wince. "She looks terrible, the poor thing."

"Why? Will you please just tell me?" Flecks of spit fly out of my mouth, freeze, and clatter to the ice.

"We owe you nothing more." The red-haired princess bares

her teeth in a greedy grin. "And now you must pay. Give us your mittens."

"These?" I hold out my hands, where Mormor knitted part of the story of my mother and me. "Why? You clearly aren't bothered by cold."

She giggles, and her elder sister jabs a long finger into her midsection. The girl hisses. "Doesn't matter why," she says. "That's what we want."

"Fine." As soon as I slip the mittens off, cold shears through my coat, wrenches at my bones, and drops me to a crouch. Before I can change my mind, the eldest princess snatches the mittens and tucks them inside her cloak.

"I can hear all the nasty things you'll say to your own daughter," she says. "They're rushing around your head, loud as shouting. All the ways you'll break her. It's better this way."

"How do you know I'll even have one?" I gasp.

"If you're smart, you won't," says the black-haired princess.

"I hate you," I say, but already they're drifting away down the fjord as if they've forgotten I exist. The bear lurches to its feet and sets off after them.

"Wait," I call, and it stops. "S-sit."

My voice isn't nearly as commanding as the princesses', but the shaggy creature listens, sinking low with a groan.

"Hold still," I whisper through chattering teeth as I climb onto its back and jam my frozen thumb into the star clasp on its collar. The metal disintegrates, and I leap away, half expecting the bear to charge and rip me to pieces. But the creature gives me a somber look and then lumbers off toward the mountains, heading away from the princesses.

Everything is silent. I am alone.

The aurora sinks lower, smokelike tendrils of gold and red licking earthward, and I'm flooded with the sense of my mother, the scent of her hair and the softness of her breath.

"Mamma," I whisper as a spiral of fuchsia unspools. It's time to call them down. The dancing lights muddle as my eyes stream freezing tears. Bouncing on the balls of my feet, I count to five. Five heartbeats until the end of me, maybe.

I can do this. I can do this.

My whistle flies out strong and certain. Instantly, the sky pulses. The lights contract, then explode, heaving downward. My hands fly up to shield my eyes from the searing light, a million times brighter than lightning and louder too, a rushing, roaring, killing sonic wave. It's been ten years, but I remember this maelstrom, and it's far more terrifying now. Every hair on my body goes rigid, the hat on my head lifts, my heels come off the ice.

Even though I can't hear it, I feel the scream burn up my throat. I'm off the ice now, legs kicking. These lights are a force of nature, stronger and more cruel than the roaring ocean could ever dream of being. I stretch my arms as wide as they'll go, reaching for the threads of her, straining to hear her breath in the midst of this vortex. But there's nothing. She's not here.

This was a trap. The lights don't care whether I live or die.

The fjord narrows below me; the panorama of empty mountains widens as I'm dragged higher. I stuff my hand in my pocket, fumbling to grasp the flare gun, but I can't feel anything except the soaring, pulling, white-hot light. Finally, I find it, but the handle catches on the lip of my pocket and my frozen fingers let go and it tumbles away.

"Help me, North Wind!" I scream. "Please! Nordenvinden, help me!"

As one, the lights suck upward, pulling me with them, and I'm certain this is the end. But then their electric grip releases.

I fall.

CHAPTER 47

Once upon a time, in a crooked old shack at the top of the world, a little girl sat on the floor with a huge sheet of paper and six pots of paint. She swirled the colors around and around on the paper: purple and black and pink, orange bleeding into yellow. After a quick peek to confirm that her mother and her friend with the sealskin slippers weren't paying attention, the girl dropped the paintbrush and plunged her hand straight into the pot of vivid green paint. She loved the way it cut through all the other colors as she swiped the paper with her slippery fingers.

The colors began to swirl all on their own. Spellbound, the girl pushed both hands into the whirlpool. To her surprise, they sank in up to her elbows. She tried to call out for help, but no sound came from her mouth. On the couch, the mother had buried her face in her hands, and her friend was rubbing her back, murmuring soft reassurances.

The paints spiraled and pulled and sucked at the girl, and then her head went underneath and all she could see was a thousand technicolor hues. She opened her mouth to scream, and the paint flooded in, acrylic and bitter and choking. It swallowed her shoulders, then her torso, and she began to thrash in the oily, saturated hues, no sense of up or down anymore.

Fingers closed around the girl's leg—her mother's fingers—and slowly, steadily, she dragged her daughter out of the paint. The girl fell onto the dusty floor, gasping for breath, shaking and covered in murderous color. She clung to her shaking mother, couldn't let go, would never let go of her again.

"Everything is spiraling out of control and I can't make it stop," said the girl's mother to her friend with the sealskin slippers. "I don't know what to do."

"Do you think it's . . . them?" The friend whispered the last word.

The mother cast a nervous glance at the window. "I don't see how they could have caused that just now. Maybe I'm doing it somehow myself. Without meaning to."

The girl felt her mother's arms tremble, and she hated it. Mothers weren't supposed to be afraid. They were supposed to have all the answers and be strong and brave all the time. The girl gave an extra-loud sob, just so her mother would hug her tighter. And she did, but her arms kept shaking. She didn't even seem to notice that the paint had smeared all over her sweater.

"I ripped out the page we changed," said the mother. "I tried to burn it, but when I threw it into the fireplace, the wind swept it up the chimney."

"Is the Nordenvinden helping them now? That rotten bastard."

Even though swearing was wrong, the girl's mother didn't admonish her friend. The girl forgot all about crying. She lifted her paint-sticky head from her mother's shoulder.

"What page?" she said.

"It's nothing," said the mother. "Why don't you go put on your boots? It's time for us to leave."

As the girl crept around the paper on the floor, careful not to touch its edges, she strained to listen to what her mother and her friend were whispering about.

"Does Peter know?" said the friend.

The mother let out a broken whisper-laugh. "No. And I hope he never finds out, because then it will definitely be all my fault."

The girl didn't understand how that was possible. She hated this entire conversation, and she began to whine that her hair was itchy and her stomach hurt.

"All right, all right," said her mother, hefting herself off the couch and also stepping carefully around the paper on the floor.

"I'll burn that once you're gone," said the friend. "Be careful, Silje."

"We'll be fine," said the mother, and the girl wished with all her heart that she believed her.

CHAPTER 48

The air slams out of my lungs as I crash onto the ice. Every synapse in my body fires over and over and over. Every bone screams from the impact. For a long while I'm not sure where I am, what's happening, which way is up. Slowly, I reorient myself as the throbbing eases and the screaming whistle in my ears quiets. I try to lift my head, but it's stuck to the ice—my arms and legs too. The stars swirl overhead and my eyelids are heavy, so deeply heavy. Everything dims and fades.

I dream that I'm lying with my mother in a cloud of snow. Whisper soft, it floats onto our faces, covers our bodies in a feathery blanket. We lie on our sides, facing each other, and my hands are in hers, a cocoon. The snow is soft as a kiss, warm as love. It piles up on my eyelids, pushing them down. I want to brush it away, but my hands are in hers and I never want to let go.

Mamma. It's not a word, just a thought.

The snow thickens, fills her ear and turns her hair white. Half of her face disappears. I want to clear it off, but I won't let go of her, I won't. My eyelids are heavy; I let them close, but I won't let go.

The snow falls and falls and falls.

Erasing.

I won't let go.

A groaning sound floats in from somewhere far away. It becomes a whine, then a roar. With a heave, I open my eyes. The sky glows orchid pink and gold over the mountains, so bright I'm sure the sun will emerge any second now. A dusting of snow has fallen, coating the ice and my body. My boot is missing, and my sock is crusted to the ice.

Against all the odds, against all the distance and forces of nature, I made it to Ekmanfjorden, but she isn't here. It makes me retch, makes me want to turn inside out. I want to punch a hole in this ice and slither down it and sink to the bottom of the ocean.

The roaring sound grows louder, impossible to ignore. A snowmobile rockets through the grainy dawn, driven by a person in a bright pink parka. Then it stops and Kaja yanks off her helmet and slide-runs across the ice to where I lie.

"Eli?" Her voice is ragged with fear.

I try to sit up, and the world smears like watercolors.

Kaja touches my bootless foot gently like she's afraid it's broken. "Half of Longyearbyen is out looking for you. Your dad and my dad are down at the other end of the fjord. Are you hurt?"

Shutting my eyes again, I take a mental scan of my body from toes to fingers to head, which aches but doesn't seem badly injured. "I don't think so."

"Where are your mittens?"

I stare down at my hands, which are mottled pink and white

and barely stinging anymore, and I wonder how many hours it's been. "I . . . lost them." A massive shiver racks my body. I've still got my mother's fingerless gloves in my coat pocket, but they won't save me from frostbite.

Frowning, Kaja pulls off her snowmobiling gloves and hands them to me. "Take these. I've got a spare set in my bag."

While she rummages around on her snowmobile, I pull on her gloves. They're nowhere near as warm as the ones Mormor made, but hopefully they'll save my fingers. My father will kill me if I lose my fingers. I'm still shivering, and I think that's a good sign. It's worse when you stop shivering.

Kaja pulls out her phone and squints at the screen. "I've barely got any signal. Hang on, I'm calling my dad."

While Kaja shouts into her phone and paces, trying to make her words understood, I sit up. The world tips, then settles. To my left the glacier looms, spilling between the mountains like someone poured it out of an enormous bowl. I've landed in a different spot from where I flew up, and I wonder how far the lights might have taken me if I'd let them.

"We'll be there soon," yells Kaja. "No, don't come. I've got her. We're fine."

We're not fine. I can't keep doing this, can't keep breaking and putting myself back together again. Every time I do, tiny pieces go missing, and they're making bigger and bigger holes. Purple cotton-ball clouds tumble through the sky. The world continues on, oblivious to my insignificant little life, my fragile, fluttering heart.

Kaja pockets her phone. "Are you ready to go?"

I shake my head.

She crouches beside me. "Hey, I get it. I know what this place is, what happened here. Can you please put my gloves back on?"

Looking down, I realize that I've somehow managed to take off and drop both of her gloves. I can't go back to Longyearbyen. This was the last place I could have possibly found my mother, and she's not here, she's not here.

"Everybody's talking about this," Kaja says, pointing at the ice. "It's thirty centimeters thick. That doesn't just happen overnight. Especially not in today's climate." She pushes her gloves onto my hand like I'm a toddler. "I know you made some sort of bargain with those girls." She holds up a finger as I start to respond. "And you don't have to tell me what you did. Really. But can I ask one favor?"

I nod, and a tear falls off my nose, making a tiny hole in the ice.

"Don't make any more deals with them. Let me take you the next time you go looking for her," says Kaja. "This isn't safe. You could have frozen to death or been eaten by a polar bear."

Hysterical laughter bursts up my throat, and soon I'm hiccupping and gasping, bent double over the absurd, thirty-centimeter-thick ice. This is the furthest thing from funny, and the laughter rips at my chest. Kaja gives me a long look that says she doesn't think it's funny either.

"I'll help you sneak out again," she says. "But I'm not letting you do this alone."

I gulp the laughter down. "I don't know what else to do." I wave at the sky, which is so muted and pale, it's impossible to imagine it ever held those lights. "If this didn't work, nothing will."

Kaja pulls me up to standing, and my legs wobble like a baby giraffe's. "We'll figure something out. Look, there's your boot."

By the sloping edge of the glacier, at its lowest point beside a jumble of boulders, my boot lies on its side. But that's not what makes the blood surge in my veins. Behind it, hobbling across the blue crags of ice and snow, is an old woman in a long black dress.

"It's her!" I shriek, slipping and almost taking Kaja down with me.

"Your mother?" She squints worriedly at the glacier.

"No, the old woman who gave me a wishing ring."

"The old . . . who?" Kaja looks like she's about to burst out laughing or crying, I'm not sure which. I don't think she's sure which.

I hobble-run across the ice, my sock crunching and sticking. "I bet she can help me—and she's not evil like those princesses."

"Eline, no!" Kaja slides after me. "I just told both of our dads that I was bringing you back. We can come here again once everybody's calmed down."

"We need to go *now*. She'll be gone later. The ice might be gone later." I cram my wooden foot inside the boot without even brushing it off. "Just give me five minutes. They won't notice an extra five minutes, right? Please, Kaja. This could be my last chance."

Kaja throws her arms up. "Fine, but we're not going up there."

We run to the glacier's edge and I cup my hands around my mouth. "Hello! *Hei! God morgen!* Excuse me!"

"*Unnskyld!*" yells Kaja, then launches into a long burst of Norwegian. The woman pauses, gives us a little wave, and continues hobbling across the ice.

"How did she even get up there?" says Kaja.

"That way." To our right, behind the pile of boulders, there's a rocky outcropping that leads onto the glacier. If I could just scramble up those boulders, I could follow her. "You've been on glaciers, right?" I say to Kaja. "Doesn't your dad lead expeditions out on them?"

"No, no, no." Kaja folds her arms over her coat. "Absolutely, one hundred percent no. We don't have any safety gear. It's way too dangerous."

"I don't care." My gloves can't grip the rocks, so I tug them off with my teeth. Slowly, I climb, oblivious to the cold stone ripping at my fingers. By the time I reach a place where I can swing onto the glacier, my skin is shredded and bleeding.

"Stop." Kaja grabs my ankle from below. "This is extremely stupid, and your dad is going to kill me. Put my gloves back on, for God's sake."

"You don't understand." My voice is shrill with desperation. "I can't find my mother. Marit is hurt, Mormor can't find her, even those princesses can't take me to her. But if that old woman gives me another ring, I can wish her back. This is the only option left, Kaja. Please, please don't take it from me."

Kaja looks back at the snowmobile and shakes her head. I open my mouth to protest, to beg, to plead, but she cuts me off. "Let me get a rope. You don't want to fall into a crevasse, trust me."

A long crevasse looms a few yards to my left. It's sickeningly narrow, and I can't see the bottom. There'd be no space to breathe if you fell in.

"Wait!" I scream at the old woman, but she just keeps moving farther and farther away.

"This is suicide." Kaja mops her forehead and starts climbing back down. "Stay there until I come back."

I honestly do mean to listen to her, but the old woman is growing faint and maybe it's just my concussed brain, but the edges of her seem to be blurring. My feet inch onto the craggy, snow-covered ice. In places where the wind has swept it clean, it gleams pure aqua blue.

"*Unn-unnskyld!*" I yell, the word lumpier than the ice on this glacier. "Please wait! It's me, Eline. The girl you gave a wishing ring to a long time ago."

The old woman stops. She swivels around, her dress swirling around her ankles, and drifts toward me. Slowly, I creep closer, testing each patch of snow before I step on it to make sure it won't give way, and finally we're both standing on the same big chunk of ice. She's only as tall as my shoulder now.

"Have you got any more of those cookies?" she croaks, watery eyes gleaming.

"I'm sorry, no."

Her dried-apple face sinks, and she starts to shuffle away. Frantically, I dig through my coat pockets and find a chocolate chip granola bar. "But I do have another kind of . . . cookie," I say, hoping her definition of baked goods isn't too strict. Quickly, I tear the wrapper off and hold it out. "Do you like chocolate?"

Before I can react, she snatches the bar from my fingers and crams the entire thing into her toothless mouth. As she chews, she shuts her eyes and groans happily. The mildew scent wafting off her turns my stomach, but I force myself to smile, to wait. Finally, she swallows and fixes her sharp little eyes on my face.

"Will you give me some more?" she wheezes.

"I gave you the only one I had." I hold out my empty hands, and she nods, gravely accepting my sacrifice. Then she takes hold of both my arms and leans me down so we're at eye level. Her sour, chocolate breath tickles my cheek.

"Where is the ring I gave you?" she says.

"It fell through a hole in the ice and I lost it," I say. "Right after I lost my mother."

She tuts, lets go of me, and rummages in the pocket of her dress. "Such a terrible shame, little girls losing their mothers."

Tears sting my eyes. The shame has been the hardest part to bear. The knowledge that I wished those lights away with my mother trapped in them. The impossible weight of that guilt.

"Now, now." The crone wipes a tear from my cheek, then licks her finger as I cringe. "Would you like another?"

"Another ring or . . . another mother?" I stammer.

She lets out a crow's caw of a laugh. "A ring, my lovely. Would you like one?"

"Please," I say. "I'd like that more than anything."

With an unsettling, gummy grin, she pulls a golden ring from her pocket and crooks her knobby finger for me to lean closer. Murmuring a low, haphazard song, she takes a strand of my hair and winds it through the ring, around and around until it's firmly stuck. The metal burns cold against my scalp.

"This will give you two wishes," she whispers. "Be careful how you use them."

I nod. "Thank you."

She sets her hands on her bony little hips. "Are you certain you haven't got any more cookies?"

"Yes," I say. "Very certain."

Muttering sadly, the old woman turns and hobbles away, her clunky shoes skimming across the glacier. In seconds, she's gone.

"Eli!" Kaja's voice rings across the ice. "What are you doing?"

Whirling around, I spot my cousin standing on the boulders we climbed up, hundreds of yards away. I can't believe I came this far out. But I'm not sorry I did. My fingers find the frigid ring tied in my hair.

I wish . . .

"Don't move." Kaja surveys the ice, then wedges some kind of anchor into the boulders. With the other end of the rope looped around her waist, she steps carefully out onto the ice. "I'm coming to get you."

I wish . . . The ring slides over my knuckle, its cold burning my skin. I understand, now, the importance of phrasing and timing everything exactly right. Clearing my throat, I let the words flood every inch, every cell, every electron in my body.

"I wish to find my mother."

The snow collapses beneath me.

CHAPTER 49

Slush fills my nose and mouth, blots out the light as the crevasse swallows me. Its sides scrape my face and back, wrench my arms overhead, and bend my knees at terrifying angles. Everything is nightmare-slow, the walls closing in and in and in, and then I'm sliding more than falling and I'm going to be crushed or trapped forever. Suddenly, the space opens up and I'm freefalling, arms whirling, fingers clawing at those icy walls that just threatened to suffocate me.

I crash down on an uneven floor. Penny-flavored blood trickles over my lips, but I can't open my eyes yet, can't quite process the fact that I'm no longer falling, can't shake the feel of those slithering walls, the choking snow. Spitting out a mouthful of ice, I press my cheek to the cold ground.

"Eli!" Kaja's frantic scream floats down the narrow crack. At the top winks a crooked gap of light. It's so incredibly far away.

I spit more bloody ice onto the ground. "I'm okay," I manage to shout.

"Stay right where you are," she yells. "I'm going for help."

Agony flares up my arm as I roll onto my back. I'm in a narrow ice cave with shadowy corners and a snow floor. I know I should wish myself out of this place, but then I'd have no wishes left. Somewhere beyond, droplets plink and water whispers.

"Eline."

I sit up, sucking in a breath as my wrecked elbow swings out. "Mamma?" My voice is muted, like the glacier is eating my words. Ice groans and settles overhead. "Are you here?"

"Yes. Are you all right?"

Slowly, agonizingly, I creak up to standing, clutching my arm to my body. "Yeah, I think so. Where are you?"

"This way."

In the farthest corner of the cave, in the direction her voice is coming from, there's a tunnel, narrow and dark.

"I should wait for Kaja," I say. "Can you come here instead?"

"I'm too weak to move. I'm sorry, Eline. I didn't mean for you to fall."

Even in the whisper, I hear the cracks in her voice, the shortness of her breath. With a shudder, I glance up at the sliver of light. Every shred of common sense says I should stay here and wait for Kaja, not go wandering deeper inside a glacier. But I don't know what's wrong with my mother, and in this instant, in this exact speck of time and space, nothing else matters. Not my cousin, not my father, not the search party or the whole town of Longyearbyen. I poke my head inside the tunnel. "Through here?"

"Yes."

My phone's screen is shattered, but the flashlight still works. Its bright beam glitters silver on the ice overhead. The snowy floor slopes downward, and I can't shake the feeling that I'm descending into the core of the earth.

The ice turns blue, and the tunnel opens up into a cave almost high enough for me to stand, with a slanted floor and walls in rippling, glassy shades of sapphire and black. I trail a gloved finger along the ice—it's even smoother than it looks. As the floor continues down, the curving ceiling brightens into a million dazzling undersea tones, shot through with pangs of gold and silver. Ahead, the passage forks.

"Left or right?" The cave nearly swallows up my words.

"Left."

This tunnel is full of the sound of trickling water. I follow the curving bend, and the cavern soars to cathedral height, its lustrous walls more like water than ice. It's surreal and painfully stunning, made even more so by the fact that I might die down here.

"Eline."

She sits in a heap at the far end of the cavern. My mother, her veins carrying the same blood as mine, her body full of my electrons. I run to her and sink to the floor, clutching my arm and trying not to scream as the movement jars my elbow. Her filthy sweater, barely white anymore, is full of giant holes. Her eyes are utterly black.

"You're hurt." She wraps both hands around my elbow, and cold radiates through my muscle and into the bone. A stiff, frozen feeling replaces the agony.

"Did you fall in here too?" I say.

"You asked me to fix everything, and I wanted so badly to do that." Her voice is a rasping husk. "I wanted to believe that bringing the whale home would work, and I wanted to save that poor creature no matter what. But it took almost everything I had left. I crawled in here to rest, and then I couldn't move." Her black eyes spill tiny beads of ice instead of tears. "I think we've both known for a long time that I'm not supposed to be here, that the only way to set everything right is for me to go back."

"What do you mean?" My exhausted heart begins to gallop. "I just got here. I just found you. That can't be right."

Pulling me close, she opens her mouth wide. There's nothing inside. No tongue, no teeth, no back of her throat, just a void. With a whimper that doesn't feel like my own voice, I pull away. She catches me before I smack my head on the wall.

"What's happening to your body?" I say.

"This isn't my body." Her black-hole eyes search my face; her mouth is set in a worried line. "My body is someplace else."

The hair on the back of my neck goes electric. "Is it up with the lights still?"

"No. I fell."

I don't want to ask any more questions because I can't face the truth: that this hasn't ever been what I thought it was. Her frigid fingers stroke the hair at the edge of my temple, just like she used to do when I was little and couldn't sleep. A shudder racks my body, and I curl the fingers of my good hand up inside my glove, wiggle my stiffening toes. My eyelids are heavy as boulders, and even though I know this is probably hypothermia and I shouldn't let myself sleep, I can't bring myself to care.

"Tell me one more story," I beg, just like I used to.

She shakes her head. "You can't stay here, Eline. You need to warm your body up, and I can't do that."

"Just one," I plead. "A short one."

Her icy sigh drifts around me like a cloud. "Just one more."

CHAPTER 50

Once upon a time, in a green house at the top of the world, a mother lay awake in the inky dark beside her sleeping husband. She could hear the stories inside the books on her shelf, whispering for her to let them out. Every night the whispers grew louder, and the mother wasn't sure she could ignore them much longer. She hadn't touched a book for nearly a month, not since her daughter had returned. She had contemplated getting rid of them all, but could never quite bring herself to do it.

The mother lay flat on her back, staring hard at the ceiling so she wouldn't see the little curls of color trailing out of her books. She could take one, just one, and slip outside. Just for a few minutes. But no, it wasn't safe even with everyone else fast asleep. She'd nearly killed her daughter and burned the house down. It was important to remember that, not the thrill of those words swirling out, the papery smell of them. Her husband had been right to send the poor child away.

Even as she forced herself to stare at the ceiling, the mother heard whispers. She knew they'd never go away. The worst part was that she didn't want them to. Since her daughter had come home and she'd stopped reading, the mother had been miserable.

She wanted her daughter to fill the void that the stories had left, but they were two separate emptinesses. Her daughter was the sun in her solar system, but the stories were the galaxy.

Sometimes the magic made the mother fly; sometimes it crushed her to dust. She couldn't control it, and she never should have shown any of it to her daughter—the last thing she wanted was for her child to turn out like she had.

And yet, and yet.

The mother eased out of bed, slid her feet into her slippers, and crept to the bookshelf. She chose the fattest, oldest tome and crept into the living room. Before she opened the book, she lit a fire, in case she had to throw it in. The mother sat on the hearth, ran her trembling finger over the leather-bound cover, and opened a sliver between the pages.

A knock sounded at the door.

The mother leapt to her feet. She wouldn't answer the door, she decided; she'd put the book away and get in bed, but as she slunk toward her room the knocking grew louder and became a pounding, a thumping, a thundering. The husband's snore broke off, and the mother's breath caught.

"Give me a minute," she whispered, waiting for her husband's breath to grow heavy and rumbling again. When it did, she crept to the door, cursing her own weak will.

There on the doorstep stood the three princesses. The mother clutched the book to her chest as if it could ward off their seeping chill. "What do you want?"

The golden-haired princess clucked her tongue. "Good evening to you too." She tipped her chin toward the mother's book. "Having trouble sleeping?"

"Does it matter?" said the mother.

The princess's laugh sounded like chains on cement. "We'd like to be paid for our services."

"What services?" The mother began to pull the door closed, slow as the setting sun to avoid notice.

The raven-haired princess wedged the toe of her slipper into the door's hinge. "We brought your mother's heart. It was no simple feat."

"I never asked you to do that," said the mother, glancing at the street behind the princesses and wishing someone would walk past.

"But you took the heart anyway," said the princess with hair like fire. "And now you must pay for it."

"So again, I ask you," said the mother. "What do you want?"

"It's not so much a giving thing as it is a letting-go thing," said the eldest princess with a serpentine smile. "Let your daughter come away with us. Let us save her from you."

"Never," spat the mother.

"We've no mothers to needle at us and blacken our hearts to match their own." The crow-haired princess peered disdainfully into the house, with its scorched carpet and bare walls. "You'll ruin this, and you know it. She'll be happier without you."

"Did you give her that fever?" asked the mother.

The flame-haired princess scoffed. "Of course not. That was a pleasant coincidence. We don't intend to hurt the girl, just free her."

This time it was the mother who scoffed, for she knew the princesses hurt a lot of things, whether they intended to or not. "You may as well leave right now," she said. "You'll never convince me. Not in a million years."

"We'll just take her if you won't let her go." The golden-haired princess's voice was cold steel. "It's no use running, no use hiding. We'll follow you. Slip underneath your doors, crawl through the holes in your drains."

The mother knew she meant it.

"Give me the night to think about it," she said.

"We'll give you until dawn," said the black-haired princess. "And if you tell anyone our plan, we'll snatch her away before you finish the sentence." She brought her fingers to her lips and blew a kiss that hit the mother's cheek like a slap. Then she linked arms with her sisters and they set off into the darkness.

The mother ran to her bedroom and turned on the lights. "We need to leave now," she said to her husband, who sat up and rubbed his eyes.

"Leave where?" he murmured.

"We need to go to the airport." The mother began pulling clothes out of drawers and tossing them onto the bed. In her haste, she caught the cord of the lamp and sent it crashing to the floor. "We have to get away from here."

"That's ridiculous," said the husband.

The mother knew she'd never convince him, knew there was no making him understand or see. Icy blocks of fear began stacking up, one on top of another, in her chest. They climbed up into her throat, and her words grew sharp. She said things she never meant, would never have said if she weren't so afraid of losing her child. She was a caged animal, her teeth and claws the only way to save them.

"Silje," said the husband. "You promised everything was better; you swore to me when Eli came back."

The mother choked down her biting words and picked up

the lamp on the floor. "I'm sorry," she said, and began to put her clothes back inside the dresser. "I'm tired, I'm sorry."

"Will you promise to call the therapist tomorrow?" said her husband, eyeing her warily.

"Yes," she said. "Yes, of course."

She turned off the light and waited a long time for her husband to snore again. The minutes ticked by, and shadows darted back and forth across her window shade. She waited and waited, and finally, her husband slept. The mother crept into her daughter's room and felt around under the bed, found the girl's toe and gave it a tug. But the girl didn't want to come out; she had become wild like a trapped animal too. As the girl slashed at her face, the mother hissed in her breath and tried not to cry. She wiped three parallel threads of blood from her cheek.

"Come with me," she whispered.

She slipped two pairs of woolen socks over the girl's feet. Long underwear, leg warmers, snow pants, sweater, fleece, coat, and two hats. She tiptoed to the closet to put on her own warm layers. Then she pulled the rifle from its safe, loaded it, and slung it over her back.

"Mamma," the girl said, pointing at a hole she'd wiped in the frost of the kitchen window.

The mother barely glanced at the window. "It's time to go." She took the girl's hand, eased the back door open, and led her out into the breathtaking cold.

She hadn't expected the reindeer, but the creature's kind eyes made the night seem less frightening. The mother lifted her daughter onto the animal's back and then climbed on herself, wrapping her arms around the girl's tiny torso and resting her chin on top of her two hats. They set off down the sleeping street.

The reindeer's loping stride grew wider as they left the out-skirts of town, its run became a glide, and soon they were skim-ming across the surface of the snow faster than a bird in flight, then veering out onto the ice of the fjord. As they flew down the corridor of ice flanked by looming, jagged mountains, the sky began to fill with color and light. A long line of ectoplasmic green, its edges hinting at pink, wavered from one horizon to the other.

"This is far enough," she whispered after they had flown down two fjords and passed a great, tumbling glacier. The animal slowed, its panting sides pressing into her legs. The mother helped her daughter down, then reached up to stroke the reindeer's velvet nose.

"Why are we getting off?" said the girl, casting a fearful look at the sky, which was now livid with streaming color.

"We'll go from here on foot," said the mother, for she saw the place, a few hundred meters away, where a tendril of crimson nearly touched the ice, and she was afraid the reindeer would scare it off. But the girl didn't want to walk, so the mother hoisted her onto her hip.

The girl caught sight of the rifle bumping against her mother's back, and she jolted. Before the mother could stop her, she had grabbed the gun barrel and was trying to wrench it away.

"Stop it." The mother's voice was sharp. The gun was loaded, and the girl knew better than to touch it. Still, her tiny mittens grasped and pushed and tugged. The mother pulled the girl off her hip and set her down.

"What are you doing?"

"You can't kill us; please don't kill us." The girl curled up fetal on the ice and began pulling at her hair.

"I'm not going to kill you," gasped the mother, though maybe what she was going to do was worse. "Please, Eline. Stop this."

"Put the gun away, get it away." The girl slapped her mother's hands as she tried to pick her up. Her breath came in short, terrified sobs. "I'll wish . . . I'll wish."

The mother took the rifle off and slid it away across the ice. "Look, it's gone, it's gone. Don't waste that wish. You might need it."

We might need it, she thought.

The girl looked at the gun, then at her mother. She held up her arms, and the mother picked her up. As the girl tucked her head into the hollow of her shoulder, the mother set off walking again, toward that curling, whispering light. For a long while, the only sound was the creaking of her boots on the snow and the slow rhythm of their cloudy breathing.

Miles from nowhere and nothing, the mother stopped.

She dropped to her knees and pulled the girl tight to her chest. She buried her nose in the girl's hats and whispered her love. Then she tipped her head back and whistled at the sky. It wasn't a song; it was a call. It was their only escape. She didn't know what would happen to them or where they'd go, but they were together; they'd always be together. Those fearsome princesses would never take her daughter.

The wave of electric light curved down, far more powerful, more magnetic and sucking and deadly than she'd expected. She tried to squeeze her daughter's hand, but her fingers began squirming of their own accord. She felt an overwhelming compulsion to let go, to save her daughter from this roaring, churning tempest of light. Suddenly, the girl's hand wasn't inside hers anymore; the child had dropped to a crouch, ripped off both of her mittens, and dug her bare fingers into the snow.

The mother gasped the girl's name. The lights swept her up. They took her away and left her poor, tiny daughter alone on the ice.

CHAPTER 51

The last word of my mother's story disappears into the smooth walls of the cave. The needle that's been pricking at me all through her story has become a razor blade.

"It was my fault," I say.

Her black eyes widen. "What?"

"The first wish. I remember it now." Ice tears roll down my cheeks, just like hers. "I wished . . ." I can't form the words, they're so awful.

My mother lays her frigid hand on my collarbone, and my tears tumble over the sleeve of her sweater. "I remember what you wished. You don't have to say it."

I wish your heart was as sad as mine. Years ago I blacked them out of the story—the words I said to her after I came home from the hotel, after our horrible trip to the grocery store—in the hopes of erasing them from reality.

"Eline, Eline," she sings. "My heart was already sadder than yours. Everything started falling apart long before then." She tips my chin up so I'm looking straight into her fathomless black eyes. "And even though nothing was your fault, I forgive you. Because I want you to move on from this, and me, and do wonderful things with your life. I forgive you."

Something unsnaps in my chest, and I'm breaking open, flooding with a million shards of devastation. But woven through it all is relief.

Finally, relief.

"I forgive you too," I say.

She closes her eyes and smiles, and for a breath of a moment, she's her old self again, not the mirror image. "That means more than you can imagine."

"I've got another wishing ring," I say. "I'll wish you back to your old self again."

Another sigh gusts around me in an icy cloud. "You can't undo what's already been undone."

Deep down, I know she's right. Gritting my teeth, I stare at the floor. "My whole life I've been missing this branch of myself that was you, and then I finally got it back and I thought I'd be whole again."

"You've got more than enough branches of yourself." Her voice is sad and certain. "Sturdy, strong ones. You're better off in this life that you didn't think you were supposed to have. The more I see you, the more I understand that."

It's not true. Nobody's better off without their mother. My need for her goes beyond anything I can rationalize: it's instinctive, it's primal, it's elemental. I'm hers and she's mine and something bound us together for this lifetime. Now it's ripping us apart.

"You're surrounded by people who love you," she says. "I couldn't have asked for more. It makes me so proud to see how you turned out."

This can't be the end. I fought so hard for her, I waited so long. *If only, if only, if only.* I'm too cold to cry now. I just want her to hold me; I just want this to never end. But the frost radiating off her is colder than the air.

"I didn't deserve to ever see you again," she says, pressing her icy lips to my cheek. "But somehow, I got to anyway."

"Can't you please stay a little longer?" Again, it's a bedtime conversation we had a hundred times when I was little. But there aren't going to be any more bedtimes.

"A few more minutes. Then you have to go."

"I don't want to."

"I know. But you're freezing to death."

Silent, I memorize the lines of her face, the sweep of her jaw and the curve of her eyebrows. I burn everything to memory. The filtered blue light around us dims, and she shifts.

"Not yet." I try to grab her sweater, but my fingers won't close.

"Use your wish. Do it for me."

I wish to stay forever with you. I wish you weren't broken.

"I wish . . ."

"Go on," she whispers.

I wish I were six years old again. I wish I'd woken Dad when you tried to leave. I wish I'd given those princesses my heart in exchange for you. I wish I'd wished the lights away faster. I wish the universe weren't so cruel.

I clap my hand over my mouth to stop all the other wishes from tumbling out. Then I take a long breath and dig out the words I need.

"I wish to find my way out of here."

On the far wall, a crack of light appears. My mother smiles, and my heart fractures like a sheet of ice.

"Tell your father I love him and goodbye," she says.

"Mamma." I bury my face in her hollow chest. Her arms wrap tight around me, my violent shivers racking us both.

"When you're ready, go to the eastern face of Tolstadfjellet," she says, pressing her mouth to the top of my head. "Bring your father."

I'm shaking so hard I can barely nod.

"I love you, Eline," she whispers into my hat.

"I love you too, Mamma."

Somehow, my leaden legs carry me toward the light. Away from her. Toward warmth and safety. Toward life.

CHAPTER 52

Stepping out of the side of the glacier and onto the fjord is like waking from a dream. The sun still isn't visible, but everything is so much brighter than it was in the cave. I shut my eyes while spots dance across the insides of my lids. Once I'm able to see again, I press my face against the crack in the ice.

"Mamma?"

No answer. My head throbs, but my arm is still numb. Several snowmobiles are parked at the edge of the boulders, and up on the glacier people are shouting. There's no way I can climb up there, so I edge backward until I can see what's happening. At least ten people are gathered near the spot where I fell, ropes are strewn everywhere, and somebody's lying at the edge of the crevasse.

"I'm down here!" My tongue is wood, and I can barely get the words out. Nobody turns to look. The effort of shouting is monumental. I slump on the ice and prop my broken arm in my lap, wishing there were someplace to lie down. I could sleep for ten years.

"You can stop looking for me now," I whisper.

I was shivering so hard in the cave that I thought all my teeth would crack, but now I'm eerily calm. At the edge of the glacier,

274

my dad is shouting and somebody's holding him back from rushing onto the ice. I wish I could tell him he doesn't have to yell and cry and break because I'm right here, but I can't. The only thing I can do is wait until they come down. Cradling my arm, I curl up in a ball on the ice. It's too hot out here, so I pull off my hat and unzip my coat. I close my eyes and the sadness fades to numb. It's too much effort to watch the people on the glacier, all that panic they're going through for no reason. It's too much effort to have any feelings right now. They'll see me eventually and then I'll sleep for a month. My eyes drift shut. I'll just rest until they come.

I wake to the smell of rotting meat, chilly slime on my cheek. A long shadow-body curled around mine, its razor claws digging into my sleeves and pant legs. My slushy blood crawls in my veins, and I can't move, can't even open my mouth to call for help.

"Your mamma is gone now, little one," whispers the lindworm, and I watch, utterly detached, as it drags its black tongue through my tangled hair. Vaguely I remember the knife in my pocket and slip my hand inside, but the pocket is empty. It doesn't matter—I'm too tired to fight. Everything inside me is too withered to care. The lindworm is right, anyway. She's gone. I am alone.

"Get off of her!" A man's voice. My father's voice.

Thundering footsteps and thrashing and jerking. My head lolls sideways, crushing my ear into the ice, my numb arm flops, and everything's moving too fast for my tired eyes to follow, but the weight is gone, the lindworm lets go with its filthy claws. My dad shouts and swears and a gun fires and my ears are ringing, singing. It all goes dark, and then something's got me again and I want to scream but my voice is gone and then I realize it's him. It's my father, lifting me off the ice, cradling me to him, carrying me away.

I'm safe.

I can let go again.

CHAPTER 53

I'm two years old, swinging with my mother at the school playground. It's summer, the wind is warm, and it smells like mud everywhere. I'm sitting on her lap, facing her so that when she's up, I'm down, and when she's down, I'm up. The toes of my purple sneakers point to the sky, then dirt, then sky again, and every time my mother drops backward, her long hair sweeps around me, curtaining me inside.

"Higher, higher," I scream. "More!" She pumps us harder. A giggle flutters like a butterfly out of my mouth, and her rich laugh joins it. Higher and higher we go, stretching out horizontal and then pushing past, higher and higher until I can see the whole town, the houses of pink and green and yellow, the stained-glass water lapping at the gravel beach.

Don't stop, I think. *Never, ever stop.*

We're almost vertical now, our feet flung high over our heads and an upside-down world far beneath us. My laughter comes in giddy, gasping shrieks, as we pause, suspended, at the very top, then keep going, up and over, all the way around. Down, down, screaming fast, with the wind licking my cheeks and ecstatic tears pouring from my eyes. Then up, up, and over the top again, my mother's strong legs pumping us round and round, faster and faster, until earth blends into sky and I can't tell up from down anymore.

I never want to stop.

CHAPTER 54

I'm lying in a bed with a cast on one arm and something prickly stuck in the other. Things are beeping, and the acrid scent of disinfectant sears the insides of my nostrils. I try to shake the prickly thing off, but someone presses my hand gently and shushes me.

"It's okay," says my dad. "You're safe."

"Where am I?"

"The hospital. You've got hypothermia and a broken arm."

I blink until my vision works. The prickly something is an IV feeding warm fluid into my arm. The room around me is painted institutional green, and a small window looks out to sloping mountains.

"You scared me half to death." Black circles ring my dad's eyes. He's aged twenty years overnight.

"I'm sorry," I mumble. "Thank you for saving me from the lindworm."

All the exhaustion jolts out of his face. "What in God's name was that thing?"

"He's from one of Mamma's stories." It's hard to focus; my brain is still swirling in dreams.

"I think it was some creep in a costume." My dad's nostril's flare. "I didn't have a gun, but I found a pocketknife on the ice beside you. The guy tried to run away, and I grabbed the tail of his suit. The fabric, the skin, whatever it was—it was all thin and dry like snake scales, and it started coming off. So I stabbed the knife into the tail, and I yelled for Álvaro to help me. He thought there was a bear and shot his rifle to scare it off. But the, the . . . guy just kept pulling and pulling until his whole skin, his costume, his suit—I don't know what it was—came off. He ran away into the mountains, this pale, naked . . . creep." He shudders. "You wouldn't believe the smell."

I would believe it.

"Thank you," I whisper.

"Never seen anything like it." My dad takes a long slurp of coffee from a paper cup. "I told the police, but I don't think they believed me."

I suspect they'll never believe any of it. But it's enough that my dad actually saw the lindworm, that he fought it off and saved me.

"I found Mamma," I say. "In the crevasse. There was a cave under the glacier and she was in there."

I wait for him to come up with a rational reason why I thought she was inside the glacier, something to do with hypothermia or concussions, but instead he holds up a folded sheet of paper covered in my mother's spidery writing.

"I found this in my bed this morning," he says. "I thought it was from you, telling me where you went." His fingers shake as he lays the paper on his knee and presses the creases flat.

I want to rip it from his hands and devour it. "What does it say?"

He picks up the letter, then sets it down again. "You could have at least left me a note, Eli."

The fact that it never crossed my mind the second time I left makes me squirm with guilt. My dad presses a button on the side of my bed, and slowly I creak upright, hissing in my breath as my broken arm slides along the mattress.

"Do you understand how close to dying you just came?" he says in a cracking voice. "Did you even care what that would've done to me?"

"I didn't think I was going to die until it was too late," I say. "I didn't really think at all."

"Neither of you ever did," he says, snatching up the letter again and looking like he wants to tear it to pieces. "It was one thing when you were a little kid, but you're old enough to take responsibility for your actions now. To know what's safe and what isn't, for crying out loud."

"I'm sorry, Dad." I close my eyes, and the room tips and whirls.

He sniffs and the paper rustles. "You're grounded for a month when we get home."

I nod. "None of this was fair to you. Not then, not now. I've been hiding everything, and it wasn't right."

He's silent for a long, long time. I want to stay with him, apologize and explain, but I'm slipping back into unconsciousness, my body too ragged to keep me here. Just as I begin to float, the paper rustles again. My father coughs, clears his throat, and begins to read.

CHAPTER 55

Once upon a time, in a red-shingled house on a little hook of land jutting out into the ocean, a wife crept into bed with her husband and lay there, watching him dream. His brown curls, the ones she used to twist around her fingers, were gone, and tiny wrinkles whispered at the corners of his eyes. Still, he was beautiful, and he smelled exactly as he used to, more like home than any house ever had. She couldn't resist kissing the tip of his nose.

The husband woke, and the wife caught her breath. She wondered if she'd changed as much as he had, if he recognized her. She wondered if he still loved her, if he hated her for what she'd done, if he'd welcome her back or throw her out.

But there was no love or hate in the husband's face. Only fear. Then his eyes snapped shut, and the wife watched his chest rise and fall, rise and fall. She waited, unspeaking, for him to decide whether it was love or hate, forgiveness or fury.

It was none of those things.

The husband rolled away. He shifted his pillow and tugged his blanket up. The tension slowly drained from his shoulder and jaw as he fell back to sleep. It was worse than fury or hate, and the wife wanted to throw herself on top of him and demand a reaction. Instead, she slid open his window and slipped outside. She went back to the tree house her daughter had built without her, curled up under the blanket her daughter had knitted without her, and cried.

The next day, she peered in the window as her husband sat in his kitchen, holding a stone that had fallen from the sky. Later, she watched as he made corn bread from scratch—the man who'd never so much as boiled an egg in his previous life. He fed their daughter in a kitchen full of objects he'd bought himself, in a house full of furniture the wife had never seen.

After their daughter had gone to sleep, the husband crept to his office and called someone else and whispered that he missed her too. Already, the wife felt her body thinning, fading, melting away, and she knew that if she came back, she'd break what he'd built. So she kept herself hidden from him, and she watched her little family, minus one. With greedy eyes, she soaked up every gesture, every word, every detail of their life on this little hook of land in the middle of the ocean.

She watched him mop the floor, fold the laundry, drive away to work and come home with bags full of groceries. She watched him pick up a stray earring on the living room floor and carefully put it away in their daughter's jewelry box. She watched him search on his computer, looking for answers, grasping for rational explanations so he and their daughter could make sense of their world, so they didn't need to be afraid, so they could keep moving forward.

As the wife watched her husband raising their child with careful wisdom and selfless love, she realized that even if he didn't see everything, he saw what mattered.

She loved him for that, more than she'd ever thought possible.

And because she loved him, she let him go.

CHAPTER 56

I have never seen my dad cry, not once in the sixteen years of my life. Not until now. His sobs are ugly and loud and his nose is running, and I want to go back and change everything, remake every decision I've made since that night the Northern Lights came to Wellfleet.

"You were trying to tell me," he says.

"I should have tried harder." I want to get out of bed and climb onto his lap, but my arm is broken and there are tubes connecting me to things.

He shakes his head and pulls a tissue from a box beside my bed.

"She asked me to tell you goodbye and that she loves you," I say. "But I guess she sort of already did that."

"Do you think she's gone for good?" he says.

Every electron in my body wants to say no, but I nod. "She was breaking. Falling apart." I hate, hate the words I'm saying. "She said her body was somewhere else, that she hasn't been in it this whole time."

He doesn't correct me, doesn't try to explain away the unexplainable. He just listens, bleary and silent.

"Right before I left, she said to look on the eastern face of

Tolstadfjellet," I say. "Do you know where that is?"

"It's a mountain not far from where you just were," he says.

"We have to go there. She said to bring you."

My dad glances at the mountains outside my window. "What are we supposed to do there?"

A wave of cold hits me all over again, and my teeth start chattering. "Find her body, I think."

He stands and peers out the window, lost in thought. I wonder if he's looking for her. I know I can't stop, even after everything.

"Your body temperature was ninety-three when we got you here," he says finally. "There's no way you're trekking out to Tolstadfjellet anytime soon. I'll go with your uncle."

It takes a monstrous effort to drag my leaden body upright, but I do it. "If you go without me, I'll never forgive you."

He returns to my bedside and pulls my blanket up, tucking it around my shoulders. "Let's give it a few days and see how you're feeling."

"We can change our plane tickets?"

"I've already called the airline. I told them I wasn't sure when we'd be able to leave."

Fatigue tugs at me like underwater weeds; I tip my head back and shut my eyes. "Okay. Good."

"Why don't you try to sleep?" he says, brushing a lock of hair from my forehead and kissing the place it covered. My mother was right: he does smell like home.

"I'm sorry, Dad. I really am."

"Don't worry about it." He smooths my hair one more time and tucks my blanket tighter. "Just sleep. You're okay, you're safe, and I'm here."

My dad has been snoring in his chair for hours now, and even though I ate some soup earlier, my stomach rumbles. It's silent and lonely in the hospital, and all I want is my mother, even that scary, hollowed-out version of her. It's been years since she's taken care of me, and this irrational, instinctive need for her should be gone by now, but it isn't; it never even faded.

Gingerly easing myself to sitting, I pick up my phone from the bedside table. A string of messages from Iris fills the screen.

> **Iris:** *Your yard is completely covered with black and white birds. I can't even see the ground.*
>
> *I didn't know what kind they were so I looked them up.*
>
> *They're Arctic terns.*
>
> *Somehow that doesn't surprise me.*
>
> *I hope you're OK*
>
> *Write back to me*
>
> *Your house is covered now too. I'm almost expecting it to fly away like in the Wizard of Oz. Look at this.*

In the photo beneath, my house and yard are unrecognizable under the swarm. I wonder if they're the same birds who took my mother over the mountains all those years ago. Maybe they came to take her back, but they were too late. We were all too late.

> **Iris:** *Now they're all gone. No sign they were ever here. Feels almost like I imagined it.*
>
> *Text me back, dammit*

Oh and also, I got into the Stanford online program. FULL SCHOLARSHIP.

I wanted to tell you in person but I couldn't wait :)

I'm not moving to Amherst. Not yet anyway.

It takes me several minutes to type a response with my one good hand and tears leaking all down my face.

Me: *THAT IS AMAZING!!!!!!! I'm so happy you're staying.*

I have so many things to tell you, I can't wait to see you again.

I want to pour my heart out to her, but the pain from my elbow is grinding all the way up into my shoulder and jaw, and I also can't stop crying. Outside the wind wails, and I miss my mother so much it's nearly dissolving me. I even miss the days before she came back, when anything was possible. When I didn't know the whole story and its sad ending.

But Iris isn't leaving me, at least not for another year. Buried deep underneath all the pain, sorrow, and loss, that one tiny fact is a seed. And it's sprouting.

As I set the phone on the table, I notice a folded square of white paper. The machine counting my pulse chirps and stutters as I grip the page in my teeth and pull the folds open with my good hand. But it's not my mother's writing, and my elation plummets. This cursive is immaculate and old-fashioned, marching in neat lines across stationery branded with the words HOTEL LUND at the top.

CHAPTER 57

Once upon a time, in a stark white hotel at the top of the world, a grandmother snuck into her granddaughter's room and found a book of stories that the girl had written. She read every single page and then went back to the beginning and started again.

The grandmother saw the pain she had caused the little girl, and it hurt her deeply, for she had only been trying to keep the girl's mind off her mother through good, honest work. Cleaning was the best antidote to sadness she knew: strong chemicals and scrubbing until one's muscles were tired and a sense of calm clarity took over. The grandmother was disappointed her granddaughter hadn't seen this, though of course such a young child couldn't be expected to understand. All the same, she wished she'd known. And she wished, more than anything, that she could have prevented it all from happening in the first place.

The grandmother also regretted the choices she'd made with her older daughter, the girl's mother. Her younger daughter had always been content to follow rules without questions, but her elder daughter was difficult, with a head full of dreams and no control over her impulses. She'd discovered the threads of magic that clung to the undersides of the world, threads that the grandmother had spent her life hiding because they could not be controlled and almost never came to any good. The headstrong daughter let the magic roll through her, untethered and wild, and no matter how many times the grandmother warned her, she didn't listen.

The grandmother knew that the magic didn't just come from books. It could be created out of anything: paint, clay, wood, string, yarn. Once, she had knitted a blanket with three princesses from her elder daughter's favorite story. She'd hoped that some of the lessons the princesses had learned would seep into the girl as she slept. She should have read the book one last time before she started to knit and bound those princesses to her daughter, for her daughter had changed their story.

The girl was particularly interested in the stars and the moon and the aurora borealis—she snuck out of the hotel whenever they were dancing in the sky. The grandmother worried, for the nighttime magic was the strongest and wildest of all. She warned and pleaded and punished, but nothing worked. The girl crept out, no matter how many locks were put on doors or bars on windows.

One night, in a fit of panic and paranoia, the grandmother wove a net from starlight and strands of her own hair, and she walked out onto the frozen fjord.

"Send me the moon," she whispered to the North Wind, and although he was a capricious thing and not always bound to listen, he obliged. The grandmother caught the moon, and she locked it in an empty closet at the top of her hotel. Then the night was silent, and her daughter stopped sneaking outside. The grandmother could breathe again, and after a few days she felt safe enough to leave the girl home while she went to buy groceries.

The grandmother had a flighty feeling in her gut as she walked home with her bags, and as she stepped into the hotel the moon came crashing down the stairs, followed by her terrified daughter. The grandmother dove out of the way, but the moon clipped her shoulder, hard, and sent her spinning.

You cannot contain me, it said as it punched a hole in the wall and flew back up to its place in the sky. Dazed, the grandmother sat among her broken eggs, and she knew the moon was right. She couldn't contain any of this, but she would protect her daughters, no matter the cost.

This was perhaps the grandmother's greatest mistake of all, for the cost of protecting her daughters was their love. She taught her elder daughter to blame herself, to hate herself when she couldn't control the magic. And as the elder daughter grew, she turned that self-loathing outward and caught her mother and her sister in its web. The girls stopped speaking to each other, and as soon as she was old enough, the younger daughter moved away. The grandmother and her elder daughter lived in an uneasy truce in their small town, smiling when they crossed paths but not speaking.

The grandmother was cautiously happy when her daughter gave birth to a beautiful baby girl, but as the years went on she began to suspect that all of her stories and threats had come to nothing. Her daughter was letting her own child play with magic. When she warned her daughter, she cut off all contact, refused to bring her beautiful baby to the hotel even on Christmas. The grandmother worried deeply. She found the golden bell that she'd taken from her daughter years before, and she called the only people who could make her listen.

The princesses promised they'd frighten the daughter. They'd twist the magic all around her, they said, make it deeper and darker and so unpredictable that she'd never want to touch it again. In exchange, the grandmother told them they could take her heart. It was a small price to pay for her daughter and granddaughter's safety.

In the days that followed, the daughter began to look unwell. Tired at first, then haggard, then so white she resembled a ghost. The grandmother suspected her bargain was working. It was worth the gaping hole in her chest.

Two weeks later, the grandmother's son-in-law knocked on her door, clutching a sobbing, frightened child. The magic had burned a black path across their living room, had nearly incinerated the house, and the grandmother realized she'd made a terrible mistake. One she was afraid to admit. One she didn't know how to fix.

The grandmother kept that beautiful little girl for three weeks, trying her best to help her, to keep her safe. On the twenty-third day, the grandmother's elder daughter knocked on her door. She held a silver box, and the grandmother knew what was inside. She saw the hate in her daughter's eyes and she wished she could undo everything, go back to those nights where her daughter slipped outside and danced with the Northern Lights, and she wished she had danced with her instead.

She'd done everything, everything wrong.

The mother set the box down on the step.

"You can have this," she said. "You can keep my daughter too, if you think I'm not safe. I only want what's right for her."

The grandmother gave the child back to her daughter, and she wished with all her heart that they would be happy, that their love for each other would remain unbroken, no matter what happened. Then she went inside, climbed into her bed, and cried for the first time in fifty years.

CHAPTER 58

One week after being released from the hospital, I'm coasting over the ice on a sled pulled by Uncle Álvaro's snowmobile, buried under a mountain of blankets, including a makeshift electric one he rigged up with battery-powered boot heaters. It snowed a few times this week, and the sled is a lot bumpier than riding on a snowmobile. The jostling of my arm, combined with the prospect of where we're going, spills waves of nausea up my throat.

On her own snowmobile, Mormor drives close beside us so that my dad, riding on the back, can keep an eye on me and make anxious tugging motions every time my blanket strays too far below my chin. He's gripping the seat, trying not to bear-hug Mormor, and every time they hit a bump, his arms fly out as he lurches backward. It'd be funny if this were any other trip.

It feels like we've been riding forever, bouncing and jostling, and just as I'm about to ask for a break so I can stretch my legs and try not to throw up, the shapes of the mountains become familiar, and my bones go heavy. The sky is a hundred shades of purple and gold, and Tolstadfjellet looms ahead, covered in snow as powdery as flour.

The slope is gentle at first, with a wide path cutting around toward the base of the mountain. As the snowmobile whooshes through the snow, my heart thumps. Invisible strings are pulling at me, but they aren't the ones I'm used to. She's here, but not the way I want her to be. Everything in me screams to go back, turn around, pretend this doesn't need to happen, but it does.

The snow deepens into drifts, and there are mountains and boulders to navigate. I'm shivering, though I'll never tell anyone. Uncle Álvaro shuts off his engine and confers with Mormor. He's trying to convince my dad of something and my dad keeps saying words like *relapse* and *temperature* and *doctor's orders*. Finally, he relents, and Uncle Álvaro turns to me.

"Eli, you're going to have to ride with me. We can't take the sled any farther."

It's impossible to read my dad's expression through his visor, but I don't need to. He's afraid. I'm afraid too.

Biting back a groan of pain as my elbow bumps the edge of the sled, I clamber out. Inside I'm twisting in a million different directions. I want the truth, and I want to hide in the delusion. I want to know, and I want to stay ignorant. I want to find her; I want this to somehow be the last piece in a puzzle that leads to her being alive and human again. I need to cling to that thread of hope or I'll never make it to Tolstadfjellet.

A channel of creamy white snow is all that separates us from the mountain. The wind twists and spins the clouds churned up by our snowmobile, which feels more like a boat than a machine. And then it's done. We're at the base of the mountain. My dad gets off Mormor's snowmobile and rolls his shoulders.

"Why don't you stay here while we look around, Eli?"

He's still trying to protect me from the truth.

"Dad, I'm fine. I'm not even cold." I speak through clenched teeth so he won't hear them rattling.

He gives me a stern squint. "I promise I'll call you if I find anything."

Anything is an absurd way of putting it. But he's already wading through the snow toward the rocks along the left side of the mountain. Mormor and Uncle Álvaro head for the opposite side, and I tuck my feet up on the snowmobile and prop my good elbow on my knee, surveying the hulking mass of rock and snow.

"How am I supposed to know where you'd be on a mountain this big?" I whisper.

The dream comes whispering back, the plummeting and burning up in the atmosphere. I woke just before I landed—before she landed. My eyes flick to a hollow tucked into the base of the mountain, straight ahead.

There.

The snow's deeper than I expected, dragging at my legs like the mountain doesn't want me to find its secrets. It'd be so easy to go back and wait for them to return without finding her, to sit and drink tea in the hotel and speculate about whatever happened to her. I could go home to Wellfleet and spend the rest of my life wondering if she'll ever come find me again. I crave that safe ignorance, but it's never going to be enough. I know why I'm here and what I need to do.

The snow is up to my thighs now, and the strings are pulling me so hard I couldn't stop if I tried. She's a magnet and I'm tiny fragments of iron. She's the earth and I'm a meteorite caught in her gravity. I'm falling, falling toward her, and I can't stop.

Snow becomes rock, turns craggy and sharp. Lungs burning,

legs shaking, I heave myself up with my one good arm. My boots catch and slip, my mitten slips and catches, until finally I reach the basin.

There's nothing here.

I slump against the mountain's side, my broken bone throbbing in time with my ragged heartbeat. The wind burns the tears on my cheeks as I press my face against the rough stone. All this time I've been searching and it always ends like this.

Then I see it: a patch of dirty white cable-knit buried in the snow. A curled-up hand at the end of the sleeve. Dream-slow, I float toward the sleeve, the hand. I push the snow away, brush the snow off, move up the shredded sweater until I find black, tangled hair. The back of her head.

"No, no, no. Please, no," I whisper, but I keep scooping the snow away until she's uncovered. Frozen. Broken. Legs bent at angles bones don't allow for.

My mother.

I knew this was coming, but I was never going to be ready for it. I thought I could avoid this ending, but I couldn't. She's been here all along, before she ever came to my house. And now I'm hollow as she ever was, my insides turned to dust and blown away on the wind. I sink down beside her and touch her matted hair.

"Can you hear me?" I say, still clinging to the desperate wish that she can use whatever magic she had to fix this. But she doesn't move. She's a broken doll.

In the periphery of my hearing, people are shouting. My dad flounders through the snow, flailing both arms. I stroke my mother's hair. I want to rewind everything. I want to go back to that night on the ice and use my wish to protect us both. I can't see how I'll ever come back from this or make sense of any of it.

I nudge her shoulder. "Wake up, Mamma. Please."

She doesn't.

My dad and Uncle Álvaro and Mormor are almost here, and I only have a few moments left of quiet before I'll have to show them this terrible thing I found. I rest my ear on her frozen back, listening for breath I know isn't there.

"I love you," I whisper into the cold bones.

I stay like that, my head too heavy to lift, until they arrive.

CHAPTER 59

SPITSBERGEN POST

BODY OF MISSING LONGYEARBYEN WOMAN FOUND AFTER A DECADE

Almost exactly ten years ago, on a frigid February night, Silje Lund vanished from the settlement of Longyearbyen, taking her young daughter with her. The next morning, an expedition group found the child, alone and alive, on the ice of Ekmanfjorden, roughly 50 kilometres away. Silje's disappearance stunned the small community where she lived. A memorial service was held, although her body was never recovered.

Until this week, that is. Just three days ago, Silje's body was discovered at the foot of Tolstadfjellet, reportedly by a family member. According to a statement released by the coroner's office, Silje was twenty-nine at the time of her death, her age when she disappeared. A member of Longyearbyen's search-and-rescue team, who wished to remain anonymous, told us that her body was perfectly preserved, most likely a result of being frozen.

But there's more to the story. Rumors are circulating that most of the bones in Silje's body were broken, as if she'd fallen from a great height. However, she had no mountaineering equipment with her, and it is unlikely that she could have climbed the snow-covered peak without it. Authorities were quick to point out that Silje's broken bones are likely the result of her body being crushed under rocks and ice, but many members of the community remain suspicious.

The coroner's office has ruled Silje's death an accident, and there will be no further investigation. But locals continue to speculate about that night a decade ago. "Nobody will ever know the whole story of what happened to Silje," said a family friend.

CHAPTER 60

The ancient church in Trondheim, made of simple stone with a steep-sloping roof, looks like something out of a fairy tale itself. The walls inside are covered in murals of saints, and above the little altar is an ornate wooden carving with gilded edges and cubbyholes holding painted statues. The straight-backed pews are packed, and people are spilling from the back all the way up the aisles. My mother's been all over the news, and people are speculating about all kinds of things. No one has mentioned any supernatural theories to me, though, just kind, heartfelt expressions of sympathy.

The minister's words float past me as I stare at my mother's casket. It seems like such a big box for her body, and some confused part of my brain keeps thinking I could walk up to it and whisper to her through the side, that she might answer me even though I know she's been lying in a morgue for days and then packaged up in this box and flown down to Norway.

She's wearing the fingerless gloves I made her, though she'll never need them now and I have no idea how the funeral home people got them onto her twisted fingers. Her body's different now, the bones all patched together and flat, her chest sunken.

They put too much blush on her cheeks, and I badly wanted to wipe it off with a tissue.

The minister has stopped speaking now, and my dad is nudging my shoulder. I don't know why I offered to do this reading, but two nights ago a poem by Sara Teasdale leapt into my brain and wouldn't let me sleep for the rest of the night. Shaky and dry-mouthed, I ease around my dad and trip up the altar's wooden steps. The space is so small that there's no need for a microphone, and my sheet of freshly printed paper wobbles in my hands as I clear my throat and wait for my voice to work.

> *Perhaps if Death is kind, and there can be returning,*
> *We will come back to earth some fragrant night,*
> *And take these lanes to find the sea, and bending*
> *Breathe the same honeysuckle, low and white.*

My voice breaks, and I cough to hide it. In the front row, Mormor catches my eye and nods slowly. *Good job*, she mouths. Keeping my gaze fixed on her flint-colored eyes, I draw a steady breath and recite the rest of the poem from memory.

> *We will come down at night to these resounding beaches*
> *And the long gentle thunder of the sea,*
> *Here for a single hour in the wide starlight*
> *We shall be happy, for the dead are free.*

Memories spill through my mind like sand through my fingers. Running with my mother to the beach under the moon, my wool coat flapping like wings behind her. Hurling stones and screaming at the sky. Narwhals and stars. Meteorites. Finally belonging to each other again, finally not being lonely. Flight and Arctic air.

Polar bears and roaring snowmobiles and ice and caverns and numbing cold. Snowy mountains and silence. Woven through it all, curling around each memory, ethereal waves of green and pink light.

In the front row, my dad's mouth is twisted in a frown that's probably meant to keep it from quivering. It's not fair that he didn't get to say goodbye. He loved her as much as I did. I've wondered a million times if she made the right choice, hiding from him. Last night, I asked him what he thought. He hugged me and told me that I needed something different than he did, and that my mother gave us both what we needed.

I fold up my paper and stare at all these people who cared about my mother in some way or another, people from Longyearbyen and Trondheim and Oslo and even Wellfleet. In the fourth row, Iris gives me a tiny wave. Her mom sits next to her, her cheeks streaked with tears even though she never met my mother. Mormor bought them expensive last-minute tickets so Iris could be here with me today.

Beside my dad, Aunt Grete is clutching Marit's hand, and Uncle Álvaro has his arm tucked around Kaja. Leaning slightly away into her own space, as always, is Mormor. Her thin face is now serene as a lake at night, and maybe, maybe, in some oblique way, I get it. Everything is in the right order again. I didn't want this to be the outcome, but it's the right one, even though it breaks me into splinters.

I step down from the altar and let my family surround me, hug me, whisper their love.

CHAPTER 61

Once upon a time, in a stark white hotel at the top of the world, a girl and her grandmother pulled a knitted blanket from the bottom of a trunk. Though the blanket was three decades old, its colors were still vibrant, peacock blue and white, and its designs were almost three-dimensional in their detail. The girl's breath caught as she recognized each face of the princesses who stood, arms linked, in front of a craggy mountain range.

The grandmother spread the blanket over the polished boards of her floor, and she took a pair of sharp silver scissors from her pocket. She clipped the bottom corner of the blanket, then picked at the edge until she held the end of a blue strand of yarn. The girl took hold of the white strand, and together they began to pull, winding the yarn into balls as the blanket unraveled.

Away went the snow beneath the princesses' feet.

Away went their slippers.

Away went the hems of their cloaks and the skirts of their dresses.

Away went their middles and their linked arms and their shoulders and their necks.

The girl paused when her unraveling reached the youngest

princess's chin, feeling an odd sense of loss even though the young women had brought nothing but sadness. She understood their wrath; she knew they hadn't been made from nothing. She hated the destruction, but it was time to end this story.

Away went the princesses' faces, their hair, their crowns.

Away went the mountains and the sky.

The blanket was no more; the grandmother and the girl held two balls of wool. They carried them into the sitting room, pulled open the woodstove door, and crammed each ball inside. The fire blazed blue, then green, and sparks whistled up the pipe.

Silence.

The grandmother smiled. The girl's hand crept inside hers, and together they went into the dining room to join the rest of their family for dinner.

AUTHOR'S NOTE

Many of the stories from Eli's and Silje's childhoods are based on or inspired by the following Norwegian folk tales:

- "East of the Sun and West of the Moon"
- "The Giant Who Had No Heart in His Body"
- "The Lassie and Her Godmother"
- "Prince Lindworm"
- "The Three Princesses in the Blue Mountain"
- "The Three Princesses of Whiteland"

If you're interested in reading them, I highly recommend *East of the Sun and West of the Moon: Old Tales from the North*, a collection edited by Noel Daniel. It contains gorgeous illustrations by Danish artist Kay Nielsen that also deeply inspired this book.

ACKNOWLEDGMENTS

To my agent, Kathleen Rushall, thank you for finding this story in your slush pile and seeing the potential in it. For sticking with it for years and through so many iterations, for never losing faith in it and making my dream come true.

To my editors, Jess Harriton and Gretchen Durning, thank you for making me feel so welcome at Razorbill, and for your support and your always insightful guidance. Thank you to Janet Rosenberg, Marinda Valenti, and Amy Schneider for the excellent copyediting and proofreading. Thank you also to Ashley Spruill and the rest of the Razorbill team.

Ioana Harasim, your art is literally and figuratively stellar, and Kristin Boyle, I couldn't imagine a more perfect cover for this book.

Margot Harrison, thank you for reading nine thousand drafts of this book and for all the support over the years. Jesse Sutanto, you always make me laugh and help me put things in perspective, and I'm so glad we got to go on this journey together. Nina Rossing, a million thanks for reading, and for your help with all things Norwegian.

I am eternally grateful to everyone who read and offered

feedback on the many wildly different drafts of this story: Addie Thorley, Angela Michielsen, Gloria Mendez, Jamie Adams, Marley Teter, and Seabrooke Leckie.

Lis Watson, I'm so glad you said yes to my completely out-of-the-blue idea to go to Svalbard. You were the best travel companion! Thank you to Vanessa at Henningsen Transport & Guiding for all the information and perspective on living in Svalbard, and to Jan and Evija at Green Dogs for the fantastic dogsledding/ice-caving trip.

Thank you to my mom, Lynn, for nurturing my love of all things book-related, and for encouraging me from page one of writing this book. To my dad, Steve, I miss you and wish you were here to read this. To my sister, Alissa, thank you for always being there for me.

Isla and Neil, thanks for changing my entire perspective on the world. If it weren't for you two, I might not have ever started writing actual books.

To my husband, Ciaran, thank you for absolutely everything.